ASHES

*The story of a man's search for class
in a classless age*

by Orvel Trainer

**PRUETT PUBLISHING COMPANY
BOULDER, COLORADO**

ISBN: 0-87108-058-3

Library of Congress Card Catalog Number: 72-91954

Pruett Publishing Company
Boulder, Colorado 80302
Printed in the United States of America
by
Pruett Press Incorporated

To Ryan and Eric

*Everyone claims some place of origin. It was the writer's privilege
to grow up among people typical of whom he writes.
Life is repetitive—seemingly alike—in any community and any
similarity of persons in this story to persons living
or dead is purely coincidental.*

Chapter 1

He listened, irritated. The jangling of the phone in the outer office gnawed at him. Today was to be a turning point in his life, and he was determined to enjoy it. Again the phone rang. Damn, where is she? Too early to be out shopping. He looked at his wrist watch—a few minutes past nine. Let it ring six times, that's my dictum. Dictum! He breathed deeply the sense of authority in the word. He rolled the word around soundlessly in his mouth.

Just then Line 3 light went on, blinking monotonously at him from the phone cradle on the polished desk top. The blinking was uncoordinated with the ringing of the phone, adding to his irritation. He pushed the inter-office button.

"Yes, Mister Potter," said a woman's voice.

"Irene, I'm out to any telephone calls this morning."

"Very well, Mister Potter." Her answer was sharp and non-committal.

Line 3 light went out.

Maxwell Irving Potter cradled the phone and swung his chair around to face the tall, wide window overlooking the city to the south. The sky was clear. Too early for the smog from the refineries, he thought. He gazed up at the sky, looking for the sun. The bunched Roman window shades cut off his view. Nervously, he looked at his watch again. Time stands still, he thought. Impulsively, he reached for the phone. Hesitating, he pushed his chair away from the desk and stared blankly out the window. He'd wait a few minutes and call her again.

A muscle in the right side of his face twitched. His eyes blinked rapidly.

Slouched down in his chair, he gazed at the horizon, at Pikes Peak looming up above the plains far away to the south. To the west and south, the city of Denver lay below him. Twelve stories up, he was. Pikes Peak out the south window and Lookout Mountain out the west one. He turned his chair to the small west window. The new Colorado State Bank Building blocked his view. Goddamned stump, he thought. A frown crossed his pink face. Be able to see Cody's grave if it weren't for that thing. Denver's dollar erection.

Max turned back to the south window. Unobscured, his view swept the dingy roofs and parking lots of Capitol Hill and on past Speer Boulevard and Cherry Creek, where they cut southeastward through the city. From the northwest corner of the building he would have been privileged to view the newer, taller and more imposing buildings—the Skyline Project and the Security Life Building. But from where he sat, his view out the south window dominated that part of the city yet to feel the demolition ball and the bulldozer blade. There was room for him out there in that part of the city. It understood him and his kind. He licked his lips and thought he was lucky to get this space when he did.

Maxwell Potter was not a big man. On the contrary, he often appeared smaller than he was—five feet, eleven inches with his shoes on. When he stood erect, his otherwise thin body protruded a bit in front. Bad posture as a child, he always apologized; left his spine bent the wrong way, as though a hinge in his middle had sprung from sitting down frontwards. His wide shoulders and deep chest were lost in the ill-fitting clothes he wore, ready-mades from the racks over on Seventeenth Street, down toward the Union Station. Tear the labels out and they won't know the difference, was his dictum.

There was something singular about the shape and the size of his head. Thinning brown hair, combed straight back over an oversized skull, exposed pink, freckled skin. His

ruddy face, clean shaven and scented, was only starting to be-
tray the wrinkles of age, and then only when he lifted his eyebrows into a frown at some real or imagined affront. But his
head was large for his body, leaving the impression that his
body had not yet reached maturity.

Max looked expansively about the office. The walls,
covered with a heavy wheat-straw paper, were rich and
warm, the light from the partly shaded windows catching only
lightly the soft-glow ribs of the paper.

Spaced carefully around the room were pictures, stu-
diously selected from his own expensive, but limited, collection of graphics, their hard black frames and white mountings standing out like so many square windows in the burnt
yellow walls. The mountings? He looked at the Daumier near
the corner, by the window. Stupid framer. Rag paper only, on
both sides. Christ, do I have to remind you every time? he'd
yelled at the man in the hardware store. Want to rot that delicate rice paper with your stinkin' sulphur? The memory of
the framing of the Daumier still upset him. Damn, if you
want a job done right, you gotta do it yourself; that was his
dictum. A feeling of pride came over him as he turned his
gaze back to the south window.

Max settled comfortably into his chair. The cushion was
new and soft. Cover it once a year, whether it needs it or not,
he thought. The chair was one of his many symbols of success; with the passage of time it had become the center of his
worldly domain. His hands clenched and then relaxed on the
foam rubber arm cushions. He stretched and yawned, his
body taut, then relaxed. For a brief moment his eyes were
closed, only to pop open again, as though to catch the world
off guard.

Again, he stared out the south window. Out there were
the satraps of his growing insurance empire, and soon it
would extend to the Coast.

He looked for Pikes Peak again but could see only the
dull, leadened mass of cloud that had moved in from the
mountains beyond. The cloud cast a shadow over Max's deter-
mination to be happy, but only briefly. He smiled again, dis-

missing the distant cloud. That day he'd opened the new agency office in Colorado Springs. That showed 'em what I could do, he thought. Only in control of the company for six months and open a new agency office right in front of their own sleepy eyes. Her old man, the fruity pill peddler. Then he remembered his wife, Phyllis.

Turning to the desk, he picked up the phone, dialed outside and then his home again. This time it was the busy signal. His irritation mounting, he dropped the phone in the cradle. The twitching of his jaw increased. His fingers drummed nervously on the soft arm cushions of the chair.

Max sat staring at the floor, his back still, his head bobbing slightly, as though in time to a distant tune.

The light on the inter-office went on. "Yes, Irene." Max held tightly to the phone.

"Mister Potter, that was Mister Lawrence Langdon calling from Portland, Oregon, a while ago." She stressed Oregon.

"I know where Portland is, Irene." Why must she be so abrasive?

"Sounded rather urgent." She ignored his retort; her voice was distant and metallic.

"I'll call him back. Maybe this afternoon." He hesitated. "Oh, did he say anything about our project out there?" She seems always to put me on the defensive, he thought.

"No, Mister Potter, he didn't."

Now she was a bit abrasive, it seemed.

"I'll call him sometime today," he promised. He was staring out the window again, his mind wandering. "Thank you, Irene." He started to put down the phone, but stopped. "And, Irene. I told the others not to come back after lunch, but would you . . . ?"

"Yes, Mister Potter. I'll see that the mail is all taken care of and will lock up the office."

"Thanks, Irene. And a Merry Christmas to you."

"Merry Christmas to you, Mister Potter."

Without hanging up, he clicked the phone, dialed 9, and then his home again. She answered after the first ring.

"Phyllis?"

"Yes? Max." There was a long pause. "You sound a bit upset, Max." Then she giggled. "Did you call earlier, say ten —fifteen minutes ago?" Her voice was warm and cheerful.

"Yes." He found his voice. "Thought maybe you'd fallen down the stairs, or something." Damned trite thing to say, he thought.

"No, darling. I was in the shower." She giggled again, her smile coming to him over the phone. He tried to relax. "You wouldn't want me parading through the house in my all-together, would you?"

"Not unless I was there to pull the blinds." He fought to control his voice. Be friendly, he thought. She spoke excitedly again. Phyllis was part of the change that was to come into his life, and he didn't want to jeopardize any position he might have with her by appearing not to be himself. Phyllis, dependable, honest, trusting Phyllis. He closed his eyes and could see her in the shower. Suddenly, he wanted her. He wanted her as Phyllis, not as somebody else. Phyllis. Phyllis. He had been drumming her name into his head for weeks, to re-acquaint himself with it, to drive the name into the dark voids of his mind where other names had been and to reassure himself that the past was now past. Phyllis. Phyllis.

"Max?" Her voice was sober now. Was there concern?

"I only called to see how you were, Phyllis." His lips were dry; he licked them. "The offices are quiet this morning and I was sitting here, lonesome."

"That's sweet of you, Max."

"Yeah. Thought I'd call." Words. Words. The line was quiet for a long moment. Perspiration stood out on his forehead. "How you coming with the cards?" He couldn't think. "Need any help?"

"Kind of late to send any more out, although I see there are several in the mail we simply must answer."

"Who?" His nervousness increased.

"Oh, that new agent from Idaho—out in Boise? And that Basco What's-his-name from Los Angeles. I never could remember his name."

"Is that all?" His voice was too high and too loud. He licked his dry lips again.

"And a lot of company trade cards—they don't count."

The line was quiet again.

Finally, it was Phyllis talking. "Did you call just to read the mail, Max?" Her voice was petulant. "I'm jealous."

"No! No!" Max Potter was trembling. This is the turning point, he thought. Not even a Christmas card. She's dead. She's dead. Tracy. He wanted to cry her name. You're dead, Tracy. You're dead. Don't ever come back. Oh, God. Don't let her come back. Only Phyllis now. Only Phyllis. Phyllis. Only Phyllis.

"Max? Are you still there, Max?"

"Yes. Yes." He scrambled to his feet. Always stand up to think. Always. "I'm sorry, dear. Something out the window —one of the new United Airlines jets." Now he was functioning. "No, I didn't call only to read the mail. I wanted to ask you out to lunch today."

"Why, darling, that would be nice." She was cheerful once more, her words caressing his ear.

"We could go to that restaurant at the top of the Security Building or . . . "

"Always life insurance, even for lunch." She laughed teasingly as she said it.

"Or—now let me finish—to that little Greek restaurant over the street at the May-D&F." He was warming up to her now.

"I'll take the Greek. It would have to be a light something, but it sounds good. And maybe we can get a good window and watch the skaters in the Plaza." She was enthusiastic. "Remember, Max, when we used to stay over night at the Hilton just before Christmas so Roger could skate until closing? And then we'd draw the window curtains and watch the snow fall against the lights display at Civic Center?"

Why did she have to mention Roger? Max was quiet.

"I'm sorry, dear. I didn't mean to remind you." They were both quiet now. Finally, it was Phyllis who spoke. "But he has his own friends now, and he was invited to Vermont for the holidays. There's next year."

"But the smart little bastard didn't have to be so blunt in refusing to come home for Christmas."

"Now, Max." She was cross. "That's not fair. It was only when you insisted that he, as you say, got blunt."

"I know, Phyllis." Max paused. He couldn't think. Surely there was more to it than that, but he couldn't think. "You're right," he sighed. "Just hard to let him go, I guess. But, I might as well get used to it."

"That's right, Max. He's a man now." The line was quiet for a moment, and then: "But how about that date for lunch, Maxwell Potter?" She was friendly again, her voice warm and consoling.

"Well, how about it? At the Greek's?"

"Yes, that would be nice." Her voice sounded younger than he could recall in a long time.

"If I'm not at the restaurant, I'll be at the stamp or coin counter just inside the store."

"I know where it is. Roger would like something in stamps. See you at two." She gave him a kiss over the phone.

He wanted to return the kiss but couldn't. "See you." He put down the phone. Slowly, he let himself down into his chair.

Phyllis. Phyllis. For the first time in his life he was free.

Suddenly, he was young again. He could see her the day they first met at the University in Boulder. She was a violinist in the CU orchestra. She was pretty—long blonde hair falling over her slender shoulders as she sat alert, awaiting the director's nod. Then the smart snap of her wrist as she brought the instrument up to her chin. Strange. It was as though he were seeing his wife for the first time since that chance encounter so many years ago. Twenty-two years. Could it be that long?

Max tried to count the years. Something like that. His mind raced through time. Married at least twenty. Staring wide-eyed at the floor, he sat, pondering those spent years. He could see himself. He saw Roger, tiny at first and then as a young man entering college. He saw Roger's mother—there was Phyllis, captured in his inner vision as in the family album. His mind hurried on. There was a woman's body he'd shared all those years, a woman's body that had brought him joy and pleasure and had satisfied his sexual gratifications. But where was the girl he'd married? Had she become only an X-factor that he could look up in an actuarial table, a typical American woman and therefore a substitute for the average female, a norm that represented the sampling of her universe?

Max felt the chest pockets of his suit coat. Shoving back his chair, he stood up. From his hip pocket he took out his wallet. He unsnapped the plastic card case. Quickly, he thumbed through the worn and blurred bits of plastic envelopes. Feverishly, he pressed the sides of the plastic envelopes and peered in between the outside cards. There was a picture of Roger and him fishing. He took out the picture. Phyllis had snapped it. Damned good picture, too. There was one of Roger in scout camp up in Wyoming and another one of Roger and him in the back yard at the old house before they moved. He looked through the envelopes again. There was nothing of Phyllis.

Lately, when he had time to think about it, Max had tried to reconstruct the years of their marriage. He had sought some focal point, or points. He had foreseen this turning point in his own life and had tried to prepare for it. He had set a date for it, the day before Christmas. If he heard nothing from Tracy McClosky by that time, the file was closed. The time had arrived, and he was ready. But was he? Until he was sure that he would not hear from her, he could not turn his back on the past. Until then he could not tear down the wall that separated him from his reality. Max was aware of that wall—he had constructed it, nerve by nerve, thought by thought, and emotion by emotion. And, Tracy hadn't even answered his letter with a Christmas card.

Max leaned his head against the window and closed his eyes. Slowly, he raised his left hand to his forehead to protect it from the cold glass. His clenched fists were white against the pink flush of his face.

Don't think about her. Only Phyllis from now on. Phyllis. Phyllis. He sagged against the window. Faintly, he could hear the jingling of the Salvation Army bell down at the Christmas booth on the street below.

Cold, Max backed away from the window and walked over to the filing cabinet nearest the door. From near the back of the top drawer he took out a bottle of Jim Beam and broke the seal. Using the cap as a measure, he poured it full. Cautiously, he walked over to the west window and looked out across Civic Center at the Christmas display adorning the front of the City-County Building. To twenty-two years, Phyllis. His face was lined. He saw his face in the reflection of the window. He raised the whisky to his lips and drank.

Chapter 2

"Yes, Irene."

"Mister Adler to see you."

"Send . . . "

"Don't bother, Irene." The voice penetrated the walls of the office. "Good morning, Maxwell."

The man was Vincent P. Adler, Executive Vice-President of Mountain-Plains Life Insurance Company. Vince Adler was a rotund, bulbous man. Just past sixty, he had the smooth skin of a child. His thick black hair, tinted weekly in the beauty shop on the second floor downstairs, gave youth to his otherwise corpulent build. Tastefully tailored in imported woolens, his person neatly groomed, Vince Adler conveyed an air of dynamism that caused the casual stranger to credit him, not Maxwell Potter, with the presidency of the company. When he smiled, strong, white teeth flashed between dark reddish-blue lips. In anger, the blackish-gray beard roots of his face brought out a granite hardness to his once finely chiseled features. Although a giant of a man, he was light and graceful in his walk. As he entered the office, he opened and closed the door without changing the pace of his step.

"By all means, Vince . . . "

"Thank you, Maxwell."

"Take a seat."

"I can't. You're in it."

"And damned well intend to stay there, I'd say."

"We'll see." Vince Adler chuckled. He didn't look at Max but seated himself in a large blue sofa chair, just past the end of the desk, against the wall by the west window. "One of these days, my boy, you're gonna see the wisdom of ol' Vince's advice and spike your guns and retire. We'll see." Vincent Adler settled firmly into the chair.

"That'll be the day." Rising easily to his feet, Max turned to Vince. "Have a piece of rope," he said, opening a cigar box that matched the wood of his desk.

"Thank you, Maxwell." Vince took the cigar, looked at it, as he always looked at the cigars Maxwell Potter offered him, bit off one end and spit the stub of cigar onto the carpet. He stuck the other end between his fat, dark lips. "Now, do you have a light?" Vince Adler sat, his big hands resting loosely on the soft-cushioned arms of the chair.

Max threw a book of paper matches to him.

"Thanks." The big man held a match to the cigar; large flowering puffs of smoke rose from before the west window.

"And, to what do I owe this visit, Mister Vice-President —the day before Christmas?" Max was at his desk again. He looked up, a friendly enough smile pulling at the corners of his mouth.

"As a matter of fact, I was just getting ready to leave for the holiday." Vince pulled on the cigar. Rich blue smoke drifted slowly across the narrow distance separating the two men. Max Potter waved away the smoke as it crowded around his face.

"Christ, I forgot," said Max, choking. "You don't smoke those damned things—you incinerate them."

"Take up the sport, Maxwell." Vince hollowed out his cheeks as he drew in the smoke, then blew it straight out in front of him. "You don't notice it that way."

Max was surprised at Vince's presence. He was supposed to be on vacation, starting last Friday.

"Wanted to go over the Oregon caper before I went away for the holiday," said Vince, at last, and serious now. He took the cigar from his mouth, inspected the long gray ash that was forming. With practiced dexterity, Adler flipped the cigar, the ashes falling in small droplets on the thick-piled, gold-colored carpet. "We gotta give that baby a lotta hard thought, Maxwell."

Max did not look up but turned to the south window. Unconsciously, his gaze scanned the horizon for Pikes Peak. The cloud mass that hid the peak was larger now. "I think I have it well in hand, Vince," he said. He stood up, still looking out the window. Why doesn't he leave? I gotta get a present for Phyllis. Max stole a glance at his watch without really seeing it. Mind's wandering. Don't antagonize him. "We've been through it all before, and I see no reason to back out now."

"I'm not sayin' to back out." Vince Adler knocked the ashes from his cigar again. "I'm sayin' there's a lot of business in the Sequoia National that we don't want."

"I know you've said that, but damnit, we either buy the company or we don't. That premium volume will give us the rating we need. For two years we've shot for *Best's 400* and by God, we're gonna make it this time."

"We might make it one year, then what? Goddamnit, that group health and accident crap isn't for us. It wasn't for Sequoia National, either. Any good, it wouldn't be up for grabs, now." His puffing on his cigar was rapid.

"All right, you got all the angles figured on this," said Max, exasperation in his voice. "We give up the group and what have we got left?" He turned from the window. "That's a good third of the premium income."

"For one thing, Maxwell, we have a charter to operate in Oregon, which we don't have now. And that's something. And through that charter we have access to the growing California market through the Sequoia outlets. Why, have you kept track of the population explosion in California alone? Those are two things that sold me on the idea in the first place. You, too, if you haven't forgotten it in this damned drive of yours to hit *Best's 400*."

"That's only part of it." Max Potter was pacing now, between his chair and the window. "There's more to it than that. We built up a case to the stockholders on how this acquisition will add to our income and our insurance in force. Getting them to drop the par value on that stock from five dollars to one so's we can use treasury stock was no easy thing, you know."

Vince Adler sighed. He took the cigar from his mouth and held it gently in his right hand. He rested both hands on his crossed knees, the smoking cigar pointing straight out ahead of him. "We've been through this so many times, Maxwell. Nobody worked harder than you to put this package together. But, after looking at the business on the books, that group stuff is a frosting Mountain-Plains can't afford. You know that. If that's the kind of business we wanted, we could have had it years ago. We're not set up for it."

"We can damned well get set up for it, then." Maxwell Potter spun on his subordinate. "Hell, Vince, that's the answer to the insurance industry—flexibility."

"Possibly, Maxwell, but specialization is what's paying off."

Max's anger was rising now. "Just because we've done well in one line doesn't mean we have to stay there. Sequoia National simply had poor management and ran out of reserves."

"Sequoia National had good management until they went into the pimping business. That's what you mean, Maxwell." Vincent Adler sighed again. "They damned well ran out of reserves, all right." His voice was loud but not unfriendly now. As he talked, he puffed, the cigar turning slowly and evenly between the thumb and index finger of his right hand. "You get a few million on the books, then go start watchin' the popularity charts. You go after the office help, the sick grandmas ready for retirement, the high school football teams and all those snot-nosed kids goin' to work today with nickels and dimes in their pockets. Good contacts, you're told. You can work it like a mine. The customers'll think of the company when they want other insurance. Hell. People think of money when they think insurance, and we won't have any to think about if we start cackling in the wrong nests." He took the cigar from his mouth and flecked the ashes onto the gold carpet.

Max stood watching. The arrogant bastard, he thought. The ashes now formed a powdery gray cloud on the light gold carpet. Max did not speak.

It was Vince who spoke. "Why do you think I pulled your ass out of the wastebasket that time when Guthry was about to call the trash man?" He looked Max in the eye, now. "To turn this into a sickness club?"

"You pulled my ass out of the wastebasket?" Max's face was red now. "What wastebasket was that, you damned fruit?"

"Ah, I thought there was more to you than we've been seein' 'round here lately," said Vince, smiling and sucking carefully on the cigar.

"I've battled the Board to save your skin every year for the last ten," said Max, ignoring the comments of the fat man by the window. "And simply because you're a damned good sales manager. Don't give me that 'I saved your ass' line." Max snorted the last words, looking his complacent vice president in the eyes. "If you weren't a good sales manager, you'd be workin' the alleys down there now with your Larimer Street cronies."

"Tut, tut, Maxwell," said Adler, flicking the cigar. "Flattery . . . " He did not finish but placed the smoldering cigar between his dark-red lips and sucked gently and evenly, the sweet smelling smoke partly blotting out his face. "You were made president of this two-bit firm 'cause you came up with what I thought then was a new idea. It wasn't until later that I realized it was because you were lazy and wasn't an idea at all. Only a rationalization of your success." He took the cigar from his mouth and looked at it. "Be that as it may, we moved from run-of-the-mill credit life to master-debtor coverage insurance. You know that. We are probably one of the most highly specialized life underwriters in the business, at least in the Rocky Mountain Empire. Now, I say buy up Sequoia

National, sell off all that group health crap. Yes, all of it. The group life with it. Pump what cash there is back into Sequoia's reserves and pray the damned outfit doesn't fold 'til we can completely absorb it into Mountain-Plains. And if your approach still has any life in it, we'll mop up on the Coast."

"Sorry, Vince," said Max, fatigue in his voice. "My mind's made up." Max had stopped pacing now; he sat down.

"You know what's wrong with you, Maxwell?" The big man spoke softly, his voice not unkind but not friendly. "You didn't get enough toys when you were a kid. This insurance company . . . " Vince raised both hands and waved them to include the whole office complex. Ashes fell from the cigar as he moved his arms. "Yeah, the whole damned building; the territory. You think you can just wind it up every morning like a toy."

"Well, it's worked for twelve years, hasn't it?" asked Max, smiling at his fat vice president. "How can you fight success?"

"Why didn't we make *Best's 400* these last two years, then?" Vince winked at Max across the desk.

"Because the sales manager began to think like Guthry," said Max, the smile gone, his face taut, his mouth a thin line across his face.

"Speaking of Timothy," said Vince, a lack of concern in his voice, "he can cause you a hell of a lot of trouble in Oregon if you don't watch your step." Vince Adler held the cigar up and looked at it. It was nearly a stub now. "Throw me those matches again, Maxwell."

"You never returned them." The tension broken, Max relaxed.

The half-burned cigar in his mouth, the fat man searched his pockets for the matches. "Right again, Maxwell." Vince Adler lit the cigar, his big fleshy cheeks the working bellows of a small forge. Blue smoke swirled about the big face once more. "I sided with you twelve years ago, Maxwell," said Vince, ignoring the short interlude, " 'cause I thought you were right. But Tim musta learned a lot working with the big companies. If his bunch can raise the capital the commissioner requires, they can have Sequoia National at the drop of a hat."

"Tim Guthry can't raise the capital; I've seen to that." He tried to inject authority into his statement. He knew it was a lie. He only hoped that time was on his side. The Oregon Insurance Commission had given until January 15 as the deadline for reorganization of the ailing Sequoia National, and no one else was in serious contention. Of this Max was certain. "He's a has-been in insurance and in everything else."

"Don't count him out yet."

"I have."

"I haven't."

"As you wish, then." Dismiss the bore and maybe he'll leave, thought Max.

Both men were silent for a moment, then it was Vince who spoke: "I guess that's the information I came for, Maxwell.

"I hope to sign the binding papers of intent the day after Christmas—at least before the first of the year." Max picked up a cigar from the box on his desk and rolled the long scented tobacco stick between the fingers of both hands. "That's what the stockholders want, and they still own the company, you know." Max did not look up.

"I know, Maxwell," said the fat man. "How well I know." There was a note of weariness in his voice.

"Was there something else, Vince?" Max was impatient.

"Oh, there's always something else, but most of it must always wait," said the fat man. Vince was finished with his cigar now. Uncrossing his legs, he lifted his fat left foot and ground the still-burning cigar into the bottom of the heel of his left shoe, the charred tobacco falling black among the gray ashes on the carpet. Unceremoniously, he threw the dead butt into the corner, between the windows. "But you raised a good point, one pregnant with possibilities. You mentioned stockholders. Do you know how many stockholders Mountain-Plains has?"

"Oh, four or five thousand, I'd guess. Why?"

"Four thousand, two hundred and thirty-eight, to be exact."

"Well, I'll be damned." Maxwell feigned surprise and admiration.

"In thirty-nine states, including Hawaii and Alaska."

"See what I've done for the company?" Max was mocking.

"And forty-three per cent of them live in Colorado." Vince paused. With effort, he pushed himself to his feet. The low blue sofa chair creaked under his weight. "And that forty-three per cent controls over sixty per cent of the vote." Wheezing, Vince Adler stepped up to the desk. After a long pause, he continued: "I learned something a long time ago, Maxwell. A smart corporate president hides the stockholders list, but a smarter vice president finds it, no matter where it's hidden." He turned to leave. "And, damnit, Maxwell," he said without warning, "if we can afford cigars, can't we also afford ash trays?" Vince crossed the office, stopping at the door. Slowly, he faced Max. "Merry Christmas, Maxwell," he said, smiling. He turned and left the room.

Chapter 3

Damned bully. He saved my ass? The crust. Max Potter screwed off the lid on the Jim Beam, poured the lid full and drank. The next time the Board brings up his name, they can have a field day with him. The ungrateful pig. Max slammed the file drawer and returned to his desk.

Without seating himself, he started opening and closing drawers. Impatient, he sat down and removed the bottom drawer to the right of the knee hole.

The drawer was large and deep, but light. Bruskly, he emptied its contents on the desk top in front of him. Three golf balls bounced and rolled across the desk and were gone. Max placed the empty drawer on the floor beside his chair. Snatching up a pair of wadded, maroon colored swimming trunks, he stretched them, turned and held them up to the light. Shaking his head, he dropped the crumpled trunks into the empty drawer and turned his attention back to the assorted bric-a-brac harvested from the sporting and country clubs that formed an important part in his empire building. A pair of run-down golf shoes. These he tossed over the end of the desk. Where the hell did they come from? he thought. His irritation rising, he scattered the debris over the top of the desk. He paused for a moment, taking in the scene. Then, with his long left arm, he swept the polished oak surface clean, the tangled mess on his desk falling into the empty drawer and onto the floor nearby. He picked up the drawer and, cautiously, slid it back into place.

The top drawer, and smaller of the two, was heavy as he removed it from the desk. With the snap of his wrists, he emptied the contents of this drawer onto the desk. There, on top of the pile, was the object of his quest—a small, square glass ash tray, dusty in the soft light. Using the right elbow of his suit coat, he polished the glass until the rich blue pigment sparkled. He pushed the ash tray to the middle of his desk and sat back to inspect it.

His eyes wandered to the junk on his desk: a broken stapler, cheap plastic letter openers from ad agencies around town, old desk calendars, paper clips and dried out rubber bands. Something dark caught his eye. Protruding from under the disarrayed desk accouterments was the butt of a gun, the waffle pattern of the black rubber handle dust covered and dull looking. Max picked up the gun. The permit! He couldn't remember whether or not it was up to date. A 25 caliber. He turned it over in his hand. A cruel little piece at short range, he thought. Reverently, he wiped the dust from the gun with his left hand. He broke it, careful not to lose the cartridges. He smelled the oil and smiled. He blew through the barrel, as though blowing away smoke from an exploded shell. Take my chair away from me, will he? For a moment Max Potter sat staring at the opened pistol. Shuddering, the spell broken, Max snapped the pistol closed and noisily raked the heap of discards back into the drawer. On top of these he threw the gun. He replaced the drawer; with his handkerchief, he wiped the lint and dust from the top of the desk. Then, satisfied with his effort, he sat quietly, looking at the square blue ash tray in the middle of the desk. For a long time he did not move.

The inter-office line lit up.

"Yes," said Max, pushing the button and lifting the receiver, his voice low, but sharp.

"The mail is here, Mister Potter."

"Bring it in, Irene." There was sarcasm in his voice.

"I thought you might be interested in the one letter . . ."

Maxwell jumped forward in his chair. He did not speak. It was Tracy; she had acknowledged his letter after all. He started to hang up but stopped. Irene didn't know anthing about Tracy. No one else knew about Tracy; it was his secret. His mind came back to the letter. "You've read it already, Irene?" A little sharper than before, he hoped.

"No." Irene's voice was cold. "It's from Mister Worley and is probably in answer to the one you dictated last Thursday."

"Yes, Irene. It probably is." Max was tired. "Please bring in the mail—all of it."

"Very well, Mister Potter."

Max cradled the phone and sat up straight in his chair. Slowly, he raised his hands to his face. I love you, Tracy. It's Christmas, remember? It's our last chance. Max closed his eyes, hard, and swallowed. I gotta let you go, Tracy. His forehead cupped in the palms of both hands, he sat, elbows hard on the desk top. I was a coward, Tracy. I'm sorry. He could see her, the way she looked only a few weeks ago, the last week in October. He shuddered. Coarse and fat now; but she hadn't always been that way. Before the war, Tracy. We could have made something of that. In time we could have come out OK, Tracy. Did she let herself go because of me? And there was his letter to her after his return home. Nothing Phyllis would have objected to; only a simple message to open communications after so many years. And now, not even a Christmas card. How long I've waited for you, Tracy. How old were you? Fourteen? Fifteen? Seventeen? He couldn't remember. But it was no good, Tracy. They never would have approved. Max swallowed hard to keep control of himself. But I loved you then, Tracy, when I knew you before the war. The linings of his nostrils smarted. It's Christmas, Tracy. Remember? The twenty-ninth Christmas without you. The muscles in his right jaw tightened; his teeth gritted—ground together. He was perspiring. And, almost aloud: "You fat bitch, you're dead, now. You're dead."

Max sagged, exhausted, in his chair. His eyes were moist. He could sense a torturous replay forming in his mind;

he shook his head. Phyllis. Phyllis. He tried to jam the replay. Don't let her come back, Phyllis. She's a stranger, Phyllis. I don't need her any more.

But the message wouldn't jam. Already the replay was beginning. I love you, Tracy. It's Christmas, remember?

Max heard the door latch click. Quickly, he dried his eyes lightly with the tips of his fingers and opened his eyes.

Irene had come and gone.

Before him, neatly placed in a row were three envelopes, still sealed. Simon A. Worley's in the middle. Max glanced at the other two—obviously bills or PR mailings. One was from a garden spray firm, the other an oil company whose name was only slightly familiar to him. Picking up the letter from Worley, the attorney, Max raked the others aside, both falling on the carpet by his chair.

Max tried to remember the reason for writing to Worley. The lawyer had been attorney of record for Mountain-Plains ever since the company's incorporation. Max held the envelope up to the light and started to tear it open. Changing his mind, he reached inside the drawer with the letter openers and brought out a long white plastic blade with a face stamped in black, the mouth laughing and the eyes in the face rolling around with every jiggle of the hand. Deftly, he slit open the envelope. Quickly, he scanned the letter.

Not waiting to finish the letter, Max reached for the telephone and dialed. He waited impatiently for the ringing to end.

"_____"

"Yes, fine. I'll hold."

As he waited he reread the first part of the letter. He sucked at his lower lip as he read and waited.

"_____"

"Yes. Thank you."

"_____"

"Simon? Max. I just got your letter on the Platte River property."

"_____"

"I know, Simon. But the city's interest in a park for that land's something recent; since the sixty-five flood."

"_____"

"To hell with the park board. I've had that land a lot longer than that bastard, whoever-he-is, has had his nose on that park."

"_____"

"But what about my use of the land? I have some rights, you know."

"_____"

"And when are they gonna build that park? From what I hear, that clean-up job alone's gonna take a long time and a lotta money."

"_____"

"Well, if they don't know, what the hell they doin' sayin' they're gonna take my land for a park?"

"_____"

"How much do they intend to pay for land down there?"

"_____"

"By the square foot? Remember, I got both sides a the stream on that lot. Hell, you've seen the lot—and the plans for the building."

"_____"

"Thanks, Simon. That building'll revolutionize construction, if not architecture, west of the Mississippi at least. Mountain-Plains Insurance Company, Home Office, sittin' astraddle of the whole goddamned river."

"_____"

"Of course we will, Simon. You have to think positively. If you'd get your head out and get on with the job, that is."

"_____"

"To hell with the city council and those zoning quacks. That's my land and there isn't any zoning limitation down there for what I have in mind."

"_____"

"I know. I know. That bastard wants a park."

"_____"

"Yeah. Well, maybe we can't straddle the river, but otherwise, there's no restriction."

"_____"

"You figured it already? How much would they pay?"

"_____"

"Between thirty-five and forty thousand! What the hell, Simon? You in with them?"

"_____"

"Whaddaya mean, what's come over me?"

"_____"

"Of course it's like me. But I know when I'm bein' taken royally."

"_____"

"OK, OK, Simon. Calm down. But thirty-five to forty thousand dollars! Hell, Simon, I got more'n sixty thousand of my own money in all that paper work—that damned architect cousin of your'n—and I'm supposed to donate it all to the city park commission for a lousy park. Christ, it was all car bodies before the flood."

"_____"

"Sure, I remember, Simon. You said: 'Don't buy it.' But it was a steal and I did buy it. Now, get that city council off my back. Soon's that West Coast deal goes through, this mouse cage we're in now's gonna be too tight. We gotta move, Simon."

"_____"

"I know you did, Simon. Appeal the decision."

"_____"

"Appeal the appeal then, damnit. Hell, I'm no lawyer. That's your job."

"_____"

"How's that? Well, when would they buy the land?"

"_____"

"Tied up indefinitely—'til they can spare the funds?"

"_____"

"You just take care of that, Simon."

"_____"

"Well, then, go find someone who can."

Max banged down the telephone. What's with Simon? Keep a man on the payroll for seventeen years and he starts gettin' sloppy. He oughta know there are a helluva lot of lawyers in the city of Denver.

Still angry, Max rose stiffly from his desk and walked over to a closet door beside the filing cabinets. Searching his pockets, he found his key case. Quietly, he unlocked the door to the closet and pulled out a tall cardboard box jammed with various and sundry maps, charts and blueprints, some neat, crisp tubes of stiff white paper; others frayed and mashed. From the box Max pulled out a round leather case, nearly four inches across, with a padlock on the zipper that went around one end of the case. He carried the case back to his desk. Taking a small key from the center drawer of his desk, he unlocked the leather case and shook the contents onto his desk. Smiling, Max unrolled a sheaf of drawings, spreading them across the desk. Before his eyes the future Home Office of Mountain-Plains Life Insurance Company came to life.

For six years those plans had been in that leather case. Not always the same plans, but plans, nevertheless. At first the drawings had been crude sketches—the projections of dreams where only junked car bodies and discarded cement slab held forth. These early plans had been rash enough. And they had nothing to do with Maxwell Potter's dreams for his insurance company. As a matter of fact, he'd had the land before he was made president of the company. The Platte River property was only a side line—at first. Perhaps low-income housing. Who the hell else would live there?

Then he'd talked to Simon Worley about the land and that he'd like to build on it some day. Too, Simon Worley's cousin, Douglas Worley Miller, out of Cincinnati, had been only recently admitted to the bar, so to speak, in architecture in Colorado and was sorely in need of a client. A very talented fellow, Simon Worley had said. Such was the beginning of Maxwell Potter's most ambitious dream, the Maxwell Potter Plaza. That was a little more than three years ago.

Maxwell pushed the button on the inter-office phone.

"Irene."

"Yes, Mister Potter."

"Please get Tom Rheinert on the phone."

"Who, Mister Potter?"

"Mister Thomas Rheinert, plant engineer in this building, Irene."

"Thank you, Sir."

Max listened to the noise of the telephone circuitry. It was amazing, modern communications. In his new building there'd be the latest—perhaps closed TV for intra-building communications. Maybe not in the insurance building itself, but in the Potter House closed circuit TV would be nice between his suite and the convention office, and the kitchen. He'd have his suite in the Potter House and his office in the Mountain-Plains Building hooked up with the latest computers and. . ."

"This is Potter—up in 1216."

"_____"

"Yes. Is Tom there?"

"_____"

"Tom Rheinert." Am I the only one he knows around here? thought Max. "Oh, you call him Rheiny? Is Rheiny there?"

"_____"

"When will he be back?"

"_____"

"I saw him working on number four elevator earlier this morning—him and the Dover man."

"_____"   *this*

"OK. Please tell him I'd like to see him as soon as possible."

Maxwell Potter was standing hunched over the spread drawings when Tom Rheinert was announced. He was erasing on one of the drawings as Tom came in.

"Come in, Tom. Come in."

Rheinert entered, drifting in like a tall ghost, his feet seeming not to touch the carpet.

Max hurried around the corner of the desk; the two men shook hands.

Tom Rheinert was tall and lanky, some four inches taller than Max. In his mid-fifties, Rheinert's gaunt face was ancient, especially around the eyes. Leathery and wrinkled, his hollow cheeks seemed to sag, exposing the jagged, yellowed teeth of his lower jaw. And the gray thin-line mustache that was never level, tugged as a weight on the bluish-black areas under his eyes. His elongated head was fringed with a fleece of hair, a white, fuzzy garland around a skull of opaquely hued skin. Cat-like in his movements, he drifted unnoticed through the labyrinth of rooms and corridors that made up the Professional Exchange Building. His face was a solemn mask as he shook hands with Maxwell Potter, President of the Mountain-Plains Insurance Company.

"Well, Tom, whataya think of it now?" With Rheinert's left elbow in his right hand, Max steered the older man over to look at the drawings.

"Not bad, since they're mostly mine." Rheinert looked intently at the plans. "You're puttin' in another landin' pad, huh?"

"Fast and efficient local transit—that's my dictum, Tom. We might take this one on the hotel outa the plans. Too much traffic up there might be unsound. But it's the concept that's important."

"But you keep movin' things like that around and we're never gonna get the engineering specs out."

"That's Miller's problem. You and me, we'll do the dreamin' and plannin'." Both men stared at the smudged top drawing. "By the time Miller's finished with the home office, we'll be ready with the rest a this for him to finish up. Won't he be surprised?" Max rubbed his hands together.

"You can bet your dear ass on that," said the gaunt Rheinert, softly, lifting a blue ash tray from the drawing corner nearest him and looking for the most recent alterations in the plans.

"Did I ever tell you I hold a degree in engineering?" said Max. Max was standing erect now, stuffing a somewhat rumpled shirttail down into his ill-fitting trousers.

"You did." Rheinert was noncommittal in his answer. He bent over the desk, scrutinizing closely the paper before him. "And what in hell, may I ask, is that?" He ran a claw-like finger along the indicated Platte River stream bed.

"Remember on Miller's plans for the Home Office— where the building sits astraddle the river? I'm suggestin' we put in a quay there along the river—like in France."

Rheinert did not answer but continued to look over the chart.

"It's gonna make the whole river front look different, Tom—the Home Office, the hotel, the apartments and all." Max was expansive now. "Better get that letter of resignation in, boy. Things are rollin'. Sometime after the first a the year."

"Humph! You're not talkin' to me about resigning, I hope," said Rheinert, straightening up. "I'll wait 'til I see those backers' money, if you don't mind."

"By the first of the year things'll be fallin' into place, you'll see."

"Anything else, Mister Potter? I got some rest rooms that's jammed up." Rheinert sniffed as he said it.

Annoyed, Max tried to ignore the man. "Yes, there is, Tom. I'd like to have you take that top drawing—the one with the latest changes. Take it with you and clean up the smudges. And draw in that quay and finish out that new landin' pad." Max moved the blue ash tray and jerked the top drawing free. He rolled it into a tight tube. "Like to have it back by the twenty-ninth, if possible." Feeling inside the long drawer of his desk, he found a rubber band. Noisily, he rolled the rubber band down over the tubed drawing; Max handed it to the building engineer. "Want to show it to the Board."

"Like I said, I got a lotta rest rooms jammed up." Without further comment, the tall man clutched the drawings in his right hand. He turned and walked toward the door.

"Merry Christmas, Tom." My voice was too plaintive, Max thought.

Rheinert opened the door and, without turning, left the office.

Chapter 4

The morning light was failing. The carpet, golden in the earlier sunlight, was now yellow and dark. Along the walls of the office the wheat straws of the wallpaper cast shadows within their textures. The luminosity of the white-mounted etchings on the walls gave way to stark contrasts of blacks and whites. A Kollwitz figure, a consumptive baby in the crib of the Weavers, trembled to the vibrations of a low-flying jet winging out over Colorado General, spewing its black fog of kerosene exhaust. Far to the south the heavy cloud mass that had earlier moved in from the mountains was maneuvering in an extensive advance along the entire front range. A white Christmas appeared imminent.

Maxwell Potter was hungry. He looked at his watch—at least four hours until he'd meet Phyllis. He couldn't remember breakfast, and the more he thought about food his hunger mounted. Something sweet. Picking up the phone, Max punched inter-office. He let it buzz. Again, he looked at his watch. Damn, when you want one of them. Try the sales desk, maybe. The light from the telephone base blinked mockingly up at him. If the enemy is smart, he will attack this country during the coffee break, he thought. He hung up.

Quickly, Max rolled up the remaining drawings, inserted them into the leather case, affixed the padlock and returned the case to the closet. With a secure snap, the closet door locked. Max swtiched on the ceiling light and, straightening himself to full height, stood before the west window inspecting his person in the reflected light from the glass. He frowned at what he saw. Smile, damnit, be happy. This is Christmas. As he went by the filing cabinet, he thought of the bottle of Jim Beam, and paused. Foregoing temptation, Max smiled, flicked off the light and stepped into the outer reception office.

Irene's office was quiet. Max stared at the emptiness. And yet there was a difference. It was the tree. Funny, he'd not seen the Christmas tree, there to the left of the door where you entered from the hall. Musta put it up this morning, he thought. Smiling, Max enjoyed the tree; happy, he opened the door and left the office.

At the elevator Max had a thought—something was amiss. It had been some time, months perhaps, since he'd bought his own coffee. He wasn't sure of the procedure. Damned, if that wasn't right. Last summer, about June or July. All coin-operated, serve-yourself center down in the basement. Feeling in his pockets, he found nothing but his key case and a chipped Boy Scout knife. After pondering the situation for an instant, Max retraced his steps to Irene's office.

Petty cash! There'd be plenty of change there. Throwing open the door, Max advanced upon his secretary's desk. Rummaging quickly through the drawers of the modularly arranged desk, his quest did not meet with success. But it is one of her responsibilities to maintain petty cash! Max protested to himself.

Then he heard footsteps. They were light, quick footsteps in the hall. A woman's walk. Through the crack behind the half-opened door he saw her coming down the hall; she was short and slender, only a girl. Max interrupted his search for the petty cash and watched her. She was blonde, her hair neatly shaped in front: a slight wave swept from left to right just above the eyes. The cut of the hair fell to the lobes of her ears, which were set with small pearls, like the perfume ads he'd admired in *Vogue*. Her dress was of a warm gray jersey, a mini skirt, and with a belt. Her hands full of envelopes, she entered Irene's office.

"Hey, you, Miss."

"Me?" The young woman stopped, startled. She turned.

"Yes, you. I'm looking for some money. You got any? Irene'll pay you back."

"No," she said, her surprise gone, "but I know where you can get a loan." The girl flashed Max a friendly smile. "Your credit any good?"

"I didn't ask you to get fresh."

"It's the season. Christmas cheer and all that." She started to turn away, but stopped. "What are you doing, playing Santa Claus to the crew with the office stamp money?" Laughing, she turned and continued on through the office, into the sales section and disappeared.

Max watched her go. Her well-formed legs, with the dress three inches above the knees, seemed to prance as she went past him. So that's what Vince dangles in front of the boys to keep their attention. That's sales: no brains but gimmicks and plenty of class, he thought.

He turned his attention back to his search for the petty cash hoard. It had to be there; Board action had provided for it. He remembered seeing it in the corporate minutes. And too, office entertainment was one of the perquisites of his office.

He did not hear her coming this time.

"You're Mister Potter, aren't you?"

It was Max's turn to be startled. He knocked the dictating machine to the floor, the recording cannister rolling across the yellow carpet and into the hallway.

"Yes. Have we met?" Max picked up the broken machine and laid it on Irene's chair.

"No, but I recognize you when I see you."

Her voice was not as high as when she had entered the office. It was, he thought, more like a melody than a voice, anyway. Why hadn't he noticed her before? "I was looking for some change for the automat down in the basement. Would you join me in a cup of coffee?" God, she looks young. Without looking at her, he started putting the things on the top of the desk back into the drawers.

"Not coffee; not that canned stuff, thank you." She stood watching him.

"You have the advantage on me." He stopped what he was doing and looked up at the young woman. "What's your name?"

"Oh, pardon me. I'm Gloria Everetts, twenty-two years old, five feet, five inches tall, slender, warm personality, punctual, capable stenographer and all-around office help and almost graduated from college." She paused in her recital; then she giggled. "Oh, and she enjoys Christmas office parties." But this time she did not giggle. "How's that for a moniker?" Her face was sober now.

"That about makes us equal, I guess." Max looked at his hands—a bottle of correction fluid in one and a box of rubber bands in the other. "Glad to meet you, Gloria." Damn, I'm more'n twice her age, he thought. "I guess you're right about the coffee. Usually, Irene, here, gets coffee for us, me, when I want it. Won't you come in? I . . ." He hesitated. But, what the hell, she said she's over the age limit, he thought. "I've been havin' a little Christmas party here in my office. Please join me." He held out his right hand to usher her in. He dropped the correction fluid onto the desk, wiped his hand on his suit coat and rose from the desk.

"But, I'm working, Mister Potter." She was being coy, now, he thought.

"So am I, Miss Everetts." He chuckled, then stopped. "It is Miss, isn't it?" He looked at her left hand as he said it. "Yes, I see you are." He stood behind Irene's desk, his right hand still outstretched toward his own office door.

"Yes, it is Miss, but a girl can always hope." She smiled at Max but didn't move.

"Well, Miss Everetts, we can hope just as well over a little bit more of Christmas cheer as well as standing here gaping at each other."

"But what about my boss? I'm a punctual and capable, etc., etc., office girl, remember?"

"Don't you worry about your boss, now. I know him like a brother." She's teasing me now, thought Max. "Anyway, he's gone for the holiday."

"Well, in that case, why don't we?" The young woman entered his office.

Max started to follow her into the office, but stopped. "Damnit," he said, snapping his fingers, his right hand shaking a bit. "Make yourself at home," he called after her. "I'll be right back." Cups, glasses, paper cups. Frantically, Maxwell Potter raced from one office to the other in the Mountain-Plains complex, looking for the proper drinking utensils. Where was everyone? Not a soul in sight. In the ad layout room he found it. But there was only one. In the cupboard above the work table was a tall fluted tumbler filled with sharpened pencils, points upward. Max grabbed the glass and dumped the pencils onto the shelf of the cupboard, slamming the cupboard door as he left. Across the hall in the men's room he washed the glass, drying it on a snatched handful of paper towels.

"You have some fine pictures, Mister Potter." Gloria was standing admiring his Edvard Munch, a small etching of a little girl.

"Oh, you know something about art?" said Max. He stopped. "Paid a thousand dollars for that little picture out in Pasadena. Hard to find these days." Pleased, he walked up to the young woman. "Munch was a very unhappy man; in love with his sister, I think it was. Too bad. He was a great artist, though."

"Yes, and you are fortunate to find one of his etchings." Because of her height, she had to look up to properly view the pictures. "Hold onto it. They're very rare."

"Oh, I intend to." More brains over there in sales than I thought. It amazed Max.

"How about that drink, now, Miss Everetts?" Max was at the filing cabinet.

"Sure, why not?" She took a few steps along the wall, still looking at the pictures. "And a Barlock; and signed. Why," and she clapped her hands, "they're all signed." She giggled again. "It must be wonderful to be able to collect fine prints like these."

"It is." Maxwell was pouring the drinks. "Money helps, but it's the studyin' and the lookin' that's the thing. Me, I'm at heart and by trainin' an engineer, believe it or not. But, the fine arts, that's what's important."

"That's what they say. I mean serious people find art—how do you say it?—acculturating." She was looking up at his Kathy Kollwitz.

"How do you want your drink?"

"One shot on the rocks."

"I don't have any ice—ah, it all melted."

"What's the choice, then?"

"Glass full, or half full."

"Half full."

"I was afraid you'd say that." Max stood before the filing cabinet, the tall fluted glass brim full of Jim Beam.

"I'll just drink what I want," she said, reaching for the glass.

"Just a minute." Max tipped the glass, the rich amber liquid running back into the bottle. "Good whisky," he said, looking at Gloria. Their eyes met; they both smiled.

Gloria giggled. "Your good whisky is filing the filling cabinet, Mister Potter." She giggled again, her face flushed.

"You're drunk, Miss Everetts." Max laughed. God, she's pretty, he thought.

Giggling, Gloria pointed to the bottle.

"Sonofabitch." Max raised the lip of the fluted glass. Spilled whisky glazed the top of the filing cabinet and was dripping in long riverlets into the open files. Setting the glass down on the cabinet, Max reached for his handkerchief and started mopping at the spilled whisky. The riverlets converged into a general flooding of the first six inches of files.

Amused, Gloria opened the file still further and looked inside, the liquor soaking new folders as the drawer slid open. "I might say, Mister Potter, you sure keep messy files." She thumbed through the damaged folders and then slammed the drawer closed. "Just like that. By an act of God, wiped out all the Aabs to Applebys. Let's drink." Gloria grabbed the fluted glass and walked over to the west window and looked out across the darkening city toward the mountains.

Max stood beside her at the window.

The traffic lights over on Colfax, where it skirts Civic Center, changed, the green lights activating traffic as they blinked eastward and out of sight among the buildings at his feet.

"Aren't you joining me?" she asked, seeing his reflection in the glass.

"Oh, yes." Max raised the bottle cap. "I can't accomplish my fall in a single drink this way." And he laughed. He raised the small white bottle cap. "Here's to a very Merry Christmas."

Gloria turned to him. They touched drinks and drank.

"Be seated." Max waved her to the blue sofa chair by the window. He sat on the corner of his desk.

She sat in the chair, a small queen on a large throne. Sitting forward in her chair, she looked at the ashes on the carpet in front of her. "Is it burnt offerings this year?" she asked, laughing.

When she laughed, a string of pearly white teeth gleamed out at him.

"Say, you're very funny." They both laughed. Then Max jumped up. "Just a minute." He ran to the filing cabinet and refilled the small bottle cap.

Gloria sat back in her chair. "You know what I was thinking, Mister Potter?"

"No, what?" He paused, careful not to spill his drink. He gulped the capful and filled the cap again. "No use making the trip twice," said Max, smiling and looking at the small white cap in his hand.

"I was thinking that when I was a freshman in college, I used to want to be a writer. I'd sharpen all of my pencils, every one in the house, and then put them in a glass just like this one."

"You're puttin' me on." Max stood in front of her before the window, the bottle of Jim Beam in his right hand. She has brains to spare, he thought. They both looked at the bottle, and then Max smiled. "The exercise back and forth was getting to me," he said, sucking in air and feigning weakness.

"Here's to your weakness." Gloria raised her glass.

Damn, I could use a girl like that, thought Max. "You know my secretary, Irene? What would you think of a job like that?"

"She's your secretary, Mister Potter? Gee, I'd think that kind of job would be great." Gloria giggled. "Here's to your weakness." She drank; coughing, she gasped for breath.

Max didn't notice. Great job, huh? "You say you are a good stenographer, Miss Everetts? Gloria?"

"I didn't say it. That's what my vita says, Max." She giggled again and looked up into his eyes.

Smiling, Max raised the bottle to a toast. "Here's to my weakness." The bottle was at his lips and he drank. Gagging and coughing, Max lowered the bottle. His face was red and he was perspiring.

"Mister Potter, your double indemnity is showing." She giggled, watching him.

Gloria finished her drink. "Well, with that I must be going." She started to rise from the deep blue sofa chair.

"Oh, you're not leaving now? We're just getting started." Max hovered above her, his left hand out flat, so as to keep her in the chair.

"But, like I said, I'm only a working girl and there's yet work to do."

"You're not working for him any more. You've been promoted. From now on, you're working for me." Max stood up. He shifted the bottle to his left hand and with his right hand outstretched, helped her from the chair.

"But my boss doesn't know anything about this," said Gloria, amused astonishment on her face.

"He will." Authority was in Max's voice. He looked at his watch. "Say, I have an appointment at two o'clock. If I'd break it, maybe we could. . . ."

Just then the phone buzzed—the inter-office light was blinking. "Let it blink," said Max. "Two o'clock?"

Gloria shifted her glass to her left hand and reached for the phone. She handed it to Max. Giggling, she pushed the button.

"Mister Potter!" It was Irene.

"Yes?" His voice was steady and low. His attention was still on Miss Everetts.

"Who, or what, has been going through my drawers, Mister Potter?"

"What does it look like that's been going through your drawers, Irene?"

"The Russian Army, since you asked, Mister Potter." There were tears in her voice. Max could almost see her chin quivering.

"Then, I'd suggest you take it up with the State Department, Irene." He paused and started to hang up. "That's in the District of Columbia," he said. With that he slammed down the receiver. Unmoved, he turned to Gloria. "At two o'clock, then?"

"Two o'clock?" For a moment there was alarm in the young woman's eyes; then she relaxed. "But it isn't even lunch, yet." She seemed to be talking to herself.

"How about it, lunch together, then?" Max held her left hand in his right. She was warm, and full of life.

"I'm sorry, Max, but I can't."

"Why not, Gloria?"

"Like I said, I haven't graduated yet. I lied to the employment agency. I graduate this spring. I'm only twenty and I'm only Christmas help. I don't want a full-time job, Mister Potter."

"But I didn't know we had any part-time—Christmas—help." He didn't believe her.

"Oh, I don't work for you, Max—Mister Potter. I'm hired by the Exchange and I'm a delivery girl to all the insurance offices in the building." She smiled. Almost curtsying, her eyes sparkling, she started to leave.

"Forget the job offer, Gloria—Miss Everetts. How about lunch, anyway?" Disappointment was creeping into Max's voice.

"I can't, Mister Potter. We're through here at noon." She set the empty glass on Max's desk. "And if I can make it, we —some of the gang—are planning a demonstration of some kind over at DU."

"But this is Christmas, Gloria."

"Thank you, Mister Potter." She was at the door now; she opened it. "Thank you, Mister Potter, for showing me your etchings." She giggled, and then she was gone.

Max looked after her and then at the bottle in his hand. Potter, you're drunk, he thought.

Lifting up the phone, he pushed inter-office.

"Yes, Mister Potter." There was indignation in every word.

"Could I have some coffee, Irene?"

"Yes, Mister Potter."

"Several cups? Black?"

"Yes, Mister Potter."

"Thank you, Irene."

"That's all right, Mister Potter." Her voice was cold.

Chapter 5

"Let me, Irene. I got it." The door opened. "Don't bother. Thanks anyway." The door closed behind him. It was Frank L. Hamper. He held a cardboard tray with two white styrafoam cups filled with coffee. "Hello, Mister Potter."

"Hello, Frank." Maxwell Potter sat at his desk, half dozing, his feet on the desk top and his chair back in a comfortable position. He looked up, surprised. "Thought you were sick, Frank. S'what Irene said yesterday."

"Was, Mister Potter, but recovered." The man named Frank placed the cardboard tray on Max's desk. Frank Hamper was a bit taller than Max, perhaps six feet tall, as he stood there in the office. He was dressed informally, a warm brown suede leather sports jacket with dark brown dacron slacks. His sport shirt was buttoned at the throat but without a tie. Neatly groomed black hair, thick, and with only a suggestion of a wave, made Frank appear older than his twenty-four years. A bad case of acne sometime in his youth prevented him from being handsome, but the rugged cut of his features and his acquired habits of dress made him one of the more attractive men in the company. "Ran into Irene downstairs and told her I was coming up." He handed one of the cups to Max. "That'll scald your insides."

Max took the cup, cautiously eyeing the second one. Hamper lifted the other cup. "Have some coffee, Mister Hamper," said Max, raising his cup. Max winced as he sipped at the hot brew.

"Thought I had the flu there for a while but seems to have passed." Hamper looked around the office. The uncapped bottle of Jim Beam still sat on the desk, along with the empty glass. "I see Santa's been here already," said Frank, laughing, his merriment forced. He looked at the blue sofa chair but didn't move toward it. "Thought you didn't touch the stuff," he said, nodding toward the open bottle on the desk.

"I'd ask you to sit down, Frank, except I don't have much time," said Max. "I gotta go buy a gift for the wife." Then he noticed the bottle. "Just a coupla the gang. You know, a snort with old friends."

"Yeah, I know how it is, Mister Potter." Frank Hamper raised the cup of coffee to his lips. "Nothing like black coffee for the flu." He sipped at the hot liquid.

Max picked up the bottle of whisky and wiped the neck on the cuff of his coat sleeve. "There's a little left. Have some."

Frank Hamper laughed again; it was a nervous little laugh.

"Go ahead, Hamper. For Christ sake, if you're gonna take charge of the Oregon office, you gotta be able to hold a drink or two." Max handed the bottle to Frank Hamper.

"A little in the coffee, then," said the young man, chuckling. He took the bottle, pouring a few drops into the hot coffee. "That's about all the Christmas cheer I can take this time of day." He handed the bottle back to Max. "Here's to a Merry Christmas." He raised the cup.

"Here's to our West Coast manager." Max raised the bottle in his left hand and drank.

The office was quiet for a moment. Finally, it was Frank Hamper who spoke. "That's what I came to see you about, Mister Potter." Frank was nervous. "That job on the Coast. I don't think the decision has been made to put me in charge."

"Of course the decision's been made. I made it—when I hired you a coupla years ago." Max was gesticulating with his hands, the words coming with some difficulty. "I mean, when the right job came along, you'd get it." Max set the bottle of whisky on the desk. "That's why we hired you."

"Adler has other plans—for the West Coast deal." Frank took another drink of coffee.

"But that's. . ."

"No!" said Frank, shaking his head in a negative motion. He raised his left hand as though to hold back Max's argument and then took another sip of coffee. Swallowing, he crossed over to the blue chair and sat down.

"Be seated, Frank." Max was serious now. He sat upright at his desk. "Sit down."

"Thank you." Frank reached forward and set the coffee cup on the desk. "At least that coffee's different." Frank laughed again, nervously, and settled back into the blue chair. Then, without warning, "I'm quitting the insurance business; getting out."

"Whataya mean, you're quittin'?" Max was on his feet now. "Look, kid, I been lookin' forward to sendin' you out to Oregon, to join Larry Langdon, and the two of you put our affairs on the track out there."

"Sorry, Mister Potter, but I have an offer from a college, to teach and to pursue graduate work in engineering."

"Engineering!" Maxwell Potter responded to the word as though it had been his winning number called out at the church raffle. "That's my trade, kid." His voice was loud and high-pitched. "I didn't know you were an engineer, too."

"It's in my vita," said Frank, sarcasm in his voice. He had given up on the coffee and sat, arms folded, in the deep blue sofa chair.

"Your vita?" said Max, puzzled for a moment. "Oh, yes." Max was calmer now. "What engineeer?" he asked, raising his heavy eyebrows and staring down at the young man. "I mean, what area? What specialization? Specialization's the thing today." Max stood there, waiting.

"Civil engineering."

"Same here," said Max, turning to the south window and staring out across the city. "Was gonna be the greatest engineer since Hoover conned the damned Chinese outa all their millions." He paused; neither of them spoke. Then it was Max again, his voice low and more to himself than to young Hamper. "My ol' man busted his ass tearin' up and rebuildin' the railroad. Wasted. Every brain he had in his head was wasted. Christ a mighty, kid," said Max, pacing back and forth before the south window, "he had more brains in this little finger"—Max raised the little finger on his right hand—"than the engineers that laid out that line had in their heads." Max turned, picked up the bottle and drank. "But he was a goddamned section hand.

"I hardly see the connection between my quitting and your father's job on the railroad," said Frank Hamper, polite enough but a little bored.

" 'Cause there ain't no money in engineerin', that's why." Max Potter had turned from the window. "But there's money in life insurance. Lotsa money."

"But how about your idol, Hoover?"

Max wasn't listening. "Then there's the math. You good at math, kid?" He gazed over at Frank.

"OK when I was in school."

"If you're good at math, stick with insurance. Actuarial work. That's the field. None of this punchin' doorbells and sellin' insurance. If you're good at math, that's the field. That bastard we hire outa Chicago to do our work. Our company alone. Whew." Max waved the bottle, the whisky sloshing around inside. "That alone'd be enough for me."

"I don't know about that, Mister Potter, but I wanted to tell you now that I was quitting so that. . ."

"But I wasn't smart, kid, not before the war. Gonna build things and be important and do things important. Used to ride the railroad on my ol' man's pass and see the bridges and buildings all along the whole Burlington line. Russia, China and all the other places I hadn't heard of would need bridges and railroads. Was gonna build up the whole country a dams and bridges." Max had run out of breath.

The man in the blue chair was quiet.

"But, you know what, kid? There ain't no money in that game unless you're the best."

"Hell, I don't say that I'm the best, but. . ."

"But you gotta be the best or it don't count." Max was panting. "My ol' man. . ." Max paused and turned to the blue chair. "Know what happened, kid? I grew up with this Catholic kid, a girl, and cute? Christ, kid, you ain't seen nothin'. An' her ol' man says nothin' doin' 'cause you ain't Catholic: and too, 'cause your ol' man's a section hand on the goddamned railroad." Max had turned back to the window. "Oh, he didn't say it to my face but the hints come to me through my girl." His arms were outstretched, his hands resting on the uprights of the steel window frame. "But I didn't get smart, kid. All during the war I go without a woman, and I'm only dreamin' when I can say 'good-by Navy' and get my hands on that GI Bill. Yes, sir. Out-Hoover Hoover and make her ol' man proud a me." Max turned to the desk and picked up the bottle.

"I think I'd better be. . ."

"Don't run off, kid." Max spun around and waved the young man back into his chair. "I haven't even got to your part, yet. You gotta get the money, kid. To hell with all that crap about ideals and commitment." Max lifted the bottle to his lips and took a drink. "Know what happened, kid?" He talked as he wiped his lips on the back of his left hand. "She's gotta three year's lead on me in college—back East somewheres—an' 'fore I can get through the second year, she marries some damned 4-F who'd been stuffin' it away runnin' his ol' man's shoe factory durin' the war."

"But. . ."

"Shut up for a moment, will ya? I'm not through." Max turned the bottle around between his fingers, thinking. He still stood by the window. "You're rough. You come in from the stinkin' mud flats a Nebraska." Max turned and looked at the young man in the chair. "No! Not you, me!" He almost yelled it at young Hamper. "But you try to do what's right—read the right books, see the right shows and meet the right people. But where's that get ya?"

The room was quiet for a long moment.

Again it was Max talking. "You know what, kid?" Max's voice was low, barely audible. "Thought I'd outlive the bastard. He was a heart case or somethin'. I'd get her that way and her ol' man'd be damned glad to see me, Catholic or no Catholic. For twenty-three goddamned years I waited." Max beat his right fist on the steel window frame. "And he died, all right," he continued, his voice still lower, "but she didn't come gallopin' to see ol' Maxie. The bitch." Max screamed the words. "Not even a Christmas card." Max rested the bottle on the metal sill of the window, both hands folded over the neck top.

The door to the office clicked softly, then again. The room was quiet for a long time.

"I love you, Tracy," sobbed Max. "It's Christmas, remember?" His forehead resting against the cold glass of the window, his hot breath formed a small but growing mist cloud over the glass by his face. Then suddenly, standing fully erect, he raised the bottle and smashed it against the flat steel window sill. "She's dead, the fat, ugly bitch. It's Phyllis. It's Phyllis, now. It's always been Phyllis." He yelled the words.

He wanted her—Phyllis. Max wanted his wife. He looked at the door. For the first time Max noticed that the blue chair was empty, that Frank Hamper was gone. Dumb bastard, thought Max. There's more money made by accident in insurance than he'll ever see in all that mud he's gonna be eatin'.

Max picked up the phone and dialed outside, then his home. To hell with lunch at two. Go home; go to bed with Phyllis. The line buzzed. Let 'er ring six times, he thought. All this damned pinin' away on a bitch you don't even know. She's dead. Her ol' man's dead same's mine. No longer important. Who'd want her now? He let the phone ring, but there wasn't an answer. Slowly, mechanically, Max let the phone fall into the cradle—very gently. Probably takin' a bath.

Max unlocked the closet by the filing cabinet and took out his coat, a military style raincoat. Buttoning up the front, he left his office. The reception office was empty as Maxwell Potter strode into the hallway. He'd go home, anyway, phone or no phone.

Like the offices and the hallway, the elevator was deserted except for Max. He took the elevator to the underground garage level. The air was cool and refreshing as the metal fire door closed behind him. Two young women, deep in conversation, brushed past him and into the building. The door opened and closed again.

Breathing deeply, Max slapped at his chest with both hands as he stood surveying the scene; it was good to be alive. He stood looking for his car; the spaces close by were nearly empty.

The attendant was not at the shack when Max got there. Two men, one short and bald and the other, perhaps his son, were in deep conversation. Max didn't recognize either of them. In a moment a light tan Lincoln pulled up before the shack.

"Here you are, sir." The attendant stood beside the car door as the driver, the younger of the two men, got behind the wheel. "Thank you, sir."

The attendant, a young man in a neatly pressed gray custodian's uniform, stepped back as the Lincoln pulled away from before the shack and into the outdoor light.

"Yes, sir?" He was addressing Max.

"My Cadillac." It was an order.

"What color, sir?" The young man craned his neck and squinted into the dimly lit garage. "This is Cadillac country, sir."

"Back in the Mountain-Plains section." Max turned his back on the young man, to look out the entrance, out toward the street. The light hurt his eyes.

"That doesn't help me much." The attendant smiled as he spoke. "You have a number, maybe; a model or a color? Maybe you named it and we might just whistle for it."

"You're new here, aren't you, kid?" Maxwell Potter was taking charge.

"Yes, sir. Just this morning. Christmas help."

"So that's it? Ah. Don't tell me." Max went into deep thought. "Let's see. You're a sociology major over at DU. Right?"

"How'd you guess?" The young attendant laughed.

"Now, see if you can do as well with my car." Max did not smile but handed the young man his key case. Max turned and watched the traffic shuttle past the entrance.

"You must be number 184, the new black Cad. Right?"

"At least they teach you to read."

Max paced back and forth before the shack. Even the fumes from the nearby cars smelled good. Max looked at his watch. Ten-fifteen. He'd catch her before she'd start getting ready. Again he breathed deeply. He held it. Good for the lungs, he thought. He'd just stay there in bed with her right through Christmas eve. Max wondered how it was that he'd ever been lucky enough to get a girl like Phyllis. All the things they'd taught each other in bed. While he paced back and forth, waiting for his car, he was falling in love with his wife all over again. He thought of their first time—before they were married. Then he heard the compression of the tires coming to a stop behind him.

"Here you are, sir." As before, the young attendant stood beside the open driver's door.

"Thank you." Max started around the front of the car. He didn't see the directional parking sign and tripped and fell. Mounted on an old automobile wheel, the sign was wheeled into place when traffic was heavy or when there was only one attendant. "Follow the Arrows" was spelled out in sharp, red letters on one side of the white sign. The word "STOP" was on the other side. At the present instance it stood between the two lanes of traffic and was a stop sign. Max went straddle of the sign as he fell. There was a groan as he went down. "Sonofabitch." Max sat on the cement floor, staring at the tear in the front of his coat, where the bottom button had torn out, threads and all.

"Let me help you, sir." The young attendant lifted, or helped lift, Max to his feet. Carefully, he brushed the floor grit off Max's coat. "They not only teach us how to read," said the young man, not particularly trying to hide his smile, "but how to pick up drunks who fall on their asses."

"It was the light. I shouldn't've looked into the light." Max kicked the sign and started for the opened car door.

"Going far, sir?"

"Why? That a study you're doin' in sociology?" Max eased himself into the driver's seat and buckled the seat belt.

"Might be," said the young attendant, closing the door. "But it isn't. They're setting up road blocks all over town checking for drunken drivers. Safest Christmas ever, says the mayor. I'd give it serious thought."

"All right, I've thought about it. Now, outa my way, kid, so's I can get on with a man's work." With that, Max accelerated the engine and the new black Cadillac leaped forward. There was a grind of metal and a flash of sparks as the "Follow the Arrows" sign disappeared under the long black front of the Cadillac. The car scraped to the gutter out in front of the garage before it stopped, the oil light on the dash board flashing red.

Maxwell Potter sighed deeply as he crawled out of the stalled car.

The young attendant, startled by the noise and the suddenness of it all, came running. "Are you hurt, sir?"

"Guess I'll walk after all, kid." Max slammed the car door. "Here." He handed the young man a ten dollar bill. "Call the dealer and have him come pick it up," he said, motioning to the car. "And see if you can clean up the mess between cars."

"See what I can do." The young man was down on his knees, looking under the car.

Max looked up the street to his right toward Seventeenth Avenue. Never a cab when you want one, he thought. He started walking.

Chapter 6

The wind had shifted around to the northwest, raw and
cold. The thawing snow of early morning had frozen, leaving
glaring patches of slippery sidewalk. High above the city,
wind-marshalled clouds fashioned a coarse, leadened mantle
of ominous blotches of blacks and ghostly whiffs of whites.
The mottled clouds hid the mountain peaks to the west.

As automobiles slipped down Seventeenth Avenue, one
way, going east, steamy exhaust clouds whizzed away in
churning spirals of angry white smoke. Heavy, ice-windowed
cars raced through the gathering chill. Monotonously, snow
cleats whispered incessantly as car tires slowed and accelerated to the pulsing movement of the heavy traffic. On the lee
side of buildings along the way the wind slackened; the indefi-
nite tonal ring of the Christmas chimes from the Cathedral
sounded to the east, down on Colfax, beyond the Capitol.

Max Potter, hunched down in his lightweight raincoat,
walked briskly down Seventeenth Avenue toward town. His
gait was unsteady but determined. At the corner of Seventeenth and Broadway he halted, stepping in between the tall,
square onyx pillars of the United Bank Building, out of the
wind. The fresh air he had so cherished only a few minutes
before in the parking garage now brought shivers to his entire
body. His face was numb.

Max thought of the whisky in his office. The burning of
the liquor still tormented his memory. A momentary flash of

warmth swept over him. He looked up the street. "Taxi! Taxi!" Max wiped his dripping nose on the sleeve of his raincoat. He moved out from the building. "Taxi!" Max stood at the curb facing Broadway, looking west, his right arm waving high above his head.

A Yellow Cab flanked across two traffic lanes to Max's side of the street. Max ran up to the cab as it pulled to the curb. Without getting out, the driver reached across the back of the seat and opened the back door. Shivering, Max crawled inside. "God, this the only cab on the beat?" The cab was warm, almost hot.

The taxi did not move, waiting. Finally the driver spoke. "Where to, Mister?" he asked, impatiently. He was watching Max in the rear view mirror.

"Home," said Max, shuddering, as though trying to shake the chill from his body. "Take me home."

"Fine, Mister," said the driver, his impatience now tinged with sarcasm. He turned, his right arm up over the back of the front seat. "But where is home?"

The driver was a little man, his eyes squinting from behind thick lenses in dull black plastic frames. His chauffeur's badge was pinned to a black stocking cap. An oversized Navy peacoat, open at the collar, gave him a wilted look as he peered into the back seat. When he spoke, his voice was high-pitched and whiny. "Where's home?" he asked again.

"I was on my way home and I wrecked my car—a new black Cadillac—and. . ."

"Look, Mack, this is a one-way street, and no parking." He raised his right thumb, indicating out back of the cab. "Christ, the cars'll be all the way back to the railroad. . ."

"108 Clement Drive," said Max, laying his head back. He sighed and closed his eyes. "That's where I live."

"OK, Mack." The driver's voice was abrupt now. "I don't wanna seem impertinent, but where in the hell is 108 Clement Drive?"

"You a sociology major over at DU, too?" Max didn't open his eyes; he sighed deeply again, licking his lips as he absorbed the comfort of the cab.

"I'm a Headstart dropout, but. . ."

"Out in Jefferson—no, Arapahoe—County." Max barely stirred.

Horns were sounding behind the taxi now.

"Look, Mister," squeaked the driver. "I'm gonna drive down past the Hilton. You sit there thinkin' where you wanna go."

The cab pulled away from the curb.

Max felt the soft, swaying movement of the cab; he wanted to sleep.

"Here's the Hilton comin' up," said the driver, nervously. Then the cab stopped. "We're in luck, Mister. A red light. You workin' on it, Mister?" There was urgency in his high, small voice. Then he turned and looked at Max. "Look, fella, give me a break. I just came on duty. I don't want no trouble." As the light flashed green, the cabby shook Max's left knee. "Wake up, goddamnit." The cab lurched through the intersection.

Max was awake. "Drive around Civic Center 'til I can think."

"Atta boy!" said the driver, his mousey voice cheerful. "I knew you wouldn't do that to me today." The driver laughed and cut the corner just past the Hilton, turning left.

Max was disappointed. Phyllis. Wanna go to bed with Phyllis. He wondered where his wife was at that moment. Probably getting ready to meet him, he thought. He rubbed his face.

"Here's the City-County Building, Mister." The cab driver was a happy guide. "See the decorations? Over ten thousand of yours and my dollars to put on that display. Seen it at night?" The cab was quiet for a moment. Again, it was the driver. "Hey, Fella, wake up!"

"Yes, yes." Max shook his head.

"You workin' on it?"

Max didn't answer.

"Here's the library comin' up ahead," called out the driver, less cheerful than he had been. "Why don't I let you out here, and you can go in and sleep and get warm, or maybe get a book and look at the pictures." His voice was kind and gentle.

"Pictures?" Max sat with his elbows on his knees, his large head resting in his hands. "Naw, she wouldn't want a picture."

"Hell, you don't have to paint one," said the driver. "Just look at 'em." The taxi stopped at the light in front of the library, giving Max time to think. "Any ideas yet, Mister?" The driver was watching Max in the mirror again.

"Yeah," said Max, his voice high-pitched. "I wonder how many a those fish die every year?"

"I'm sorry, Mister, I don't read you!" He hesitated. "What fish?"

" 'Member coupla years ago? Kids put all that soap or detergent, or somethin', in there and killed all the fish?"

"Where's that?" The driver looked over his shoulder. "What fish?"

"You sure you're not just Christmas help?" Max had his hands on the back of the driver's seat and pulled himself up so that his head was just behind the cabby's. "You new 'round here?"

"Me? No!" There was surprise in the driver's voice. Then he giggled. "Hell no, Mister. I was born in a washroom at the Shirley Savoy, honest Injun." The driver moved his head away from Max's breath. "Now, where ya wanna go, Mack?"

"United Bank Building."

"But that's where I just picked ya up," protested the taxi driver. The cab eased away from the light.

"See if there's any dead fish there now," said Max. He wiped his nose on his sleeve. "Cold weather'd freeze the ass off a fish in that shallow pond." Max nudged the driver's shoulder with his right hand. "Ever think 'bout that?"

"I'm tryin' to picture such an event, if that's what ya mean," said the driver, a lightness in his voice again.

"Wonder how many fish die there in the winter, compared to summer." Max's voice was somber.

"I think they drain the water out in the winter," said the driver, a new interest in his voice. "Goin' by the Capitol now, Mister."

"Statistics and prabability's my business," said Max, fully awake now. "I'm president of a insurance company—Mountain-Plains—ever hear of it?"

"Yeah, and I'm Santa Claus," said the driver, giggling.

"That's right, buddy. President," said Max, sighing. The air in the cab was close. Max pulled open his tie and unbuttoned his collar. "Buddy, know what time a year more people die?"

"No, when?" The driver was noncommittal.

The taxi changed lanes to the left.

"The ten days after Christmas." Max said it with authority. "Read that once. The ol' farts wanna see one more Christmas and then they cash in. Ain't that a helluva note?"

"Sure is, Mister." The taxi slowed and made a left turn.

"United Bank Building, it is, then?"

Max was quiet.

"Hey, Mister, you still awake?"

"Yeah."

"United Bank Building, still?

"Naw, don't wanna see no empty pond." Max had settled back into his seat. "Know where Arnie's massage parlor is, out on east Colfax?" He spoke with resignation in his voice.

"Before lunch?" The driver turned to look at Max again. "You'd face those whores 'fore lunch?" The taxi braked suddenly for the next light.

"Lunch?" Max sat upright. "Hell, I gotta meet my wife for lunch."

"OK, now we're gettin' somewheres." The driver revved up the engine. "Just tell me where you're gonna meet her and we're there."

"May-D-F."

"See how easy it was, buddy?"

"Gotta be there by two o'clock."

"That's a coupla hours yet," complained the cabby. The taxi lurched forward. "Look, Mack. You got my stomach goin' now. Just give me a place, will ya?" There was desperation in his voice.

"A place where I can buy a gift. Gotta get Phyllis a gift."

"Get it after Christmas. Cheaper that way. My wife's gone and won't be back 'til coupla days 'fore New Years. She'll get her present then and won't know the difference." The driver was silent for a moment. "Course I ain't got mine, either, for that matter," he said.

Max wasn't listening. She has a fur piece. Perfume? She'd like that. That's what I got her the first Christmas, he thought. Get her a name brand—one a those bottles with the name signed on it. Suddenly, he remembered the girl at the office, Gloria Everetts. All of them are signed, she had said. That'd make a good present. A picture for Phyllis.

"Driver, take me to a place called La Bouquet, near Larimer Square."

"It's gonna be a beautiful day, after all," said the driver.

Max smiled and settled back into the warmth and comfort of the cab.

Max slammed the cab door. "Keep the change," he called out. The Yellow Cab pulled away from the curb and was lost in traffic.

La Bouquet was part of a lusty replica of an imagined frontier Denver, a portion of the preserved Old Town. Up a span of overly restored steps, the art gallery nestled among the upstairs stanchions of a former warehouse, now dusted off and decked out profusely with genre art of the Old West.

The far-off jangle of a bell sounded as Max entered.

"I'll be down in a minute," said a voice from the low mezzanine above the rear of the main room of the gallery. It was a woman's voice.

"No, hurry," answered Max, cheerfully.

Awed, Maxwell Potter stalked the canvases of the gallery. Shiprock, the lodestone of the desert, silhouetted there with the roseate sunset at its back. Ah, The Massacre. Bloodthirsty redskins.

Max stood back the correct distance and admired the careful detail of the yukka needles and the buffalo grass there under the belly of the chief's fallen horse. God, that's pretty, he thought. For a moment he was lost in reverence for the artist's works. Such pictures! He was glad that someday he might bestow a purchase upon this same gallery. He could see the new offices of the Mountain-Plains Insurance Company, veritable pallets of the creator's touch, the quintessence of the artist's dream. Max looked at the names on the canvases; the canvases were all signed. No signature, no purchase; that was his dictum. O'Brian, Smith, Yashida. Why couldn't Rembrandt have painted something like that, or Picasso? These were all unknowns. All unknowns. Too risky.

"Can I help you?" The woman's voice was closer and more festive than before, yet restrained.

"Yes, Sally." Max turned to the woman. "I brought a . . ."

"My name is not Sally, sir," said the voice, disdainfully.

The woman was short and robust, somewhere close to sixty, probably more than less. Sheathed in a tight-fitting, blue jersey dress, she was not as tall as Max's chin. Her hair was dyed blue-silver. Crystal, cord-strung beads hung generously from her arched neck, a large many-faceted crystal imparting the cleavage between her stunted breasts. When she spoke, gold platework glistened among the white pearls of her teeth. Although not tall, she had an air of masculine strength about her.

"Now, what was it, sir?" A measured smile crossed her finical composure.

"What happened to Sally?" asked Max, puzzled. "I did my business with Sally." It was almost with a pout.

"There isn't such a person here, sir," said the woman, coolly. "How can I help you?"

"You new here, lady?" asked Max, suspiciously. He stared down into the woman's face.

"Six months, if that's new!" She turned and walked away, toward the back of the gallery. "Please feel free to browse around." Her back was still turned toward him. "We have other examples of prints and watercolors in folios and cabinets upstairs." The woman began a retreat from the room.

"Just a minute, Ma'am," said Max. He felt faint; the room was getting hot. He was perspiring. "I don't wanna buy a picture. I already got one. I just wanna pick it up."

"I'm sorry, sir," said the woman, swinging around to face him, more starch in her voice now, "but we don't loan out any of our pictures."

"No! No! You don't understand." Max pulled at his open collar. God, I wish she'd turn down the heat, he thought. "Some time ago . . ." He brought out his handkerchief and mopped at his face. "A picture—a Rainwire, I think the name was, and I asked Sally . . ."

"If there was a Sally working here, she certainly isn't here now." The woman stood, straightening her shoulders. "I can hardly know what you might have discussed with someone who was here before me." She looked him in the eyes and did not flinch. "Can I?" she demanded, harshness in her voice. "If you didn't buy it from us, I can hardly . . ."

"That will do, Maud!" It was a man's voice.

The voice was low and calm. It came from the darkness to the left, from under the overhanging mezzanine at the rear of the gallery. Max raised his eyes. In the dim light of an open door stood a stout, black-bearded man. Dressed in a dark suit, with vest, he appeared as a squat, massive statue. President Grant at a horse-judging show.

"I was only informing him that . . ." Her voice was strained.

"That will do, Maud," said the man, crisply. He did not move.

"Well, thank you!" The woman called Maud turned, and with an angry stomp, brushed by the man with the beard and was gone.

"My name's Potter and I . . ."

"That clinical bitch. Thinks she knows everything there is to know 'bout art." The pitch of the man's voice was low and even. Standing in the door, he looked in the direction Maud had taken. "She's a fraud if you ever saw one and . . ."

"Look, I brought a picture in here and gave it to Sally and asked . . ."

"Know what she did?" asked the man, stepping into the room.

"Sally?" asked Max, encouragement in his voice.

"No, Maud." The stout man with the beard bit off the end of a cigar and, turning his head, spit the cigar end through the open doorway and into the hall. "She hauls off to Taos and brings back all these goddamned desert oils." He made a flourish with his right hand, the one with the cigar, to indicate the entire room. Pausing, he methodically searched his vest pocket. "Gotta match?" he asked, looking at Max.

"Don't smoke." Max could not muster the usual pride in the statement. Gotta get outa here, he thought. That whisky doesn't sit too well. Drinkin' in the morning's always bad for my stomach. The man with the beard was talking again.

"She knows it's the mountains and the cow scenes, and those goddamned aspen. They're the ones that sell . . ."

"Look, I don't give a damn 'bout Maud." Max was trembling. "Now don't say a word 'til I finish." He paused, breathing deeply. "I had a picture, a print, and a friend tells me to bring it here to have you evaluate it." Max gazed around the room. "And I gave it to Sally . . ."

"But we don't . . ."

"And she says to come back in a week or so." Max stared him down. "Musta been a year ago and . . ."

"Why, of course . . ." The man paused. Scratching his head, he walked past Max to a large folio in the far corner. "We kept all the old customers' stuff back here."

"And I wanna pick it up," said Max, not moving.

"Now, what was the artist?" asked the man with the beard.

"Some Frenchman—Rainwire, or something like that."

"Oh, yes. Renoir." The bearded man pulled at the string that held the folio. Opening the large cardboard flaps, he rummaged through the unmounted pictures inside. "Your name was what?"

"Potter," said Max, shifting his feet nervously. "I'm president of Mountain-Plains Life Insurance Company, and . . ."

"Potter?" said the man, interrupting Max. Then he was quiet again.

"I like to collect art and my friend suggested I . . ."

"Yes, here we are. A Renoir dry point." The man lifted the picture out of the folio and held it up to the dim light from the windows out front. The heavy plastic that encased the picture shimmered in the light. "Says here on this paper to check the signature for authenticity."

"That's right," said Max, hesitantly. "I buy only signed pictures."

"Good policy, sir, if the artist really signed it," said the bearded man, taking the cigar out of his mouth and scrutinizing the picture more carefully. "She's a beauty, isn't she?"

Maxwell Potter breathed deeply before answering "Collect only the best, that's my dictum."

"Well, you can't beat Renoir, I guess," said the stout man. He carried the picture to the front of the gallery and held it up to the light from the window. "You gotta watch out for these gyp joints, thought. Christ, some a these places'll sell you anything and tell you it's something else." He squinted at the picture. "But this is a Renoir, all right; you can tell by his style. Beautiful." He stood in apparent awe of the picture.

Maxwell Potter was proud of his property. "How 'bout the signature?" asked Max.

"What's it in, ink? Looks like it might even be in the plate." The man held the picture up closer to his eyes.

Max felt sick. "It's not signed in the plate," he said, his voice nervous. "The man said he never signed the plates."

"Don't know much about these foreigners," said the stout one. He turned from the window and stood looking at Max. "Wouldn't take much for an unscrupulous dealer to just sign 'em as he saw fit, would it?"

"But the other pictures in my office!" Max didn't want to think of them. As though made of wax, the pictures in his office began to melt and run down the walls, blurred and ruined.

"A man's gotta be careful." The bearded man looked at Max. Max's face was white now. "But you leave it here a while," he said, holding the Renoir print in his left hand and waving it. "And soon's we get settled I'll give it another look." He stuck the picture under his left arm and started searching his pockets for a match again. "Don't want a forgery on our hands, do we?" He winked at Max as he said it.

"Thought my wife would like it for Christmas," said Max, disappointment in his voice. "But if it's a fake . . ." He didn't finish.

"Don't feel so bad," said the bearded man, tossing Max's Renoir print on top of a table of carelessly thrown together print reproductions. "We got lots of pictures." With the unlit cigar in his mouth, he strode over to a large oil, framed and leaning against the wall. "How'd you like a nice desert scene?" He tapped on the picture frame. "There, look at it. All the goddamned Sioux nation in that picture."

"But who painted it?" asked Max, bending over and looking at the signature. "De Va . . . something."

"What the hell, you want a name or a picture?"

They were both silent; then Max spoke. "Only big names. Gotta stick with it." He was determined.

"Maybe that's de Vinci, for all we know," said the man, a slight smile on his face.

"He didn't sign his pictures, either," said Max, again bending and looking at the canvas.

"Well, you come in again and we'll probably have a name you'll like," said the bearded man. "And we'll look at that Renoir again." He took the unlit cigar out of his mouth. "Maybe Maud'll know something 'bout him."

Nervously, Max looked at the man. "Pardon me, but you got a rest room handy?" Max wiped his face again and put his handkerchief in his coat pocket.

"Right this way, sir," said the man with the beard. He ushered Max into the hallway. "First door on the right. That's it."

The far-off jingle of a bell sounded.

The bearded man looked up toward the front. "Can I help you, ma'am?" he asked, disappearing into the gallery.

Chapter 7

The seat was cold. Max sat with eyes closed, his elbows on his knees, his head resting heavily in both hands. His breathing was quick and unsteady.

Office parties, he thought. He swallowed, fighting the bitter, burning taste in his mouth. His stomach ached. No longer perspiring, his skin was cold.

Max opened his eyes. The stall was clean and white. Too clean and too white. From off to the right a light cast faint shadows over the thin partition of the stall. On a hook on the door were his jacket and raincoat. The paint on the floor of the stall was gray, shiny and new. Battleship gray.

What's worse than a girl with paper falsies? A woman with a cardboard box!!!

If you want something . . .

Max's eyes wandered along the shadowy wall of the stall. Scratched words, sanitized under the new paint, laced the shiny surface. Knew better'n to drink, thought Max. The pain in his stomach spread upward into his chest.

Don't throw cigarette buts in the urinal. It makes them soggy and hard to light.

Max closed his eyes.

Columbo's balls were round-o
They hung down to the ground-o.

Graffiti!   Graffiti!   Graffiti!

The boys laughed.

" Look at them big tits!" cried the boy holding back the door. He was straining his neck to look over the heads of the others.

"Wait'll the janitor sees that!" said a tall, red-haired boy standing between the toilet stool and the wall opposite the one with the picture. They all laughed again.

"He'll be mad 'cause you scratched the paint," said the boy by the door.

"Think he'll tell ol' lady Hamill?" asked another boy, squatting, and looking at the picture being scratched into the paint of the rest room wall.

"Write us another poem, Max," said the boy squatting on the floor.

"Whatta ya gonna write, Max?" The voice was from outside the stall.

Four boys watched quietly while Maxwell Potter carved lettering into the hard gray enamel with the pen blade of his chipped Boy Scout knife. The sharp steel blade cut noiselessly into the paint, the boys moving their lips as the words formed:

OL MISSUS HAMILL HAS THE ASS OF A CAMMILL

The tall boy with red hair giggled.

Max finished.

All four boys picked up the wording and chanted the lines, "Ol Missus Hamill has the ass of a camel."

"Shhh . . ." cautioned the voice outside the stall. "The girls'll hear you and tell."

"You know what they can do," said Max. Max sat back and looked at the picture and the just-finished verse. His head was big for his body. Fine strands of brown hair fell uncombed over a wide, smooth forehead. He shook his head sideways to the right to clear the hair from his eyes. Squatting beside the other boy, close to the stool, Max's shoulders were square and strong. His interest was on his art work and on the wall writings. With the tip of the knife blade he picked flecks of paint from the lettering. "Now I'm really gonna write her a poem."

Other boys were sticking their heads into the stall, giggling as they read the verse and looked at the picture.

"Roses are red, violets are . . ."

"That's too old, Max," said one of the heads sticking into the stall.

"No! I got it. Roses are . . ."

"I got it, Max!" said a new voice, shrill and excited. "Grass is greener and so's your wiener."

All the boys laughed.

"Not me, you dumbbell," said Max, laughing. "Ol' lady Hamill."

"Not much'll go with Hamill," said the new voice.

"How about ol' lady Howells?" It was the boy squatting beside Max this time.

"Ol' lady Howells, how is your bowels?" Another voice had joined in.

"Not worth a damn, she said to the man." It was the red-haired boy's turn. He laughed, then continued: "But if I'd eat cabbage and less rutabaggage my stomach will, a lot longer last me."

"That's too hard to write," said Max turning up his nose.

The bell range.

"Comin', Max?" asked the serious boy squatting beside him in the stall. He stood up, looking furtively at Max. "We'd better get back to geography or ol' lady Hamill will come in here and get us and then we're in trouble."

The other boys had left; only running feet outside the door now.

"Yeah, I'm comin'." Maxwell Potter stood up, still looking at the picture. With a fast motion of the index finger on his right hand, he closed the blade of his knife. He backed out of the stall, still looking at the picture on the wall. Giggling, he turned and ran across the room to the hall door and out.

An apple a day keeps the doctor away.

The only light in the room now came in through the open kitchen door. He could hear voices in the kitchen.

"How's he now?" It was the ol' man's voice out in the kitchen.

"Delirious most a the day since you went to work, Paul." Her voice was low and soft and worried. "It's festered more'n it was this morning." She paused. "Can't we take him to the hospital, Paul?" She didn't plead; just asked.

"That'd cost money, Gwen. And we don't have any," said the ol' man. His voice was strong, but the words came slowly. "No, Gwen," said the ol' man, resolution, yet defeat, in his voice. "I gotta do it myself." The voices in the kitchen were quiet, and then it was the ol' man speaking again. "Those Catholic heathens'd only bless him and put him out in the hall. We haven't got the right kinda money." They were both quiet again.

Something sliding on a board. That'd be the ol' man putting away his lunchbox. Every night he put it on the shelf behind the stove. The ol' man always left something of his lunch. But not tonight, probably. No one to eat it.

"I've thought about it all day, Gwen. I gotta do it."

"I know, Paul."

Then, they were quiet for a long time.

When they spoke, it was the ol' man again. "Here, scrub these up and put 'em in that shallow pan. Better boil the water. I slipped 'em outta the tool box on one a the section cars. And get that razor my dad gave me. They can boil while I eat supper. Out like he is, he won't know it's hap-penin'."

The boy lay on the couch in front of the darkened window, his head toward the kitchen door. A shadow filled the room, and the ol' man stood by the couch looking down at the boy. He stood there in the near darkness for a long moment. A rough hand patted the boy's head once, twice, and then was gone. The shadow entered the kitchen again and the ol' man ate his supper.

Voices again. It was the ol' man speaking. "Get your Lysol and put some in the pan a water with the pliers and razor." His voice was steady, matter-of-fact. "And get the peroxide outta the pantry." The hinges on the pantry door scraped as the door opened, and then closed. "You hold his shoulders down," said the ol' man, "and I'll do the rest."

The lamp was brought in from the kitchen and put on a small table, with the light back out of the boy's face. The pan with the tools in it and the peroxide were brought in and put on the small table. The light in the room trembled when the pan bumped the wood of the table top. Again the ol' man stood looking down at the boy.

Max looked up. "It hurts, Daddy," he said softly. "I heard you tell Mamma you had to do it. Do what, Daddy?"

The ol' man didn't answer but turned to the table. It was the mother who spoke. She stood at the end of the couch, behind the boy's head. "He's gonna take the sliver outta your hand, Maxie." She paused before continuing. "It's gotta come out, Maxie. It's dirty and black and almost clear through your little hand."

Max jerked upright on the couch. "Don't Daddy," he screamed. "It hurts, Daddy. I won't play in the brickyard again, Daddy. I won't go there no more." The boy screamed and tried to jump from the couch. "Don't touch it, Daddy!"

Grabbing the boy by the shoulders from behind, his mother forced his head down into the pillow. Quickly, the ol' man straddled the boy's left arm and reached for the pan on the small table. He grabbed the razor and flipped open the blade.

"No, Daddy! Don't, Daddy! Don't!" The boy's screams echoed from the walls of the room.

Throwing the razor onto the table, the ol' man snatched up the pointed-nosed pliers from the pan. The boy tried to rise up from his bed, but the mother was on top of him now, holding him onto the couch. With his left arm held in the vise of the ol' man's legs, Max could only scream and thrash about with the body and legs as the ol' man probed for the sliver in the small hand. The screams were no longer words but were the anguished gurgling of an animal in pain.

The pliers fell to the floor. Seizing the opened bottle of peroxide, the ol' man sloshed part of the contents into the open wound and then, tipping the bottle, poured the remainder into his mouth. Choking, he spewed the foaming peroxide onto the floor. Holding back the thumb on the small hand, the ol' man bent over, pressing the open wound to his own lips. The ol' man shuddered as he sucked on the bleeding hand, his leg grip on the small arm relaxing momentarily. Only moans came from the boy on the couch now.

Suddenly, the ol' man jumped to his feet. Ignoring the boy, he grabbed the shallow pan, the hot water splashing out, and with his face buried in the pan, the ol' man vomited, staggering around the table and into the kitchen.

The ol' man had done what he had to do.

Goddamn the ol' man.

If you want to get a kick, try . . .

The silo was deep. Maxwell Potter looked up the ladder to the top, at the clean blue sky and the low sheep clouds moving across the ring of blue from the northeast. Then he looked down again at the brown chipped stuff at the bottom. The rusty rungs of the ladder were little more than thick crusty stains on the cement walls of the silo pit. The boy clung to the ladder. Already, he could smell the silage. He closed his eyes and gripped the rung nearest his head. His pants were wet; he couldn't help it. Maybe that was the way you were supposed to feel. Slowly, he let himself down, his feet feeling for each rung below. He paused.

From upwind of the silo came the sharp reports of a rifle; then the boom of a shotgun. That'd be the ol' man and Jake Blugon, the owner of the farm, practicing for the turkey shoot the Elks was holdin' on Thursday, Thanksgiving Day. Can't use rifles in the turkey shoot, but the ol' man can't afford shotgun shells for practicin'. The guns sounded far away. Better hurry 'fore they catch me in here, thought Max. A few more steps.

The brown stuff in the silo was packed hard on top but was springy when you jumped up and down on it. Scattered across the surface were faded, empty red shotgun shells and clouded, dusty brown beer bottles, some broken where they had been thrown against the cement wall, the pieces sliding to the bottom in shiny heaps of glass. The circular wall cliff of the silo was stained, the molasses-colored stain rings close together like the rungs of the ladder. Max started counting the rings. Supposed to be over a hundred twenty. But, then, Red usually exaggerates things. The rings trembled and ran together as Max tried to count them. The ladder wobbled when he reached for it. Red hadn't told him what to expect; only that goin' down in the silo made ya feel good, like gettin' drunk. Red had been drunk once, with a friend of his mother's.

Max backed away from the ladder and lay down on the hard brown silage. He could hear the guns again; they sounded closer. It was the ol' man's rifle that time. Something, like a big noisy mosquito, sang around the silo pit, then fell on the crisp brown stuff. Max tried to keep his eyes open. The sky, up at the ring, was dark now, up where the blue had been. Then the stars came out. There's the ol' man's gun again. Max could hear the falling bits of glass, then the ol' man's voice. It was excited and far off, but it was the ol' man's. The wet pants were cold.

Feebly, the boy sighed as gentle hands lifted him from the hard brown stuff at the bottom of the silo. "Come on, boy." It was the ol' man's voice. Sounded like he was cryin'. "Hold on, Maxie. We're gettin' ya outta here."

What's worse than a girl with paper falsies?
A woman . . .

He held the box of groceries close to his chest and looked in through the small square glass in the door. The wire mesh of the screen door played tricks with his eyes. He shook his head, drops of sweat falling from the end of his nose. His breathing was quick, but not forced.

Carefully balancing the cardboard box on the two-by-four railing that was around the stairs landing, he took out a carbon-copy bill for the groceries from his shirt pocket. "Don't let go them goods 'til you collect for them," old Addlesdorf had ordered. Four dollars and thirty-nine cents was what the groceries came to. Grocery bill in hand, he reached for the door, to knock on the screen door and tell her the grocery boy was here. He couldn't reach the door without letting go the box. Again he tried to peer through the small glass in the door. No good. He could take the groceries back to the store, but then old Addlesdorf would be mad. Or maybe he'd laugh. Max didn't want the old storekeeper to laugh at him.

"I'd go up there myself, Max," the old grocer had said, "but I don't need business that bad." Nervously, the old man had stuffed the sacks of food into the box. " 'Sides, that's what I'm payin' you for." Old Addlesdorf had wheezed as he spoke. "Now, if she give ya any trouble, or says anything out a the way to ya, just tell me." He hadn't looked at Max as he spoke. "Now, get them groceries up there. Tell Lohena they're just like she called in last night." Max had almost made it to the door. "And be sure she pays you in cash." There was sarcasm in his voice when he said it.

What had old Addlesdorf meant by that last statement? The thought bothered Max as he stood on the landing. Had the old man laughed at him? He didn't want anyone laughing at him, not where a girl, or a woman, was concerned.

Max set the cardboard box on the worn boards of the landing. Gotta get that meat in outta this sun, he thought. The screen door was unlocked. He opened the screen door and tapped on the inside door. He listened. Quietly, he tried the knob of the door; it was unlocked. Max picked up the box of groceries and stepped inside.

A fetid odor escaped from the unaired room. In the corner to the far right of the room and facing him was a chipped and once-white kitchen sink. Dirty dishes and bits of food were piled up to the water faucets that jutted from the wall above the sink. The punctured and crumbling plaster around the faucets was wet and moulding. The faucet on the left dripped, the large drops of water splashing into the dishes and spoiled food in the sink.

An open butter dish sat on the table in the middle of the room to the left of the door, the rim of the small white plate chipped and greasy. Large house flies crawled around the plate, their blue-black bodies sharp against the oily butter. Strewn around the room were soiled assortments of clothing. A man's white shirt, torn and dirty, lay on the floor by the table. Torn and wadded newspapers and trash-filled paper sacks rose in a pile from the floor up under the sink. The ice box, a dark, deeply marred oak chest, sat in the corner opposite the sink, against the outside wall, just beyond the only window in the room. A pool of water stood near the middle of the floor in front of the ice box; an irregularly formed finger of water disappeared under the oak chest.

Max stepped over the rivulet of water and set the box on top of the ice box. He started to open the ice storage compartment. Pausing, he listened.

He could hear it plainly at first, regular and even. Then it changed and was double, uneven and out of step. It was both a snore and a sigh at the same time, followed by even breathing again.

Cautiously, Max moved over to the partly opened door and looked in. On a table near the door and against the wall were glasses and soft drink bottles; in a waste basket by the table the necks of two whisky flasks protruded.

Then in the mirror above the table he saw them. They were both naked, lying on a bed in front of the window. Max turned his head away from the mirror and peered from behind the partly opened door.

She lay on her back, the dirty striped ticking of the mattress rumpled under her weight. Her face was red and bruised; and her hair, dark and stringy, was matted under her head. The man lay on his stomach, his left arm over her middle, his face against the pit of her left arm. Unevenly, they snored and sighed, their bodies moving only slightly as they slept.

The room was hot and smelled of the sweat from their bodies and from the stale air and rotting food in the kitchen. Flies, like those in the butter dish, crawled over the woman's legs and stomach. The man's legs and arms were hairy; his head was shiny except for a line of gray hair in back. The woman's right leg twitched now; the flies on her leg stopped crawling, waited, then crawled again.

Max stood and watched. She was as old as his mother, maybe older. Then he thought of old Addlesdorf. He'd always delivered the groceries here himself. Why not this time?

The room felt hotter now than when he'd come in. Better not stay.

Quietly, Max closed the door to the bedroom.

Out on the landing again, the air was cooler.

The bill and the groceries! Max turned and looked through the glass in the door. And old Addlesdorf. Let him collect it the best way he can, thought Max.

As he descended the stairs, he looked east, out over the roof tops of Thatcher. The hot air danced over the black tar of the roofs.

Maxwell Potter didn't hear Maud enter the restroom. Suddenly, the stall door swung open, Max's jacket falling to the floor.

"Oh, my God," gasped the startled Maud.

"Wrong again, old girl," said Max, looking up, himself startled, but smiling. "Come in! Come in!" Then he saw his coat on the floor. "That floor's dirty, Ma'am." Max reached for his coat. "Would you . . ."

"Well, I never . . ."

"I'll bet you have," said Max, sardonically, picking up the coat and shaking it. "If you hadn't painted out all the funnies on the wall in here, I coulda read . . ."

But she was gone. The restroom door slammed shut.

Goddamned wench, thought Max.

Max washed his face at the sink; the water, cold on his pink flesh, felt fresh and clean. Drying his hands on the paper towels, he looked at the thin scar line below the thumb of his left hand. Goddamn the ol' man.

Max stepped into the hall. The far off jangling of a bell. Another customer. Comin' or goin', he wondered.

Chapter 8

The art gallery was deserted when Maxwell entered, his topcoat hanging over his left arm. He looked for the stout, bearded man. Impatiently, he gazed toward the front of the shop, out the large windows, onto Larimer Street. Snow was falling, the large flakes spiraling in wide arcs past the windows. Motor traffic in the street was light; figures moved rapidly along the sidewalk in either direction, hurrying with their last-minute shopping. A white Christmas after all, thought Max. Unconsciously, he began humming, the words tumbling around in his head. Max crossed to the far corner of the room, to the pile of print reproductions on the counter. Fumbling through the pile, he lifted out his Renoir print.

"Can I help you, sir?"

"I was just gonna take . . ."

"Fine print, there," said the man with the beard. "Authentic looking signature, you will notice."

"But I thought Renoir . . ."

"Signed only in the plate?" The bearded man's face was flushed. His breath was strong with whisky. "Not always. You can see he really signed that one. A beauty, isn't it?"

"But, a while ago . . ."

"Gotta be careful buyin' prints. Now, a reproduction's a different matter," said the bearded man, ignoring Max. He rubbed his face with his calloused left hand, paused, and then looked toward the back of the room. Nervously, he glanced toward the entrance to the hall. "Now, if I was you . . ."

"Look," said Max, wagging the print in front of the bearded man's face. "You gotta frame for this?"

"I'd buy a oil a them Indians over there," said the bearded man. He pointed to the desert scene leaning against the far wall. "Now, that's a conversational piece a art if I ever saw one."

"Look, goddamnit," said Max, exasperation in his voice. He grabbed the stout man by the right arm. "I wanta get this framed."

Startled, the man looked at Max, his nervousness increasing. Again he glanced toward the entrance to the hall. "Sure." He took the print. "Under the counter over here." He led the way to a low counter beyond the large oil painting that leaned against the wall. Looking at the Renoir print, he slid back the cabinet door, the one to the right. Broken and chipped frames protruded from the middle shelf of the cabinet. "Here," he said, motioning toward the frames, "we oughta be able to pick something outta that." He laid the print on the carpet. "Here's one that'll . . ."

" Is that your picture?" It was Maud's voice. She stood in the hall entrance, arms akimbo. From down the hall came the sound of water filling the stool tank in the rest room. The bearded man seemed to shrink before the opened cabinet door. Maud's voice was low and calm, almost cold. She stared fixedly at Max.

"I'm waitin' on this customer," said the bearded man, not looking up, anger in his voice.

"I wasn't talking to you," said Maud, haughtily, her eyes flashing at the squatted, bearded man now sorting through the pile of assorted frames and pieces of frames. "But, instead of throwin' out this drunk bastard, you bring him back in here and . . ."

"What drunk bastard?" snapped the bearded man, interrupting Maud and looking at Max. "He ain't drunk." Curiosity showed on his face and in his voice. "You the guy back in the can she's been blubberin' about?" His voice was edgy and high pitched.

"Look, do I get my picture framed or not?" asked Max, struggling into his topcoat, his own voice rising. "I gotta lotta shoppin' to do."

"Not in here," cried Maud, excitedly, looking at the Renoir print on the floor. Deftly, she lifted her right foot and brought it down hard on the print, her sharp shoe heel jabbing through the picture. With that, she jumped up and down on the print with both feet, her shoes grinding the crisp paper into the soft carpet. "No one's gonna insult me in my own home," said Maud, turning and looking Max in the eye. She then stalked out of the gallery and into the darkness at the back of the room and was gone.

Both men stared at the torn print. "That insufferable slut," said the bearded man, his hairy jaw sagging as he stared after the departed Maud.

"She's your problem," said Max, shaking himself from his silence. "What about my picture?" The man didn't move. Max nudged him with his left foot. "The picture, damnit! What about my picture?"

"That was your picture already, wasn't it?" said the bearded man, picking up the battered print from the carpet and smoothing it out against the counter front. He held it at arm's length and peered at it expertly. "Wouldn't look too good," he said, frowning up at Max. Shrugging his shoulders, he rose slowly to his feet. His face was dark under the coarse beard. He tossed the ruined picture onto the counter top and wiped his perspiring face on the sleeve of his right arm. "She used to be a hot bitch in bed, but now she takes it out on the customers." His voice was low, his glance furtive. "Sh . . ."

Max picked up the picture. "That was to be my wife's Christmas present," he said, turning the unmounted picture over and over, inspecting the holes.

"Well, you said you liked this Indian picture, didn't you?" said the bearded man, stepping back and pointing to the bright oil leaning against the wall at the end of the counter. "Fix her up with that."

"But I can't read the signature," said Max, squinting his eyes and bending over the painting.

"Oh, you're the one on the name kick; now I remember." The bearded man warmed up to Max. "De Vagos painted this one," he said, gaiety in his voice for the first time. "I didn't take you seriously a while ago." He patted the ornate frame with his left hand, his face beaming warmth, a smile topping the black beard. "She'd love this one. And what the hell. You want a picture, not a name." He was all confidence now. "Why a picture like this . . ."

"I'll take it," said Max, standing back, his eyes moving quickly, his gaze sweeping over the bright objects on the canvas.

"Great!" said the man with the beard, patting the picture frame again. "More Indians per square foot than any you'll ever see again," he purred. "And look at the detail. Look at the guts a that horse," he said, turning to Max. They were both quiet for a moment. Then the man with the beard spoke; the words were firm and hard. "That'll be four hundred dollars, please." He looked up at Max and smiled as he spoke.

"Like hell it'll be four hundred dollars," said Max, a threat creeping into his voice. "That print your hot piece a tail just trounced cost me nearly five hundred—four ninety-five to be exact—and . . ."

"Why, that piece a scrap paper," said the man. "You saw it in with them reproductions, didn't you? Hardly tell 'em apart."

"Look. You deliver that Indian to my wife and we'll call it square," said Max, ignoring the man's protests. A note of conciliation had surfaced in Max's voice.

"This may be Christmas, fella, but I'm no Santa Claus," said the man, scratching his beard and with emphasis in his voice.

Max had his wallet out now. Taking out a card, he handed it to the shorter man. "Look at that and then tell me what you're gonna and not gonna do." He was contemptuous of the man now. "Where's your phone?" he demanded, fatuously. "Ya think I gotta take this crap from you."

"Phone's in the hall," said the man, waving his right arm, his eyes scanning the card he held in his left hand. "So, you're president a Mountain-Plains Life Insurance," said the man, an affected air of relief in his voice. "I thought you were gonna turn out to be a building inspector."

Max was dialing his number; the dialing ended. The gallery was quiet, then Max's voice. It was loud and strong: "Simon?"

"_____"

"Yes, I'm glad I called, too. It was my idea, you know."

"_____"

"Larry Langdon? I told Irene I'd call him."

"_____"

"Yeah." Max's voice was authoritative. "I know Larry's worried. And Frank's worried. That's cause they don't know all the details."

"_____"

"Frank quit this morning. But he'll be back," said Max, confidently.

"_____"

"It's that damned Vince. He's got these two kids scared to death."

"_____"

"To hell with the competition!" yelled Max, angrily.

"_____"

"Whatta ya mean, what's come over me lately?" His breathing was labored. "I'm my same sweet old self, only I'm just startin' to get people organized. That's what's the matter."

"_____"

"You leave the details to me," growled Max. "We've got that deal all wrapped up and you know it."

"_____"

'Well, I know it."

"_____"

"Well, you just keep your wig on and ol' Maxwell'll take care a the chickens." Max gloated as he spoke. "Anyway, I didn't call to talk about business; not as such."

"_____"

"No. I'm down near Larimer Square. An arty dump called La Bouquet."

"_____"

"No, it's not a strip joint." He emphasized joint, sarcasm in his voice. "Arty like you put on a wall."

"_____"

"La Bouquet. And I want you to prepare a suit against him for the damages I . . ."

"You can have the Indian picture." It was the stout man with the beard. He tugged at Max's sleeve. "For fifty bucks and the damaged Renoir you can have the Da Vagos, or whatever his name is." The man looked up at Max, Max's business card clenched tightly in his fist.

"Just a minute, Simon, we have a supplicant." Max lowered the phone and turned toward the man. "For fifty dollars?" shouted Max. "Why, I should boot your ass out that front door and make my own choice free, seeings how you fixed my print."

"But I didn't do it," exclaimed the man, an embarrassed smile above the beard. "And, she'll get mad as hell, my givin' her pictures out." The man glanced down the hall and then into the darkened end of the gallery.

"Well, I'm madder'n hell now. And, she's not gonna be any happier my haulin' her down there to City-County Building." Max's voice was calmer now. Got the little bastard on that one, he thought.

"Twenty-five, and we deliver," said the bearded man, his voice almost a whisper.

"Even, Steven and you deliver—to my office. It's there on the card." He stood still, holding the receiver. Phyllis wouldn't want all that violence in the living room, anyway, he thought. Max waited. "What'll it be, suit or delivery?"

"We'll deliver it," said the man, turning back to the gallery. "Maybe Maud can fix up that Renoir."

"Fine. Fine," said Max, jubilantly. "That's what I like to see. Mind over passion, that's my dictum," he crowed.

Turning, Max lifted the phone. "Simon? Forget the suit! He sees the light a day."

"_____"

"Look, Simon. I'm the president a the company, remember? I know . . ."

"_____"

"Tim Guthry can't swing enough dough, or savvy . . ."

"_____"

"I know, but he can't get enough support to win over the commissioner and . . ."

"_____"

"I know. Larry'd believe anything Vince told him on that score. We're gonna buy that company and we're gonna keep all the business 'at's on the books. You start the papers like I said. Vince'll fall into line when the whole thing's over."

"_____"

"You'll see. And tell Larry those phone calls cost money."

"_____"

"I'll call sometime today—to wish him a Merry Christmas. Now, I gotta go get a present for Phyllis, first."

Noisily, Maxwell Potter hung up the phone and stepped into the gallery. "Be sure to cover that painting so's it won't get snowed on," he said, standing over the bearded man. The man was again squatted in front of the open cabinet, struggling with the assortment of old picture frames, shoving them back onto the shelf inside the cabinet door.

"I'm in the business, remember?" said the man, not looking up. He had retrieved his cigar, the rich, blue smoke curling up around the counter top.

"My secretary"—Max relished the words as he said them—"will be there to receive it." Probably thinks a secretary's something to stand up to and write letters on, thought Max.

"We'll deliver it when we close up this afternoon," said the man superciliously.

"Good," said Max, buttoning up his raincoat. He fumbled for the missing button, where he had torn the coat when he fell in the parking garage. What a bunch a smart bastards they turn loose in this town on Christmas, thought Max. "Merry Christmas." Smiling, Max stepped past the squatting figure; the blue cigar smoke choked him as he passed. Never make a enemy needlessly, that's my dictum, thought Max.

The air was cold and fresh as he descended the steps leading from the art shop. He paused and breathed deeply, his chest muscles expanding fully to the luxuriant Christmas feeling that was engulfing him. Good for the lungs, he thought; gets down into all those little sacs.

Large flakes of snow blotted against his eyes and nose. Again he breathed in deeply the cold, moist air. Up and down Larimer Street, beyond the restored buildings of the square to the east, and up the street toward the mountains to the west, the falling snow blurred the otherwise drabness of the scene. Gone were the tramps and the winos. Even the trucks were gone now. Max had forgotten when the street had looked so beautiful.

Continuing down the steps, Max turned up the street, heading east. He thought of his De Vagos painting. Beautiful. De Vagos. His mind stumbled a bit over the name. It sounded familiar. But, all those Dago names sounded alike, he thought. At least it was an American scene. Why was it no American artist ever was famous, except Whistler's Mother? The question had always bothered him, particularly so since he'd started seriously collecting art four or five year ago. Only those damned, morbid Kraut artists make the grade. It ranked him. Fakes! He thought of all those expensive prints on his office wall. What's her name, Everetts. She liked them. Fakes, probably all fakes. She's a phony if I ever saw one, thought Max. Christ! All that money.

A chill swept over him: somebody just stepped over my grave, he thought. Max tried to laugh at his father's old joke. Suddenly, the beauty of Larimer Street had disappeared. Cold water from the melting snow in his hair crawled down around his collar and down his neck. He turned up the collar of his raincoat, his shoulders hunching down into the lightweight garment. At the corner he turned south, along Fifteenth Street toward town.

Over the city the furry softness of the storm held in the glow that is Christmas in the city; string lights above the streets, and bunting and lights in the windows of the store fronts, were caught up in the gleam of shiny cars that slipped quietly through the snow. As he walked along Fifteenth Street, his mind wandered to his first Christmas away from home. It had been here in Denver. How many years ago? Then he thought of Roger.

Smart little punk. The time'll come and he'll wish he'd been home for Christmas. Vermont for Christmas! What the hell's a kid a mine doin' goin' to Vermont for the holiday? If he can't come home, maybe he'd like to work his ass off scoopin' coal during vacation. A thought was forming in Max's brain. But you don't scoop coal any more, he thought, dismissing the idea. He kicked the snow off the toe of his shoe. All the guts. Wantin' me to buy him a new set a skis so's he can spend his vacation in Vermont with his friends. What the hell he thinks money's for. Next thing he'll be wantin' a car. Get through college and get a job. Then's the time to be king, if you can. Not gonna be any society pimp in my house. By god, that shut them both up when I said that, he thought.

Maxwell Potter sloshed along through the falling snow, the white flakes adding grayness to his thinning hair. His shoulders were bent inwardly to the warmth of his coat, his eyes downcast as though searching the very steps he was taking. In the torn topcoat, with the bottom button missing and the cloth dirty from the parking garage floor where he had fallen earlier, Max appeared not unlike the other men bumping along Fifteenth Street, some on endless trips to nowhere.

Glancing into the streaked, steamed-up glass of a shop-front window, he saw himself. For a brief moment he felt free. Go down to the Mission and get a free Christmas dinner. It seemed a lifetime ago, he thought. That first Christmas away from home. Skidrow! How close he'd come that time. The feeling of freedom that he'd felt a moment ago was gone now. Thirty-three years scrambling and slugging to get away from Skidrow but only a cheap taxi ride back. He was cold, shivering.

Chapter 9

He felt the bump and saw the small, brown paper sack in the snow.

"I'm sorry, sir," she said. "That was clumsy of me. I mean—these walk lights and the snow." Her voice quavered as she spoke.

Max looked up; momentarily, he stared at her, startled from his thoughts.

She smiled, the snow on her steel-rimmed glasses at first clouding the lenses. Then he could see her eyes; they were warm and happy eyes, yet pale and watery in the failing light. Her face, now white against the cold air, was lined and drawn. Framing her cheeks, and with a scant triangle in the middle of her forehead, was a brightly flowered scarf, loosely knotted under a wrinkled and receding chin. On the right side of her nose, on the flare of the nostril, was a small shiny wart, pearlike, and set in a face of cold marble. Wet corners of wrapped parcels protruded from under each arm. Her body, clad in a heavy brown and white tweed coat, was short and thin.

Max smiled. Stooping, he picked up the fallen sack, carefully wiping off the wet snow. "It was my fault, ma'am," he said, returning the small package to her. "I guess my mind was out there among the snowflakes."

"Merry Christmas, sir," said the woman, smiling wistfully again. Bowing slightly, she was soon lost in the jostling crowd of the street.

Max turned and looked after her. For a moment he saw in the small woman his grandmother, or was it his aunt, on his father's side? Or his own mother? No, she'd never gotten that old.

He sniffed the air where the woman had just stood. The perfume! It was when he had stooped to pick up the dropped sack from the snow. The scent was a soft, feminine smell, clean and old, from his childhood, or his youth. For a moment he stood on the street corner, his eyes closed, the consuming loneliness of the crowded street disappearing. Warm, soft, sweet smelling. Perfume! He was surprised at the simplicity of it all. Perfume for his wife's Christmas present. Max looked up Fifteenth Street toward town. There on the corner, down at the end of the next block. A drug store.

The best they had, thought Max, standing at the curb, inspecting the package he had just purchased. Thirty-four ninety-five for the perfume and body powder. Not bad, he thought, frowning, if you don't bathe very often in it. He inspected the wrapping, holding the small square package up close to his eyes and then shaking it. He listened; two distinct movements from within. Risky practice, lettin' 'em sell you the already wrapped ones instead a makin' 'em do it in front of you, he thought. Max shrugged, pulled loose the intricately tied bow and ribbon from the package and slipped the present and bow into his right-hand coat pocket.

Again, he sniffed at the air around him. Only my imagination, he thought. White Christmas. Again the song came back to him. Max was humming, the words tumbling around in his thoughts. He could hear the bell of the Salvation Army worker over on the corner by the newspaper vending box. Still humming, the song forming silent words on his lips, Max dropped a dime into the red kettle. Never lose a vote of faith, he thought, bowing to the woman ringing the bell.

She wasn't looking. The Christmas tune died on Max's lips.

Stiffly, he stepped from the curb, turned, and started across the street. The DON'T WALK sign was on.

Max pressed his hand against the Christmas present in his pocket; it was warm against his leg. Phyllis! It will be good to get home to her, he thought. For the moment he forgot about their luncheon date. Get home to her. She'd be waiting for him. All these years of marriage, thought Max, and she's more beautiful than ever. A woman like Phyllis keeps a man in shape. A sort of paid up love policy.

Max jumped, but not soon enough.

The roar of engines closed in upon him. Max jerked up tall as the engines roared past. Too late; his face was covered with water. The engines! He wiped at his eyes with his left hand while he fought the water with his right. He could smell the exhaust. Get me out of here. He wanted to scream it. Water in his face again. We're number two, thought Max, suddenly. Five, six, seven. But we're number two. Max felt for his Mae West. I'll drown. A cold wave of water washed over his face. Max shook his head; the carrier still going by. They don't see me; they don't see me.

The faces all looking forward; looking only to the front. That one, up against the glass. And the eyes! They're in formation by now, thought Max. Not without us.

If I could only see. Only the ship going by. And the eyes! If I could only see the leader. The roar of the engines.

Gasping, and wiping water from his face, Max dashed between the roars of the engines and fell panting against the lamp post at the far corner of the intersection, his knees against a wooden box stacked high with the late morning *Post*.

Then the engines stopped.

Wind's changed, thought Max. He grasped firmly to the lamp post, his body limp against the cold upright, his eyes closed. "They've gone off and left me," he sobbed, clutching the post.

The engines again, farther off this time, and going in a different direction. Slowly, his hands tiring, Max slumped until he sat on the newspapers, his eyes still closed, his right hand still firmly grasping the lamp post. With his left hand he rubbed his eyes.

"Max, get me outta here." Benny's voice was lost in the roar of the engines. "Max . . ." There it was again, but lost.

Shaking. Plane's coming apart. Baxter, can't you fly this thing? Put the fuel to her. Past the island. Lift her up, Baxter. There's the flagman. Baxter, didn't you see the goddamned flagman? Only the water. Eternal father, strong to save, protect us from the . . .

Rising. Pit nearly full. Head hurts, can't move. Get out! Hatch cover gone, so get out. Sandwich and loose cigarettes up from below. Benny's sandwich and cigarettes. Lucky Strike green has gone to war. Now kick off! Pull the Mae West.

Mister Baxter. Mister . . . Sir? And the eyes. All white; face up against the glass. Hard-boiled egg eyes. Dying eyes. Choking, and blood comin' out. Water bubblin' in. Sir! The foam. Pink foam on the glass. Water goin' in. Mouth open and water ogin' in. Bubblin'. Bubble, you sonofabitch. Baxter, the flyin' bastard. A cigarette. One a Benny's cigarettes. Keep it. See ya sometime, Benny.

Max swallowed. Chilled and shivering, he clung to the wet lamp post. He shifted his position on the pile of newspapers. Far away, the roar of engines shuttled back and forth through his consciousness, his thoughts running after the engines and falling as spent shell casings into the watery pathways of his mind. She wouldn't even let me tell her about the Navy.

Pride of the Yankees was showin' at the Fox. Gary Cooper as Lou Gehrig. Tracy said she'd go, and a malt after the show. Borrowed a car, and after the show we'd have a malt down at Dairy Land and then drive down by the river. Moon'd be just right—almost full yet. All planned out.

Surprise her. Joined the Navy today. God, it gives a man a good feeling. Most of the men from here goin' into the Navy. Bob Wait, Golden Glove champ of all Chaushasha County, went last week. And the coach goin' next week. Army, though; coach'd been drafted. Surprise her, all right. Joined up. Not wait for that draft board to get their hands on me. A clean

place to sleep and good food. The draft board can keep all
that dirt and mud of the Army. 'Nough a that here. Jeffrey
can have it.

Jeffrey! Jeffrey! Jeffrey's leave. Comin' home on leave.
Only thing Tracy'd been able to talk about. So she had a
brother in the Army. Now he was comin' home. A pain in the
ass if there ever was one.

All planned out. We'd drive down by the river. Park
there under the cottonwoods, just east a the road, where it
crosses the bridge. Cool there this time a night. Learned to
neck there; not with Tracy, though. Older girl from the high
school; she liked to pick up boys from the junior high in her
ol' man's car. It'd be nice to sit there with Tracy and neck and
look out at the moon on the churning water of the river. The
August crickets sound the best. They know it's 'bout over for
them, and they wantta make the most of it. Tracy'd like sitting
there, too. So many things to tell her 'fore gettin' on the train
for Omaha in the morning.

Gotta go to Omaha in the morning. Sounds big and
important, sayin' it like that. Gonna learn a trade, and that'll
help me get through college. But not without Tracy. Your ol'
man'll be proud a me someday.

God, there's a lot to talk to her about 'fore getting' on
that train.

Remember, Tracy, how I met you? Up at the "Y" that
time. Went there to see Jeffrey. Didn't know he had a sister.
You'd been in the Catholic school, remember? And I didn't
know you even lived. But I owed Jeff a nickel and wanted to
pay him back. I didn't belong to the "Y", but he did. I swam
in the river in the summer. Anyway, when I asked for him,
they said he wasn't there, but someone called you. Some girl's
party upstairs. That'd make it 'bout five years now, Tracy.
Wonder how she'll take that, knowin' I've liked her five years?
That oughtta mean something to her.

And your ol' man, Tracy. I know from what you've said,
and the way he acts sometimes, that he don't—doesn't—like
me much. Not just 'cause I'm not Catholic but 'cause my ol'

man's poor. At least that's what my ol' man says 'bout your ol' man. But it won't always be this way, Tracy. I'm gonna become a flyer, and then a engineer. President says the country's gonna need a lot of pilots. And when I get out I'm gonna make money, you'll see. And he can't tell you what to do after you're a woman, and you will be when I get out. If you really like me, Tracy, he can't make no difference.

God, will she listen to all that in one evening?

And your mother. She's beautiful, Tracy.

And my ol' man, and my mother and then college. That's a lot to talk about 'fore gettin' on the train to Omaha in the morning.

All planned out.

But Tracy wasn't at home when the doorbell rang at seven-thirty, just like I said I would. Graduation suit on for the last time, and fifty cents worth a gasoline in a borrowed car. Nobody at home except Grandma, and she was in the wheelchair. Family'd gone out to take pictures—have a family portrait made—Jeffrey bein' home and all. And then they'd gone to dinner. Might be a little late, but I could come in and wait.

For more'n two hours listenin' to Grandma. More'n two hours bein' pumped. Lot a good it did her, though—pryin' ol' woman. Two hours a waitin', wastin' what little time there was left 'fore gettin' on the train.

Forgot Jeffrey. That's the slip-up. Damned ninety-day wonder. A dog-face officer in the infantry. Hoped he'd get his ass shot off but not on my time.

Finally, at a quarter to ten. Tracy insists on walking to the movie. Only a few blocks, she says. And about her brother. Jeffrey! Jeffrey! Jeffrey! Did I know he is a Second Lieutenant already?

And the movie! Gary Cooper or Rin-Tin-Tin? How'd you tell? How can you talk to a girl in the goddamned movies? Got sick during the movie and had to go to the bathroom three times. Let's leave—we know he dies. But, she wants to stay. About one o'clock when the show's out and she gets scared.

Never been out past twelve without special permission. She runs all the way home, like I was chasin' her.

But, Tracy, I need to talk to you.

She can't hear.

She's waitin' at the porch door for me. Her hands are soft and warm. For the first time, maybe she'll kiss me. Tracy, I'd like to . . .

Then the door opened and her ol' man's standin' there.

"It's past twelve o'clock, Tracy. I'll speak to you in the morning." Hiram McClosky, hidden mostly in the shadows of the porch, waited until she was gone.

"Just a minute, Potter," said McClosky, his voice excited and menacing, "I'm not through with you."

"But it was late when we started and I—we . . ."

"Shut up," said McClosky. He was close to Max now. "I'll do the talking. When you take my daughter out, I expect you to have her in no later than twelve. Do you understand that?" Hiram McClosky's voice was muffled but clear. For a moment neither of them spoke, and then it was McClockey again: "Anyway, she's goin' off to college in a few weeks and I won't allow her to see you again. Do you understand?"

Forgot the car and walked home. Sent the car keys home from Omaha. Too many things to think of before gettin' on the train.

"Hey mister! Mister! You dropped this when that car 'bout hit you." It was a boy speaking. No taller than Max as he sat on the pile of newspapers, the boy smiled as he gave up the crushed package. "Sorry it got so messed up," said the child. A dark blue nylon windbreaker, with parka drawn tightly around the face, hid all but his eyes, nose and dark red lips. Snow blotched his face, competing with the many freckles, now burnished red marks across his wet nose and around his eyes. "Merry Christmas, Mister," said the boy, turning; he disappeared up the sidewalk to Max's back.

Max sat staring at the thing the boy had handed him. Only a suggestion of the Christmas wrapping was intact. Like melting ice cream from a child's cone, a creamy pink liquid dropped from the package corner, running down the front of Max's topcoat. The bath powder and perfume. Shaking the ruined Christmas package, Max inspected the contents, listening carefully for the bottle of perfume. And then he felt it fall; the bottle lay in the snow at his feet. Stiffly, he bent and picked it up.

As he wiped slush from the bottle in his hand, the cuts in the once-jewelled surface were grime-filled, a coarse rock from a placer's trough. Max looked at the bottle but didn't see it. Almost instinctively, he raised the bottle to his nose, to sense its fragrance. Then he jerked, the hand holding the bottle turning white as he gripped the small vessel.

Mrs. Baxter's perfume! That's what the ol' lady's perfume was, thought Max. Only ol' lady Baxter was rich and that ol' lady wasn't. Max looked down Fifteenth Street to where he had bumped into the old woman. Mrs. Baxter—Mr. Baxter's mother. The pilot's mother. A widow. Ol' man a judge in Oklahoma, or someplace. But had died 'fore the war. Ol' lady Baxter, that's what that perfume reminds me of.

She'd come down to San Diego after the crash. Nice ol' lady, though, as rich ol' ladies go. Went to dinner with her. Somewhere out of La Jolla. Never been there 'fore she took me there. Had walked by, and had seen it from the bus comin' in from the beach to the nickel snatcher over to North Island. But never dreamed of eatin' out there. Not until we went there. She'd come down to San Diego after the crash.

A fur. Still see the fur around her shoulders. San Diego's chilly in early December but not cold and the fur'd looked out a place. But she'd worn the fur—four stuffed looking, button-eyed pups around her neck. And she'd smelled like money itself. A light, nice smell, like the ol' woman. Come to pump me. Knew she was comin' and that she'd pump me 'bout the crash. Planned to be sick when she came down to San Diego, but got the days mixed up. "Max Potter, report to the M.A. shack." And there I was havin' wine and dinner with her and lookin' out over the Pacific.

Rich looking, ol' lady Baxter. Shorter than me. Musta been shorter than her son. Baxter, the flyin' bastard.

Somewhere in the second glass of wine she starts pumpin'. The wine was a bitter Chiante. "Choose the wine," she says, beckoning the waiter to the table. Afraid of wine: once a wino, always a wino. But she insists. Chiante—the name'd sounded right. Only you eat it with spaghetti. Makes your lips pucker.

Then she says it: "How did Larry get killed?" Probably not just like that 'cause a the wine. But she asks it, softly, and her voice is calm and cold. Her eyes look like the button-eyed dogs around her neck.

The question is a surprise. Knew she's gonna have to ask it, but still it comes as a surprise. How do you tell a mother her only son got killed? Even a prick like him. Embarrassed, fumbling with the glass. Afraid to look at her. Larry Baxter, the flyin' bastard. Sounds different, looking at the cool, dry-eyed mother across the table. Rich ol' lady like her couldn't take it. Wonder what it'd be like to have a rich mother like that?

Lie to her. Lie for the sonofabitch. Safest pilot in the squadron, Baxter was, I tell her. Baxter—Larry—personally inspected the plane before every flight and made sure the engine was in perfect condition. A genius with engines, especially airplane engines.

Yes, Larry'd been good with mechanical things since he'd been a little boy.

Christ, what crap.

And then she pumps some more.

Tell her about the time Baxter bailed out and let his torpedo bomber go down with the gunners still inside? A rich bitch like that? Think she'd believe it? Why upset her?

More lies.

Larry'd held the respect of not only the other pilots, but the enlisted men all'd wanted to fly with him. But the men'd been assigned to him and he'd not been one to show favors.

Her eyes demand more details. And the wine and all. There was this gunner named Benny. He and the ordinance men'd probably loaded the plane wrong, or something. Always hard to keep your eyes on that ordinance bunch. Baxter'd—

Larry'd—talked to Benny before 'bout the plane, but with some people there's no hope, and Benny was one a those. Larry'd keep thinkin' Benny'd shape up. 'Course there's no tellin' what happened, really, but there'd been that problem with Benny.

That's what cut, those lies 'bout Benny. Benny what? Can't even remember his name. But lyin' to ol' lady Baxter 'bout Benny was almost too much.

But fate catches up with even the greatest among us, I tell her. She seems to like that. Saw it in a movie somewhere. Christ, what crap. Larry'd gone down with his plane tryin' to save Benny—tryin' to pull him out. Poor dumb Benny.

At the nickel snatcher to North Island that night the ol' lady's lips'd been warm and friendly. A good-by kiss on the cheek. And she'd smelled like money itself. God, to be one a those stuffed dogs around her neck. A rich ol' woman like that.

Benny's mother. Never did . . .

Max jerked upright on the pile of newspapers, the pain in his ribs blinding him for a moment. Then he was jabbed again.

"Ge . . . Ge . . . Ge . . . Ge . . . Get off . . . off . . . off . . . off . . . off my Chr . . . Chr . . . Chr . . . Christmas money. How . . . How . . . How . . . How the he . . . he . . . he . . . hell ya . . ."

Max looked up. The eyes of a gnarled, troll-like man stared at him from a cold and placid face.

Chapter 10

"I'll take care of it, Shelton." It was a studied, almost restrained voice, soft and without excitement.

"But, my . . . my Chris . . . Chris . . . Chris . . . Christmas mon . . . mon . . . mon . . . money" whimpered the man called Shelton, motioning toward Max and shaking his clenched right fist at the wet figure sitting on the stack of newspapers.

"It'll be all right, I tell you," said the voice, soft, yet stern. The voice was at Max's right elbow now. "Up the street there, Shelton. Some customers," said the voice. "I'll take care of this."

Shelton turned to the pedestrians crossing with the traffic light from the south. "*P . . . P . . . P . . . Post,*" whined Shelton.

For a long moment a snow-shrouded figure stood staring at Max, their eyes finally meeting. The eyes of the man with the soft voice were popping, thyroid eyes, buried under a heavy knit, once black, stocking cap, the kind common to men of the sea. It was frayed where holes had been cut or burned in the soft fleece of the wool. In the yarn above the left ear, the cap was soiled with food, and the crown was hard-crusted under the softness of the snow. The brows above the eyes were thin, light wisps of hair. The face was bloated and smooth. Stooped shoulders, now a rounded shelf of flaky whiteness, hovered over a trembling frame. A gray, and much stained, topcoat of herringbone tweed, the stripes stretched wide and uneven, was buttoned snuggly under a soft-hanging chin. The coat bulged out around the middle and under the arms. Coiled around the man's neck was a faded, maroon-plaid wool scarf, the large firm knot at the throat holding his head out and upward. His teeth were yellow, with only the incisors visible in his lower jaw as he opened his mouth to breathe, the steaming air coming out of his mouth in short puffs. The man's rough, chubby hands made paddling motions as he flipped his short arms to ward off the chill. Looking at Max, the man circled slowly around to the front, a large, turtle-like man swimming in a sea of white snow crystals.

"You and your friend over there crawl out of the pond at the zoo?" Max asked, scornfully, staring at the stooped figure before him. "Or, did you get your holy days mixed up?"

The old man was quiet. A wide yellow tongue slid through the empty space between the two lower incisors as he licked his gray lips. Then he smiled. "Still the same old Maxie Potter, eh?" he said, nervously, the words soft and little more than a whisper. "Still the same old spunk, eh, kid?"

"You have the advantage, as they say," said Max, a kindling of interest showing on his wet face and in his voice.

"It ain't been that long, kid," said the old man, a sardonic note in his voice. "Maybe a war or two," he said, suggesting a shrug with his flipping arms, "but not that long." The smile widened as he watched Max. "Unless you've completely forgotten all your old friends."

"Friends?" said Max, mockingly, still looking the stooped figure in the eyes, the scorn in his voice turning now to mock suspicion. "You some more of the Christmas help from D.U.?" Max remained seated on the wet newspapers, the crushed Christmas package still clutched in his left hand. A smear of wet bath powder formed a pink, diffused cloud on the front of his wet raincoat. In his right hand was the gift bottle of perfume. He slipped the bottle into his raincoat pocket. "Or are you one of our salesmen?" asked Max, sarcasm in his voice. He waved his hand, the one with the crushed package, as though to push away the face before him. A stream of pink water streaked the front of the old man's coat.

"Nope!" said the old man with finality, pinching his nose hard with his right hand and then wiping his hand on the side of his topcoat. "I'm the man who brung ya to this town a long time ago and tried to make a man outta ya." He was serious now as he spoke. His round, bloated face was turning gray like his lips. He watched Max. "Ya wouldn't believe that, wouldja?"

"Like hell you are," said Max, his interest in the old man failing. "That old coot died a long time ago." Max started to rise.

"No! No! Don't get up, Maxie," said the old man.

Max leaned back against the pole and stared at the man.

"Arzie Beatrice—AB they used to call me, remember?" A nervous smile tugged at his lips as his bulging eyes flicked over the younger man's face.

Max sat up, his face red. "But you're fat, and what did you do with your gold teeth?" Max's eyes searched the old man's face.

"Ever learn to hold your hooch, kid?" asked the old man, laughing. There was no humor in the laugh. "Or don't they call it that in high society these days?" The laugh and smile were gone now, and a faint gleam flashed in the green eyes.

"But you were an old fart when I knew you, AB," said Max, laughing, ignoring the old man's words. "Damn, I wish all our policyholders were like you."

"Ever find that ax I gave you for a present that time, Maxie?" asked the old man, nudging Max on the right shoulder. "Ten or eleven years old, ya musta been," he said, chuckling but without humor. "That was an expensive piece of hardware, kid."

"But, you can't be AB," said Max, excitement in his voice for the first time. "My Ma . . ." His voice stopped; his gaze fell from the old man's face. "But, I guess you'd know 'bout that," he said at last.

"Yeah, kid," said AB, nervously shuffling his wet shoes in the deepening snow. He looked away as he spoke. "I was the one that cut her down out there in the shed after Paul died." AB's voice was barely audible. "No note, no word to nobody, nothin'."

Then both men were quiet.

The traffic light changed again. AB moved in close to Max as the crowd jostled past them on the corner. His breath, short and wheezing up close, came out in puffs of steam in the cold morning air. The breath was foul and smelled of bad teeth and cheap food.

It was the old man who spoke. "This ain't no place to talk, kid." Turning, he waved to Shelton, now hawking his papers on the other corner, to the south, across the street. Motioning for Shelton to come back over, AB turned again to Max. "Let's get over into a doorway so's we can talk," he said, jerking his head, motioning for Max to follow. With his arms flipping at the cold, snowy air, his head pulled down into the bulk of his bulging topcoat, the stooped figure turned his face into the storm and started up Fifteenth Street, his pop-eyes blinking at the falling snowflakes.

AB pirouetted, flipped his right arm up above his head, indicating for Max to follow. He smiled, the yellow tongue moving between the lower incisors. Turning again, he drifted among the shoppers moving up Fifteenth Street. Max watched as the old man disappeared momentarily in the holiday crowd, only to see him emerge, occasionally looking back over his shoulder.

Max rose from his perch on the newspapers. From his pocket he took a handful of change and dropped it on the stack of damp papers.

"Th . . . Th . . . Th . . . Thanks," said Shelton, waving to Max, smiling. "Mer . . . Mer . . . Mer . . . Merry . . ."

Max didn't wait. Without looking, he threw the ruined Christmas package into the snow and followed the old man up Fifteenth Street.

At the corner of Fifteenth and Stout, AB stopped and waited. Turning, he saw Max and flipped up his right arm again for him to follow and then disappeared to the left, down Stout to the west.

AB was standing in front of an abandoned two-storied brick building when Max caught up with him. The windows of the building were boarded up on the street level. Now marked for demolition in the wake of the Skyline clearing project, the building had once housed a stationery and used book store. Along the front of the building, just above the jagged glass shards that still held fast to the metal casings of the window openings, bold gilded wooden lettering, broken and hanging from loose nails, suggested primitive printing, symbols of a world now gone. A wedge-shaped doorway, the glass opening in the door boarded up like the windows, was set back into the building a little more than a tall man's reach. The old man stepped back into the doorway as Max walked up. Max followed into the doorway and stood beside him. The floor was dry and hard.

Suddenly, AB darted out to the middle of the sidewalk, looked for a long moment up toward Fifteenth Street and then stepped back into the protecting doorway. He stamped the snow from his wet shoes.

"I'm here, AB," said Max, humor in his voice for the first time. He nudged the old man with his left elbow. "You saw me come."

"So I did," said AB. The corners of his mouth twitched nervously. Again he darted onto the sidewalk and looked up toward the corner. The street where they stood was deserted. Again he stepped back into the doorway, still looking up toward the corner.

Max was quiet. He stood, half leaning against the door, the collar of his raincoat up around his neck. Water from the melting snow on his face and hair streaked his thin face and neck. He leaned there, his eyes closed. His teeth chattered.

"You should of come home, Maxie," said AB, his voice no longer soft. It was harsh now. "He died askin' for you, kid." The old man looked up at Max, standing against the door. The nervousness had left his voice. "Ya could of saved your Ma's life if you'd of come home, Maxie."

They were both quiet. The old man stood staring into the spiraling snowflakes beyond the doorway.

Finally, it was Max who spoke. "What life?" It was more a statement than a question.

"The only one she had, Maxie," said AB. His voice was soft once more.

Neither spoke.

AB darted onto the sidewalk and looked up toward Fifteenth Street. He stood there, flipping his arms against his sides. Then slowly, as before, he stepped back into the protecting doorway.

Max had his eyes open now, but he didn't notice the old man. "I was at Jacksonville, Florida. In the Navy," said Max. "I couldn't . . ."

"The Red Cross said you could come home or I wouldn't of sent you the telegram," said AB, interrupting Max. His voice was argumentative.

"But there was a war on," said Max, "and . . ."

"So there was, kid," said AB, his yellow tongue passing between the two incisors. The old man's voice was low, as though talking to himself. "Did ya win it, eh, Maxie?" he asked, sucking in the last words. He wheezed as he breathed.

They were both quiet again.

AB beat his arms against his sides. He was shivering; the loose-hanging skin under his chin was trembling. Stomping his feet on the worn stone floor, he peered around Max, up toward the corner again. "I saw ya get outta that cab down on Larimer. Lotta changes there since the old days, eh, kid?" AB was standing close to Max again, beating his arms against his sides. "How long did ya last that time, Maxie? 'Til Christmas?"

"Two days past Christmas." It was Max's voice, far off.

AB rubbed his rough hands together. The knuckles were blue; as he flexed them they turned white, then red. "Knowed ya was in Denver," he said at last. "Knowed it for a long time. Seen how ya made it big, in the papers and all. And a classy woman, too." AB stood back and looked up at Max. "She's all right, Maxie. She knows her class." The old man paused, his breathing difficult.

"No Thatcher woman, you can bet your dear ass," said Max, disgust ringing in his voice. Again he stood with his head leaning against the nailed-up door, his eyes closed.

"Ya used to be a good fighter, kid," said the old man, matter-of-factly, ignoring Max. "A good two-minute rounder. Other kids couldn't touch ya. Ya had class in the ring, Maxie." He was puffing now, the steam hissing from his blue lips. He bent forward and looked up to the corner again. "Ya stayed where ya belonged you'd of had class, kid."

"I've done all right, AB," said Max, almost arrogantly. Still leaning against the door, he didn't look at the old man. He stood motionless, his hands deep in his raincoat pockets. "An education, my own company, a kid in college, and, as you say, a classy woman." He paused for a moment. "What would of been your odds on that happening when ya knew me as a kid?" he asked, nudging AB. "Huh, AB?"

"What education was that, Maxie?"

Max didn't answer, but stood, eyes closed, his body relaxed against the door.

" 'Member how your Ma'd read to us all every Saturday night?" said AB, ignoring Max. "Paul—he'd get the corn ready and she'd let us choose the story. Street and Smith's. God, I got to know every story they'd write. 'Member Maxie?" There was an air of excited melancholy in AB's voice now. "She's the only one that could read. Sometimes you'd go to sleep on the floor. 'Member that kid that lived out past the brickyard? Scared to go home some nights. One time your Pa had a take him home, he was so scared of the dark." AB sighed as he finished. "There was a lotta love in your Ma, Maxie." He did not look up but stared into the storm.

"Look, you musta wanted something other than to tell me what a great family I had," said Max, impatiently. He stomped his feet. "It's cold standing here," he said.

"Ya get used to it, kid," said AB. The old man's face was dark now.

AB stepped out onto the sidewalk again and looked up toward the corner. Then, quietly, he moved back into the doorway.

"Your ol' man deserved better'n he got from you, Maxie," said AB. The nervousness had returned to his voice. His yellow tongue licked his blue lips.

"Now, wait a min . . ."

"Don't get huffy with me, Maxie," said AB, interrupting his younger companion. "Ya got it comin'." AB cupped his hands and blew puffs of steamy air on the stubby fingers. "Blood poisonin'," he said, dragging the words out. He rubbed his hands together. "Ever see it kill a man, Maxie?" He looked up at Max. "It's a pretty sight." There was bitterness in his voice. "That kinda death robs a man of his dignity. He stinks, Maxie. Did ya ever see a man sweat and stink 'til it makes you puke to be in the same room, Maxie? He kept askin' for you. He didn't needa die, not like that, kid." AB was panting, his breath coming hard. "Rail slipped off the buck and cut his leg. Not bad. On the shin bone. But it musta hurt, 'cause he cussed up a storm when it happened." The old man hesitated, and then continued. "A week went by and nobody'd paid any attention to him. You get bunged up all along puttin' down those damned railroad ties. Then on a Monday morning we found him layin' there in the snow along the tracks. Wonder he didn't freeze. Thought he had the grippe or somethin', and the boss, ol' Frasier, the bastard—'member him?—he took Paul home, took his clothes off and put him in bed. Thought he was growin' a new set of balls. Only there was three of 'em, right up there in the crack of his ass, practically." AB was perspiring; his bloated face was pink for the first time. "The doc looked at him," said AB, sighing, "but it was no use. He lasted four more days. And all the time he keeps askin' . . ."

"OK! OK!" yelled Max, turning on the old man. "That was his idea, bustin' his back on the goddamned railroad. So what the hell, a lotta people die. He knew he wasn't gonna live forever," said Max, shoving the old man aside and starting to leave.

"Just a minute, Maxie," said AB, nervousness in his voice again. "Like I said, I knowed for a long time you been in town. I've been waitin' to have this talk." He pinched his dripping nose and wiped his hand on his coat.

"You fraud," said Max, stepping back and looking at the old man. "You got an angle here somewhere," he said, looking into the bulging eyes staring out at him.

"Like I said, kid," said AB, not looking at Max, his body trembling. "Ya got a classy wife and a good job." His wide tongue licked his gray lips. "It wouldn't help none if people knowed about what a . . ."

Whirling, Max grabbed the old man by the front of his coat, slamming him hard against the boarded-up window opening. "Now, what exactly did you have in mind?" asked Max, his voice menacing.

"Nothin', Maxie. Nothin'," moaned the old man. "I just . . ."

"You stop me on the street. You wanta talk old days." Max tightened his grip on AB's coat. The steam from the two men's breathing filled the doorway. "Now, what do you want?" shouted Max angrily, shaking the old man.

"Money!" said AB, desperation in his round, watery eyes. "I gave your Ma thirty-five dollars just before Paul died." He gasped as he spoke, his neck outthrust with his humped back up against the wall. "When I saw you get outta the cab, I sent Sharky—a friend a mine—to figure the interest." AB's eyes moved, staring past Max. "He ain't back yet."

"What about my kid?" asked Max, suspicion in his voice. "You been talking to my kid?" He jabbed his two tight fists into the old man's chest; he didn't release his grip on the coat.

"No! No!" said AB, fear in his voice now. "I've seen him, but I didn't talk to him."

"Look, you start buggin' my kid, or anyone, 'bout me and I'll kill you. Understand?" Their faces were close; the old man's breath smelled of garlic and fish. The top button on his coat was missing now; the coat was open at the throat. "A man's life is his. Forgotten. You tear it out and you burn it like a page out of a book. No credits, no debits. And all you get for it's a pile a ashes." Max looked into the bulging eyes. "Just because you never made it outta your stinkin' lot," said Max, contempt in his voice, his mouth turned down at the corners, and his breathing deep but quick, "don't plague me with your goddamned sentimentalities." He let go of the old man's coat and turned to leave.

"Just the thirty-five, Maxie," begged AB, his face blue again and trembling. "I gotta live, too." He was slumped against the door.

"Why?" asked Max, looking at the old man, his eyes steady, "what'd it get you?"

Pulling his raincoat collar up around his neck, Max stepped into the storm, up toward the corner on Fifteenth Street. He didn't look back.

Chapter 11

Max turned the corner, down Fifteenth Street toward downtown and Civic Center. He walked briskly, but aimlessly, his eyes downcast, open but not seeing. His mind was lost in the whirlwind of himself, tossed and spinning on end, pivoting on the chance meeting with AB, a friend of so long ago. Those years of so long ago—slabs of stone that weighed upon his soul.

Don't look back, he thought. There is no past. Life's new every morning. Don't need to look back. Regret is double jeopardy. Only the present. No looking back. Plan for the future. Don't keep paying for something you didn't buy. It was a prison and I escaped.

Max congratulated himself on his escape. They were his wardens: his parents, the people he had known then. They were the accusers, the judges, the jailers and the guards. They were the accessories, before and after the fact. And it had been their game, not his. Redemption. The Golden Rule. Pray and believe. Pray and ye shall have. All passwords of that prison.

Within the walls of his confinement the dampness of his life chilled the flicking warmth that was his soul; the cracks and crevices of his inner being squeezed in upon the moving force that drove him. Far back in his memory, beyond the slabs of stone, there groped a feeling of excitement, of lightness of heart, a quickening of the pulse. But the feeling was primitive in his being and for many years had been foreign to him. Only at night, as the mind creeps into the memory crevices of the past, was he haunted by the faces in his life.

The snow fell evenly now. The spiraling flakes, sharp crystalline symbols for writing on the wind, etched in whiteness the cornices and window ledges of the decaying buildings that walled the street. Driven by the wind, chalky patches of snow blurred, altered and left hidden the many shop signs along the way, their messages betrayed only by the smells and mingled voices as doors opened and closed upon the sidewalk.

In the alley, sheltered from the wind, a yellow striped cat feasted on the remains of a bird. Gaunt and suspicious, the cat looked sideways at the footsteps in the snow; sharp teeth tore away the flesh, the feathers of the bird now forming a blue-gray carpet on the snow.

Suddenly and quietly, as though shot from a child's sling, the khaki-clad figure slid over the top of the Chevy, thumped softly on the hood of the car, slid, bounced off the lamp pole, and fell to the sidewalk, both feet lying in the gutter between the Chevy and the car in front. It was a man in Army uniform; he lay still in the snow. A dark brown sock covered his left foot; the shoe was missing.

Max stopped, looked up.

Shiny wet, slipping to one side, righting itself, then slipping again, a cream-colored Lincoln went by. The driver, a dark lump behind the wheel, was alone. Three cars down the gutter, the Lincoln crashed, the sharp explosion of shattered glass and fragmented metal startling the Christmas shoppers on the sidewalk. Spinning, tail out into the street as it hit the car at the curb, the Lincoln was itself struck in the right side by a long yellow taxi and swept on with the traffic. Other cars turned out past the wreckage.

Now traffic was halted entirely in the right, outside lane. Horns blared. Already a crowd was gathering at the curb, staring at the wrecked machines.

Under the right front wheel of a stopped car, where the alley entered the street, a man's brown shoe lay, only the sole and one side visible in the slush of the street. The driver of the car honked the horn. Two children in parkas in the front seat pressed their faces up against the windshield, looking at the stopped cars ahead. The horn sounded again.

Max stood at the alley, staring.

The man on the sidewalk was on his hands and knees now, his head down. A lock of blond hair fell forward into the snow. Where his face had lain, the snow was pink; then small icy red spots formed cherry dots in the snow. As the man pushed himself up, the dots in the snow stopped. Then he was on his feet, standing in the gutter, leaning against the lamp pole. He was tall, his matted blond hair partly hiding the high cheekbones of a finely shaped face. Not past nineteen; perhaps twenty.

Blood was running in a thin, irregular line from his left ear and down his neck. A pink spot was worming on his snow-covered shirt front. The narrow blue of his eyes contrasted sharply with the white chalkiness of the snow that caked the front of his uniform. He was without coat, the brown shirt sleeves splotched and wet from the grime and snow of the sidewalk.

Except for the thin line of blood on his left jaw and neck, the young man's face was white like the snow. He shook himself, his tall frame uncoordinated as he pushed away from the pole. Looking at his shoeless foot and at the blood-spattered snow, embarrassment seemed to engulf him. He swatted at the snow that still clung to his shirt front.

Passersby looked disapprovingly at him, some continuing to stare at him over their shoulders long after they had passed. Others ignored him in their hurried steps, or were attracted by the wrecked machines in the street.

A squat, round man in a black felt hat and gray tweed topcoat was directing traffic past the wreckage in the outside lane.

A momentary smile flashed across the ashen young face of the soldier as he stood in the gutter, his shoeless foot now spongy and trembling. Jerking, he stood upright. Bewilderment, then panic swept over his face; his mouth fell open to speak. Holding out his arms, he lurched across the sidewalk, missing Max, and staggering into the alley. He stopped and turned. Startled, he again reached out for Max, this time only his left arm outstretched. His right hand quivered at his side; then it was rigid.

Frightened, he looked at Max. The narrow blueness of his left eye was gone. With only a large black shiny round hole where the flicker of a smile had been only a moment before, the eye now stared straight ahead. The right eye, alive and darting from side to side, searched Max's face and the alley. Fear swam in the watery narrow blueness of the eye.

Again he tried to speak; his left hand clawed at his throat. His hand came away red and wet. The red line below his left ear was wider now. Much like the monacled eye of a jeweler inspecting a fascinating gem, the right eye searched the moving, sticky fingers of the left hand. A scream, silent and breathless, formed on the young face, then faded; the right eye closed.

Slowly, like a candle before a flame, the tall body towered for a moment over the right leg, sagged, and then bent. Without a sound his body fell, slumped against the coarse brickwork of the building, then over onto the soft white mat of the alley, his face in the cold wetness of the storm.

Max sat in the snow in the alley, his left shoulder up against the brick wall. Cradled in his arms, he held the fallen soldier to his chest, the cold shoulders chilling through his jacket. Around the damp body Max gripped his own raincoat. Faintly, he could feel a pulse in the man's right arm where he gripped it under the coat.

Hurry! Why don't they hurry? thought Max.

He looked into the wet, still face, the fixed left eye staring, wide but unseeing. The right eye was closed, as though asleep.

Why don't they hurry?

Max looked over his right shoulder toward the street. The honking had ceased; traffic was again moving.

Again Max looked down into the young face. He thought of his own son. And of the war years. So many young faces. Benny. Benny who? Don't look back. Pages outa a book. Burned pages.

His face is Roger's age, thought Max. It could have been my own son. The muscles in Max's jaws tightened. Gently, Max pulled the raincoat away from the soldier's mouth and with his left hand combed back the long strands of blond hair from the cold, white face. His grip tightened around the young man's shoulders.

He was being watched; he could feel it. Behind the half-closed lid, the right eye was alive. The left eye. He'd gotten used to it—wide and staring. But the other one! And he was trying to move his lips. The effort was feeble.

Then Max sat up and listened.

Far down the street, toward Larimer, coming up Fifteenth Street with the traffic, he could hear the wail of a siren.

"Hear that, fella?" he whispered, squeezing the cold right arm. "Hear that siren? They're comin'." Looking over his shoulder toward the street, he flexed his left leg. "Hold on, son."

That'd be Stout Street, thought Max.

The siren was loud. Then the wailing slowed, nearly stopped. Max shifted his left leg under the heavy body.

"Hold on," he repeated.

The siren was at the alley now. They'd have to get through the crowd.

His knee under the raised head was numb. He looked back as the siren started past the alley; it was a police car, probably answering a call to the car wrecks. The police car stopped. Max could see the rear bumper through the crowd that flashed by the alley opening at the street.

We're trapped, he thought. Like in a box or a camera. Flashes. Glimpses. But nobody looks in.

"They'll find us, fella," whispered Max. "They'll find us."

He bit his lip. The taste of blood sweetened his mouth. Max could feel the eye watching, judging. He looked down; the live eye was half open. Slowly it moved, looking at Max.

Then the gaze faltered, the eye looking up the cold, stormy alley. But it didn't close, not completely.

Talk, thought Max. Talk to him. Keep him alive.

"You're gonna make it all right, son," said Max, an attempt at cheerfulness in his tired voice. "You're still young. Too young to die. When you're young, you're not ready. You'll know when you're ready, all right. I saw the ribbons on your chest. I wasn't in the Army myself during the war, but I know they didn't give those bars to no USO commandos." He chuckled as he said it. He was frightened by his own voice.

The eye was watching his face again. He could feel it without looking. He shifted his right leg under the raised head.

"You weren't ready to go, that's all."

Then he thought of Benny. Benny's mother and father'd come all the way to San Diego to celebrate his nineteenth birthday. An Italian dinner, with everything just like in Italy. It had taken two days to gather up all the dandelions, mushrooms and other required ingredients. They'd gone to a little out-of-the-way restaurant to cook it. And Benny died. And at nineteen. Benny What's-his -name.

"You're young and . . ."

Shut up! Shut up! Quit bullshittin' him. Max fought back the words. Nobody saw us! He's gonna die. And nobody saw it, nobody but me.

Max gripped the young man tightly again. He closed his eyes, resting his face on the matted blond hair.

"Oh, God, let him live," he whispered, gently cradling the cold firm chin in the trembling fingers of his left hand. He wept quietly as he said it. For a moment the words flickered in his memory. Then they were gone.

He was quiet for a long moment.

"If you're Catholic, son," he whispered at last, concern in his voice, "He might not have heard me." He pressed his face tightly against the boy's damp hair. "But I did the best I could."

The alley was quiet. The bustle of the street to his back was lost to him. Max sat in the wetness of the snow, waiting.

Releasing his grip on the young man's shoulder, Max felt for the pulse once more. The blood was quiet; the arm was cold. The right eye was closed, relaxed. No longer bright, the other eye stared into the loneliness of the cold afternoon sky.

"Merry Christmas, son," whispered Max, pulling his cramped leg from under the heavy body, "wherever you are."

Max rose to his feet, still looking at the fallen soldier in the snow. He bent over him, picked up the raincoat, shook it and stepped back for a final examination.

His left leg was asleep. Gritting his teeth, he closed his eyes and paused, leaning against the brick wall. Trusting his weight on his leg again, he turned, not looking at the man in the snow.

The police car was still there at the alley. He could see it through the crowd of bundles and legs as the Christmas shoppers hurried past the opening to the street.

Across the alley from the quiet figure in the snow, the yellow striped cat tore at the remaining flesh of the bird. Gaunt and suspicious, the cat looked sideways at the police cruiser slicing through the crowd and into the alley. Frightened, the cat grabbed up the bird and ran. At the corner of the building it stopped, turned and looked back, then disappeared up Fifteenth Street toward the wrecked buildings to the north.

A squat, round man in a black felt hat and a gray tweed topcoat sat in the front seat of the cruiser with the policeman. He sat quietly as the officer spoke into a microphone. The stop lights on the cruiser flashed red—sharp and bright. The policeman got out and bent over the figure in the snow. He held a man's brown shoe in his right hand.

Max glanced back up the alley. The officer was in the police cruiser, talking into a microphone again. While he talked, he handed a small slip of paper to the squat, round man sitting beside him. The man took the paper and looked at it.

Chapter 12

"A martini," said Max to the short, elderly man in white shirt and black bow tie behind the bar.

The room was dark. In the booths along the front, to the right of the entrance as you came in, and on past the end of the bar, vague, almost static, shapes sat outlined against splashes of amber light that emanated from windows of imitation bottle glass. The room was close, the air rancid.

The slumped figure of a man sat at the end of the bar, his back to the windows. On the shiny surface before him was a small whisky glass and a large tumbler of water. He sat hunched forward over the bar, his shoulders draped with a loose-hanging green suitcoat. The dark figure was faceless in the shadows of a wide-rimmed summer hat, the straw soiled and without shape. Only the lobe of his left ear was visible in the light. He sat quietly. Then a hand appeared above the edge of the bar. Unsteady fingers grasped the small whisky glass. The man drank, sipping in long sucking noises. He raised the right arm, sniffed and cleared his throat. With the whisky glass still in his left hand, with his right hand he raised the tumbler of water, his hand trembling as he did so. Coughing, he set both glasses on the bar, his body convulsed, fighting the phlegm in his throat.

"Your martini," said the bartender, matter-of-factly, placing the stemmed glass on the bar in front of Max. His voice was thick and foreign, but friendly. Max dropped a dollar bill onto the bar. The bartender turned; the bell sounded in the cash register. "Thank you, sir," he said, laying a dime and nickel by Max's glass. He turned and disappeared through a narrow door at the far end of the bottle rack that lined the wall behind the bar. A long mirror formed a back to the bottle rack. The man at the other end of the bar, with his back to the window, had stopped coughing now. Max watched him in the mirror behind the bar.

The room was quiet.

Then Max heard her voice. She was seated at the far end of the bar where the bartender had disappeared through the narrow door. One waitress was standing there, at the end, past the last stool, when Max walked in. Now a second waitress had joined her, taking the last seat. Her nasal voice, though not loud, was penetrating and abrasive. "What made you catch on to him in the first place, Fay?" she asked, tapping the end of a newly lit cigarette on the edge of a bent metal ashtray and looking up at the other waitress.

The two women wore tight-fitting, lavender satin costumes, with narrow straps over the shoulders and a three-inch gray fur strip at the hem. The fur strips came just above the knees. In the dim light of the room the two women looked enough alike to be sisters: deeply lined smile wrinkles around the mouths and in the dry skin above the cheek bones, near the eyes; blonde, short-fitting wigs and flat, little-girl breasts.

The seated one raised her chin, blowing a cloud of smoke into the stale air.

"He's trouble. Always looking for a fight," said the waitress named Fay, shrugging her bare shoulders. "He comes in here, gets a few drinks under his belt and then gets tough." She screwed up her face as she said it, shrugging her shoulders again. "Made a big man out of him, I guess." She shifted her stance, leaving her left elbow on the bar. "One night he said, 'Don't goddamn me, Fay, I wont stand for it.'" Her voice was serious. "'I didn't,' I said." Then she smiled. "'I said, "goddamn, comma, Warren."' Jesus, that made him mad." She laughed a dry, humorless laugh. "He's a pain," she said, shrugging her thin shoulders again and sighing. "And that dish he brings in here."

"Yeah, he's a phony if ever I saw one," said the one seated at the bar. She drew heavily on the cigarette, then exhaled as she spoke. "One night he sat right over there in the corner . . ."—she turned, motioning with her left hand toward the corner table opposite the entrance, lighted by a spot lamp hanging from the ceiling—"stroking her boobies right in front of everyone." She choked, short puffs of smoke punctuating her coughing. "Yes, by God," she said, her coughing under control, "practically had 'em out there on the table playin' with 'em."

A siren sounded at the alley corner, next to the bar, the flashing emergency light dancing momentarily on the false bottle glass windows and the ceiling of the room.

That'd be the ambulance, thought Max.

He started to rise from his place at the bar, then stopped.

No good now, he thought. Too late. If it's gonna happen, it's always too late, from the day you're born.

He held the glass in his left hand, stirring the olive around and around in the oily looking drink with his right index finger.

The mortality table's gonna get you, no matter what, he thought. Him growin' up and all those campaign bars and he has to go like that. Life expectancy at age nineteen. Statistics. What chance's a guy got?

Max felt the cold air, then the front door closed. He looked up.

Two men entered. He could see them in the mirror on the wall, behind the bottle rack, the thick wooden shelves of the rack slicing their reflections into long, irregular, moving splotches of flesh and clothing as they walked up to the bar. Their heads were obscured by the bottles on the top shelf. One of the men was slender, the other was heavy and bounced as he walked. Both wore chocolate-colored corduroy blazers, with coarsely knit collars.

"Coupla beers, Fay," said the heavier of the two.

They sat at the bar, the heavy one taking a seat next to the waitress and the other one near Max, an empty stool between them.

Fay had slipped around behind the bar.

"So we're not talking 'bout lap dogs." It was the slender man talking now. "I don't consider a French Poodle a lap dog, though," he continued, throwing two one-dollar bills on the bar. "But lap dogs or no lap dogs, that's not the point." He reached for his beer. "I just can't believe that a Poodle can be bred by—let alone give birth to—a St. Bernard."

"You saw the picture in the *Post,*" said the heavy one. "Same face, same head, same other markings as the St. Bernard." He lifted the glass of beer to his lips, drinking half the glass before stopping. "Big as a horse. Lived right next door to the Poodle." The man belched, then wiped his mouth on the back of his right hand. "I'm satisfied he did it."

"Only a week old when that picture was shot," said the slender one, shrugging, "and the pup's 'bout as big as the mother."

"So, there's your proof," said the heavy one.

Both men were quiet now, sitting there drinking their beers.

Talk, talk, talk! thought Max. What about the man in the alley?

Max lifted the long-stemmed glass to his lips and drank.

Nineteen. No older'n twenty. Could have been my own son, damn his hide.

Max thought of Vermont. And Benny? Benny . . . ?

Musta hit the kid hard—that car, thought Max. Just like takin' a shell. Blow you right out of your shoes. The guy out north of town, that time. Head on with that semi-trailer. Same thing happened. Went through the windshield and landed in a field. But both shoes were still on the floorboard, strings all tied and natural.

Max drank again. He sat absently, holding the toothpick in his right hand, twirling the large green olive on the end of the stick.

Wonder if he was really dead when I left him? he thought.

He lifted the glass and drank again.

"Another martini," said Max, addressing no one in particular.

"Have a beer," said Fay. It was an order. She stood behind the bar, the fingers of both hands resting on the curb of the polished bar top. "I don't know how to mix a martini."

"Neither did the bartender," said Max, staring coldly at the waitress, "but he got paid for one." Max finished his drink. "Another of the same," he said, still looking at the waitress.

"Look, fella," said Fay, her voice not unfriendly, "have a beer. If I mix you a martini, you'll be in your cups like ol' gramps down there," she said, indicating the old man at the end of the bar, his face still dark under the wide rim of the straw hat. "This isn't my specialty, back here."

"What happened to the old man?" asked Max, looking in the direction the bartender had taken, through the narrow door.

"Damned if I know," said Fay, shrugging her bony shoulders. "Beer or not?" she asked, raising her eyebrows. The friendliness had left her voice. She waited, her hands resting quietly on the bar.

"No wonder people want to pick a fight with you," said Max, straining his long, slender neck and looking down the bar towards the other waitress. "The mystery is, how'd ol' gramps get the drinks under his belt in the first place," he said, laughing. "Certainly not in here," he said, still laughing and slapping the bar.

"I was wonderin' when the smart asses were gonna come in off the street," said Fay, a smirk replacing the smile of a few moments before. "Only, you start a fight with me and you'll find your ass back out on the street again." She waited. "Beer or not?" she repeated, finally.

"Say," said Max, his face lighting up, "are you a sociology student at D.U.?"

"Me?" exclaimed Fay, her voice shrill. "Why, that's about . . ."

"She?" It was the other waitress speaking. "You know the old adage: 'You can lead a whore to culture, but you can't make her think.' "

Fay ignored the other waitress. "Beer or . . . "

"I don't want . . . "

"Do all of us a favor, Fay, and fix the bastard . . ."

"Potter's the name," said Max, looking down the bar and smiling, "but, for a stranger, that's close."

"But I don't even know what he wants," said Fay, anger in her voice. "There's martinis and there's martinis." She leaned back against the bottle rack, her bare arms folded across her flat chest. She stared into the space before her; the laugh wrinkles around her mouth and eyes were lost in her tired face.

"Look, fella, please tell the Mother Superior whether you want gin or vodka," said the waitress seated at the end of the bar. Her voice was patronizing.

"Let's try gin," said Max, sarcism in his voice, "and see what she puts in it."

Fay took his glass from the bar and turned to the row of bottles on the shelves along the wall.

"Vermouth, Fay. Vermouth," said the other waitress, laughing, criticism in every syllable. "Her at D.U.?" she laughed humorlessly, her voice dry. Cigarette smoke clouded her face.

Fay reached for a bottle on the shelf.

"Not the sweet!" The other woman's voice cackled as she laughed. "Oh, that'd make a martini, all right."

"OK, so you're a smart ass, too," said Fay, turning back to the bar, a bottle of dry vermouth in her left hand. She set Max's empty glass down on the mixing screen and looked searchingly up along the bar toward the windows.

"Always, vermouth and gin or vermouth and vodka," said the other waitress. She shook her head. "But not the sweet." She drew heavily on her cigarette. "The man says gin. So it's one to four—one vermouth to four gin." She laughed again, choking as she did so, the smoke screening her face. "Hell, I'd fight, too, if you mixed my drinks," she said, still coughing, the words wrapped in smoke. "And, if he wants it extra dry," she said, her coughing stopped now, "just wave the bottle of vermouth over the glass." Slowly she knocked the ashes off her cigarette into the ashtray. "It's that easy," she said, raising the cigarette to her lips again.

"Maybe so," said Fay, picking up Max's glass and dropping it into the discard bin under the bar. The crash of shattering glass startled Max; he rose from his stool to look over the bar to where his glass had gone.

"If he wants a martini, he'll either wait 'til Shorty gets back or he'll have to mix it himself," said Fay, wiping her hands on her costume and again folding her arms across her chest. "What'll it be, fellas?" said Fay, turning and looking at the other two men. "Two more?"

"Make it three," said the slender man, the one nearest Max. "One for your friend here." He turned to Max, smiling. "Don't tempt her. If you can't make it until Adolph gets back, you'd better switch to beer."

"A beer, then," said Max, defeated. "Any beer. I don't really give a damn."

"We call it draft beer," said Fay, smiling and friendly again. She placed three glasses on the bar, the foam from the beer wetting the glass-like surface. "This I can do," said Fay, still smiling.

"Say 'thank you' to the Mother Superior," said the waitress at the end of the bar, sarcasm in her voice.

The wail of a siren cut through the stale air of the room. It was close by, in the alley. It was going away.

"Hope they get that mess cleaned up soon," said Fay, motioning with her head toward the front of the building. "A wreck like that's bad for business. Any man big 'nough to step up to the bar sees a wreck and, bang, he's right back in his sandbox, playin' with cars. A fire or a car wreck'll do it ever time."

The siren could still be heard. Goin' east to one of the hospitals along Seventeenth Avenue, thought Max.

"More'n just a car wreck this time," said the heavy man at the bar. "Heard someone was killed."

"No kiddin'," said Fay, a note of excitement and a new interest in her voice.

For the first time Max looked directly at the two men seated with him at the bar. Then he gazed down at the dying bubbles of foam on the polished wood of the bar. Mechanically he drank his beer. Looking up again, he could see the two men in the mirror behind the bottles, their faces peering out between variously colored liquors on the bottom shelf of the rack.

The heavy man was blond, with long, shaggy sideburns framing a chubby, round face. Irregular upper front teeth flashed in the dim light as he yawned. Without a hat, his hair was pasted to his large head, his hair wet with melting snow. Holding his beer glass in his right hand, he wiped his nose on the back of his right hand.

The other man, the slender one, was dark with thick brown hair parted on the right and with well-clipped, thin sideburns running down his wide face, almost to the edge of the protruding jawbone. Poor orthodonistry had left him with a gummed, grandpa look. His eyes, partly hidden in the darkness of the barroom, sparkled as he sat staring into the nothingness behind the bar.

Both men were in their mid or late twenties.

The chrome pouring spouts on the shelved bottles were shiny horns now with the reflection of the bottles in the mirror.

Max rubbed his eyes with the long slender fingers of his left hand; his eyes were tired and heavy. He looked away from the mirror, at the old man at the end of the bar, near the windows. The old man's head lay on the bar now, his straw hat, a dirty yellow harlequin crown against the amber light of the window, clung to his fallen head. The whisky glass lay on its side on the bar, to the left of the man's face. With arm outstretched on the bar, the right hand still clutched the half-full tumbler of water. The old man snored, his body and head still and dark.

The young man nearest Max was talking. " . . . and that's probably the police taking away the body."

No one spoke. The men sat, slowly drinking their beers. Then it was Max who spoke.

"I saw him get it," said Max, whispering the words. "This Lincoln plows into him and smashes up all those cars." He sat looking into his glass. "Kid couldn't have been more'n nineteen, twenty years old. 'Bout the age of my own son."

"That damned phony, Kirby," said the waitress seated at the bar, a newly lit cigarette bobbing up and down in her lips as she spoke. "I'll bet he missed the whole damned show."

"You bet he did," said Fay, laughing, "but when he sits back there at the table tonight, you'll be told that it was him that called the police and it was him that's the star witness to the whole thing."

"Not a word outta him," whispered Max, more to himself than to the others. "Tried to cry but couldn't even do that. 'Bout nineteen or twenty. Coulda been anyone."

"We didn't see it ourselves," said the slender man, looking at Max in the mirror between the bottles, "but we saw the ambulance turn in out there just as we were comin' in here. Too damned cold to wait, but that's what someone said. Man'd been killed in the wreck."

"No one give a damn," said Max, ignoring the other. "He reached for me. I coulda helped him."

Max raised his glass without seeing it and drank.

"Knocked him right outta his shoes—hit him so hard," said Max.

"Kirby—this Warren Kirby we've been talkin' 'bout— he'll have something to say 'bout this, all right," said Fay, laughing her humorless laugh. "After he reads it in the papers, that it." She folded and unfolded her arms. "I only hope the police hauled his ass off to the dryin'-out tank and they keep him there for Christmas. He's trouble."

There was a noise at the back of the building. A door slammed shut.

"Careful, Paula," said Fay, motioning her head toward the narrow door at the far end of the bar. "Here comes Shorty."

Paula turned, easing herself to her feet. The cigarette had disappeared. She set two empty beer glasses on the bar as the bartender entered.

"Too bad," said Adolph, sadly, his squat figure coming up behind the bar. "He was a good boy. And so young." His thick, heavy voice was far off. He seemed not to notice the others in the room.

Fay was out from behind the bar now, helping Paula over at the booths by the windows.

"Three beers, Adolph," said Paula, setting three empty glasses on the curved end of the bar. Reaching over the bar to the mixing screen, she grabbed a bar cloth and returned to the booth near the door, just to the right as you enter.

"He sometimes gave the girls a bad time but not any more," said the old bartender. "But he was a good boy."

"Crowd 'bout gone out there in the alley, Adolph?" asked the heavy young man, trying to make conversation with the bartender. Adolph didn't answer. Slowly, he drew three glasses of beer and set them on the bar in the amber light from the street. "Yes," he said, finally "they're going." He didn't look up.

"By any chance, did you see Kirby out there any-wheres?" asked Fay, sliding a round tray of empty glasses and beer bottles across the bar. "Someone a while ago said they saw him out there in the gutter, drunker'n a coot."

"I saw him," said Adolph, taking the money off the bar and turning toward the cash register. Paula picked up the three glasses of beer, disappearing from view in the mirror. The old bartender squeezed his nose hard, then wiped his hand on his apron. "He won't be in tonight," he said, his voice tired. "They hauled him away."

"There's a Santa Claus after all," said Fay, standing at the end of the bar and looking out across the dimly lit room.

"The wench," said Max, gazing into his beer, his voice low and weak. "At least her Kirby can still get drunk and cause trouble."

The empty beer bottles clanked softly as they fell into the bin below the bar. The old bartender wiped the round tray and put it under the bar, the metal thumping the hollowness of the wood.

Chapter 13

"Three more beers, Adolph," said Max, tossing a five-dollar bill on the bar and waving with his left hand to indicate the two men with him at the bar.

"Much obliged," said the heavier of the two, "but the beer's on us."

"Yeah, we want to get you off martinis," said the other man, the one near Max. His speech was slow and deliberate.

The bartender filled the glasses and placed them on the bar, one at a time, starting with the heavy man. He picked up the five-dollar bill. The cash register bell chimed. The old man laid the change on the bar in front of Max.

"Well, the next one's on us," said the heavy man.

The men were quiet except for their drinking.

Then is was the slender man speaking: "You said you could have helped the guy that was killed," he said, turning to Max and looking at him for the first time. His voice was friendly; his eyes were steady and without warmth.

Max looked at him but didn't speak.

"Why didn't you, then?" asked the slender man, his gaze not moving from Max's face.

"He died before I could do anything," said Max, shifting his eyes to the glass of beer in front of him. "He just lay there in the snow and died."

"Then you couldn't do anything for him," said the slender man. "You can't have it both ways." His voice was no longer friendly but matter-of-fact. "He was going to die, and that's that."

"But I coulda helped him somehow," said Max, a slight whine in his protesting voice. "He tried to . . ."

"Bullshit, the guy was Jesusly gonna die, an' you weren't gonna save him, either." It was the heavy man speaking. His voice was loud, yet confidential. He was standing now, the nearly full beer glass in his right hand. "A guy gets killed and you old farts blubber 'bout what you coulda done to help him." The man moved along the bar and took the stool to the right of Max.

"Careful who you're bullshittin' and old fartin'," said Max, his voice high pitched now. He began to rise from his stool, fumbling in his right coat pocket as he did so. "I'll have you know that I'm president of . . ."

"No offense, fella," said the slender man, on the left, reaching for Max's left arm and easing him back onto the stool. "Cruncher, there's, only trying to make conversation." He smiled, his pale cheeks wrinkling where thin lips cut the sallow skin of his hollowed-out face. "Only he gets all upset with a put-on."

"A put-on?" said Max, starting to rise again.

"The Professor's right," said the man called Cruncher. "A put-on." The air whistled between his teeth as he said the words; bubbles of beer pelted the back of Max's neck.

Max wiped at the bubbles as he turned to face the man.

"But you don't even know me," said Max, the whine in his voice sharper now. "How in the hell is helping a dying man a put-on?" He took a long drink of beer from his glass.

" 'Cause you're hangin-out all over the place," said Cruncher. He had set his glass on the bar. "You mention you gotta kid, right?"

"Roger," said Max, calmly, his voice low and firm.

"Roger? How corny can a guy get?" snapped Cruncher.

"Now, just a minute," said Max, slamming his right hand flat upon the bar, anger in his voice. "I haven't even had the pleasure of an introduction and you start all this personal stuff."

"Who's personal?" asked Cruncher, a note of patience in his loud voice. "You got a kid. And you said somethin' 'bout bein' some president a somethin'. So you got a wife and some fancy dude house somewhere. Right?"

"That's what I mean, all this personal . . ."

"That's the put-on," said The Professor, the man on the left. "We know you really don't give a damn about your fellow man." He breathed deeply, then shrugged his shoulders. "Only in war does a man really care about helping his fellow man."

"Oh Christ, here we go with another hero of the wars." It was Fay speaking. She stood at the far end of the bar, her bare arms folded across her flat chest. "Was you with George Washington, dearie?"

The room was nearly empty now.

"You broads stay outta this," yelled the heavy man, Cruncher, suddenly leaning forward and looking down the bar at Fay. He raised his left hand as though to strike her.

"If you was, War Hero," continued the waitress, ignoring Cruncher, her voice shrill and laughing, "you shoulda waited. They built a bridge across the river." Her voice cackled.

Adolph stood in the shadows behind the bar sucking quietly on his cold pipe. He was asleep, or appeared to be.

"Doesn't it strike you as ironic that in battle a man will risk his very life to save another man, a total stranger?" It was The Professor speaking.

Baxter, the flyin' bastard, thought Max. Baxter, save his fellow man?

"But you set that man down in a city, or in regular civilian life," said The Professor, "and he might not raise a finger to save a man, even an acquaintance."

Benny. Benny What's-his-name, thought Max. Goddamnit, how could I ever forget Benny's name?

"He's Jesusly right," said Cruncher, jabbing Max had in the ribs with his left elbow. Beer slopped from Max's glass onto the bar. "You old farts are a put-on when you grieve for mankind. You got the whole world messed up. Look at war! Why we gotta fight the goddamned wars?" There was a frantic urgency in his voice. Again he jabbed Max in the ribs. Cruncher's voice was noisy and excited. "Huh?" he grunted.

Max lowered his right elbow to protect his ribs. Benny . . . ? The thought wouldn't leave him.

"Well?" Cruncher wet his lips as he waited.

" 'Cause a the Democrats, right?" said Max, his voice calm, but laced with sarcasm.

"See what I mean, fella," said Cruncher, disgustedly. "You were born in the wrong century." He raised his beer glass and drank; his fleshy face was red. Perspiration wet his forehead.

"What do you know 'bout war?" asked Max, looking first at Crnucher and then at The Professor. He pulled at his collar; the room was suddenly warm. "I was in the war, through the whole Pacific campaign." He pounded the word "Pacific" into the bar. "Let's see you beat that!" He wiped the bottom of his glass along the bar, then drank.

"A lemon sucker if I ever saw one," said Cruncher, sneering as he said it.

"You don't have to fight in a war to see the incongruity and hyprocrisy of the reasons why men fight."

Max turned to the speaker, the man on his left.

The Professor was staring into the mirror behind the bottle rack as he spoke. His voice was even and deliberate. "I believe it was Lee who once said: 'Thank God war is so terrible or we'd get to love it.' " He turned and looked at Max. "Know what he meant by that?" he asked sardonically.

Max shrugged his shoulders, not speaking. He lifted his glass. The foam was warm on his lip.

"There's something in war itself that meets the needs of men," continued The Professor, again looking past the bottles on the wall in front of him. His voice was low and purposeful. The grandpa mouth added age to the face that looked out of the mirror from between the bottles. "It can't be had in peace, and every generation longs for it. Walt Whitman was on it when he said, 'Oh, with the love of lovers bind us.' And James was looking for it. But no one's come up with James' 'moral equivalent to war'."

"Three more beers," said Cruncher. He slid a five-dollar bill across the bar.

"No, I'll get mine," said Max, his right hand reaching into his coat pocket.

Cruncher's left hand clamped tightly on Max's arm. "You see, fella," he said, "we gotta have our wars 'cause a man ain't got no other way a showin' another man that he loves him."

Max shook his right arm free. Fumbling in his coat pocket, he pulled out a dollar bill. Adolph set the fresh glasses of beer in front of him and picked up the five-dollar bill "No, I'll pay for my own," said Max, reaching across the bar for the bartender's sleeve, his voice high-pitched again.

Adolph was at the cash register now. The bell sounded as the money was rung up. He turned and laid the change for the five on the bar.

"Here, I can buy my own drinks," said Max, tossing a dollar bill onto the bar in front of Cruncher.

"Keep it," said Cruncher, flicking the bill back along the bar.

"Apologists for war," said The Professor, still contemplating the space behind the bar, his voice low, as though now talking to himself and ignoring the other two men, "ponder the question of why each generation must have its holocaust. It is said that every war produces its legions of old men. And the war was the watershed of their lives. And the young men? If not formal war," he continued, sloshing beer around in his glass, "they must incite civil strife and disorder. Confrontation, with violence as an end in itself, is the goal." The Professor turned and looked at Max again, his eyes cold as before, his thin lips forming a line between his sunken, gummed jaws. "Why?" he asked, quietly shouting the question, his voice tense now.

The room was quiet except for the snoring drunk at the end of the bar near the window. His breathing was little more than sighs as he lay limp on the bar. Max and Cruncher stared at their half-empty glasses but did not answer.

"Because," said The Professor, seeming oblivious of the others at the bar. He pounded again. "Because society will not admit to the underlying female moral structure upon which Western civilization rests. This civilization, in maintaining the wife-mother reverence in Western man, emphasizes man's maleness as sire of the next generation and as guarantor of continuity of the race. But in doing so, the resulting societies tend to rob men of their manhood."

"Halleluiah! Halleluiah!" laughed Fay from her station at the end of the bar. "Maybe the libs got something after all." There was a cheerfulness in her voice that had not been there before.

Paula placed two empty glasses on the bar, down by the sleeping drunk. "Two," she said.

Adolph took the glasses.

"You miss the whole point," said Cruncher, leaning forward and looking down the bar at Fay. His voice was low but angry. "The liberation a broads got nothin' to do with it." He raised his glass and drank, sucking in the liquid. "Now shut up and listen to the man," he said, looking at Fay again and shaking the foam-rimmed glass in his hand as though it were a judge's gavel. "He's got this all figured out."

"So, men go to war, or plan for war." It was The Professor speaking again. "In war," he continued, his voice crisp but not loud, "men exclude women from the game and devise strategies that defy society's interference with their expressions of manhood. Negotiations to avoid war reinforce the causes of war. And peace treaties, arising from the same female drive for immortality through the race, simply allocate time and resources for the continued struggle of man for his manhood. Only in the heat of battle is a man permitted to openly display his real love for a fellow man." The Professor lifted his glass and drank. A light feather of foam coated his thin upper lip. "But in doing so," he said, wiping his mouth with the back of his left hand, his voice lower now, "he has to kill another man, another army and another society." Pausing, as though musing over the words he had just spoken, and moving his glass back and forth along the bar, toying with the wetness of the slick surface, he reached his left hand forward on the bar, three fingers up. "Three more, Adolph," he said.

"I'll get these," said Max, fumbling with his topcoat again.

"They're on me this time," said The Professor. He laid two one-dollar bills on the bar.

"No! Really! I want to pay for my own," said Max, holding a dollar bill in his right hand and waving it at Adolph.

"Relax, fella," said Cruncher, again jabbing Max in the ribs. Max sucked in his air but didn't move. "You still got your mind on that martini."

"But I must pay for my own drink," said Max, angrily.

"Let the little orphan pay for his own drink, then," said Fay, again laughing her shrill cackle. Setting an empty beer glass on the bar, just past The Professor, she reached across the bar for a wet cloth. "One more, Adolph," she said, her voice solemn now.

"Keep your money," said The Professor, a gummed smile parting his pale lips. "It's my turn."

"Look, no one's gonna buy me drinks if I don't want 'em to," said Max, the whine back in his voice again. "Here!" With his left hand he stuffed the dollar bill into The Professor's right jacket pocket.

"It's already paid for," said The Professor, his voice again cold, the smile gone. Calmly, he took the dollar bill from his pocket and laid it on the bar in front of Max.

"I'm not gonna be any common bar pick-up," said Max, pushing the money aside. He started to rise.

"No offense, fella," said The Professor, again reaching for Max's left arm. "I was talking about war." Gently, he pulled Max back down onto the stool. "Look at it philosophically," he said, casually, looking across at himself in the bottle-cluttered mirror. "One shouldn't court his own death, but when it happens to someone else, it's done. The whole thing is a matter of timing. All the wars! So what? Everyone out there on the street," he said, almost scornfully, and motioning with his head over his right shoulder toward the windows, "even the youngest—give them ninety-five or a hundred years. A matter of timing. It isn't that we die, but how and why we die that's important." He took a deep breath, then drank from the fresh glass of beer. "It's the 'why' that is perhaps more important than the 'how'," he said at last, after a long pause.

The cheap scum, thought Max, biting his lower lip as he breathed deeply. Think they can come in here . . .

"In my discussion of war," said The Professor, his voice low but excited, the words pronounced with a certain incantation now, "homosexuality doesn't necessarily mean body contact between participating males. It can mean simply the elimination of women and femaleness from their inner lives. They might gang-bang the same woman, or frequent the same whore, but there's no contradiction here. It simply. . ."

A loud thump on the bar interrupted him. A short, heavy boot, with a leg in it, lay on the bar in front of Cruncher. The leg was a shiny tan, but without flesh.

Bolts held the foreleg to a stump that ended just above the knee. Slowly, Cruncher unlaced the boot, the long strings slipping softly through trembling fingers.

"Please call a taxi, Adolph," said The Professor.

The bartender walked to the far end of the bar.

Cruncher was pulling the tongue loose in the unlaced part of the boot.

"In repeated wars," said The Professor, ignoring the others at the bar, "men must seek out greater and greater fetes of glory. They must up the ante, as it were. Women and children are not idle victims of war, but are necessary to the godliness of war, to the search for an acceptable expression of love of man for man. Both must be sacrificed with the stronger surviving, dedicated to future jousts. Maybe James' search for a moral equivalent to war was aimed at identifying this homosexual drive." The Professor shifted his position on his stool, sipping absently from his glass.

"Keep on goin', Professor," said Cruncher, his voice, like his fingers, trembling now. "Tell 'em why we gotta have the wars." He pulled the bolt from the knee joint of the leg and laid the two pieces of leg on the bar. Without pausing, he pulled at the toe of the sock working the brown woolen knit off the hard, flesh-colored foot he held in his trembling right hand.

"Look at Napoleon," said The Professor, finality in his voice and ignoring Cruncher, "by these standards the greatest homosexual of them all." Again he sipped on his beer. Wiping his mouth on the back of his hand, he continued: "All the peace treaties, the United Nations, the great sums spent on international understanding, on armaments and disarmament—all lost until we better understand this universal moral drive for manhood."

Suddenly, a cold draft swept along the bar. "Someone want a taxi in here?" called a loud but friendly voice from the open door.

"Over here," said Adolph, the curved-stem pipe still in his mouth. He motioned the taxi driver to the bar.

Cruncher sat at the bar; his head and left arm lay sprawled across the boot and the disassembled parts of the foot and leg. His massive shoulders shook as he wept quietly into the brown heavy woolen sock he held in his tightly clenched right fist.

The Professor was on his feet now. "When I'm ready, driver, you take his right arm." In his left hand was a large paper grocery sack. Carefully, he lifted the unlaced boot from the bar and dropped it into the sack. Then the foot. Then the pieces of the leg.

The taxi driver lifted the clenched right fist from the bar. "Let's go, fella," he said, his voice soft and with warmth. Gingerly, he pulled the sock from Cruncher's hand and dropped it into the paper sack.

The Professor and the taxi driver turned the heavy Cruncher around and together lifted the nearly limp body from the high stool. "OK, let's go," said The Professor, his voice even and without emotion. "You take your leg," he said, thrusting the full paper sack into the stiff fingers of his companion. "OK, driver, take us out to Fitzsimmons." The Professor's voice was cold and matter-of-fact.

The three men left the bar, their arms interlocked for support; the empty pants leg, dangling loosely from under the chocolate brown corduroy jacket, flapped easily in the wind as the door opened and the men passed through.

"Well, did you ever see such gall?" said Paula, wiping the bar where Cruncher had sat. She shivered. "And for Christ sake, was that taxi driver born in a barn?" With deliberation the waitress closed the barroom door.

Chapter 14

"How about that, Adolph?" said Paula, standing at the end of the bar. "Putting his filthy shoe on the bar!" Again she wiped at the place on the shiny wood.

The bartender didn't answer. His short, dark figure worked methodically behind the bar. He dunked a dirty beer glass down over the scrubbing brush several times, then down in the rinse water and then placed it on the drip mat just to the right of the beer taps.

"That's the trouble with this work," said Fay, reaching for a bar cloth by the drip mat, "all the cheap skates in town come to a dive like this." As she stretched for the cloth, the front of her fur-trimmed costume hung loosely from her gaunt frame.

Max looked at the woman, at the fur trim of the costume and at the dry, wrinkled skin of her chest. The chest was ribby and flat. Better nipples on a dog, thought Max. He stared at her. Not like Tracy's, he thought.

"Like that, do you?" said Fay, looking at Max, his stare still fixed on the loose hanging front of her costume. Max's face flushed. Fay paused for a moment, her body poised over the bar. "When you're through looking," she said, laughing her dry, raspy cackle, "just put a coin in and push one of the buttons and see if the tail light goes on."

"Quit hustling the trade," said Paula, a cigarette in her right hand. The sarcasm was back in her voice. She stood looking down along the bar from her station at the far end. "I'm sure the man's boot looked as tempting," she said, blowing a thick cloud of smoke as she spoke, "unless our customer here was nursed on the buttons of his father's army tunic."

"A martini, Adolph," said Max, ignoring the two sparring women. "Extra dry and smooth," he said, slowly and raising his right hand as though stroking an imaginary cat. He watched the old man as he reached for a clean stemmed glass. "How do you keep any business around here?" he asked, motioning with his right hand to indicate the two waitresses. "They'd be a plague on a pest house."

The bartender shrugged his stooped shoulders. Sucking deeply on his cold pipe, he shrugged again. Slowly he raised the bottle of gin. "Married the bitch," he said, not loud but firmly. He poured a jigger of gin into the stemmed glass.

"Really!" said Max, incredulously. He turned and looked for Paula. Her cigarette lay in the ash tray, smoldering. "Which one?" asked Max.

"I don't know," said Adolph, shrugging again. For the first time, a smile seeped through the sour, drawn face. "Sister bitches, and I'm an old man."

"All he remembers is the change in the till," said Fay, laughing and placing the cloth and three empty glasses on the bar. "One of these days Paula and me is gonna draw straws and decide which one married him. The winner walks outta here and never looks back." She cackled as she laughed. "Three more beers, Adolph, and hold the head this time."

Max felt the cold air on his feet again. A chill swept over him. He felt his pants and raincoat with his right hand. He shuddered.

"Your martini," said the bartender, setting the stemmed glass on the bar in front of Max. He picked up the dollar bill from the bar. The cash register bell rang.

The room was filling up now. The drunk was gone from the end of the bar near the window, his place taken by a young man and woman. The woman's face was hidden in shadows against the faint light from the street. Her hair was long and dark, partly covered with a too-small clear plastic head scarf. Pellets of water clouded the crinkled plastic; her threadbare coat was buttoned to her neck. The young man, tall and blond, wiped drops of water from his face as the snow in his hair melted. A heavy frost still clung to the narrow fur collar of his brown leather jacket. The jacket was new and smelled of wet animals.

Max watched the young woman as he toyed with his martini glass. Must be about twenty-three, four, thought Max. Better clothes, and do something with that hair, she'd look something like Tracy at that age. How the hell would I know what she looked like at that age? thought Max. Know what she looks like now. He sipped at his martini. And what she looked like then.

He thought about all the years in between, how he'd looked for her in crowds. He'd not really looked for her, but out of the corner of an eye he would see her on the street, even in foreign countries, but then when he'd try to find her, she'd be gone.

In his letter to Tracy he'd tried to explain this to her. How many times had he written the letter? On the backs of envelopes in his pockets he had scribbled phrases and then sentences. For two days he had worked to put the letters together. What parts had he thrown away and what parts sent? He couldn't remember. He was embarrassed as he remembered the letter, especially the parts he might have sent and should have thrown away.

What the hell, he thought. His neck and the skin around his hairline felt warm and wet. Only because the letter didn't work, he thought. If she'd answered it, I'd a been damned proud I wrote and sent it.

Wonder if she even knew what I was talking about, thought Max. He smiled. He was perspiring; he could feel it running down his sides, like cool bugs all marching in one direction over his ribs.

Max sipped again at his martini. God, I hope she's read Dante, he thought, 'cause that was the best part, at least the best part of the heavy stuff. Max shifted his position on the bar stool. Beatrice! In love with the same woman all his life, this Dante. See her in crowds. Christ, lit 52. Surely she read that. In love with her all his life but didn't let her know about it. That's what my life's been without her. If she even read the goddamned letter, she ought to get something outta that part, he thought. His own living hell, like Dante's inferno.

Great Books! That was the course at C.U. Not lit 52. Good course except that part on the Bible. The Bible as literature! Without ol' Crabnackle the Bible was flat. Catechism Crabnackle. Clymer S. Crabnackle. Methodist for method. Ol' Crabnackle. The Trinity: F.D.R., Joe Lewis and Crabnackle. Humanities 52, that's what it was. Musta had a course at Nebraska close to hum 52.

All his life looking for Beatrice, thought Max. Damned fool could have had her several times but every time missed the boat. Max shuddered; the martini tasted bitter. Not him, though. He'd sent Tracy Christmas cards, and once he'd sent her a birthday card. He'd signed the letter, though. The cards were really for me, he remembered, to keep Tracy alive in my brain. Even with other women, they'd always been Tracy. As long as he could write something, even her name on an envelope, he'd be keeping her alive. But the letter was different.

It was good to see you again, Tracy, thought Max. How in hell could anybody object to a start like that? Twenty-nine years. That's a long time, Tracy, to be away from you. Or had he thrown that part away?

Max set his martini glass on the bar and counted on his fingers the years since he had last seen her, before their meeting in October.

Goddamn him; he ruined it for me. We weren't important to him. Wasn't good enough for his sweet little girl. Heard he wasn't as well off when he died as people had thought. But, for twenty-nine long, damned years I coulda worried about it. Glad I didn't put that in the letter, thought Max.

Max picked up the glass and sipped at his bitter martini.

Remember the dance I took you to that time, Tracy? Hum 52. Coulda had her several times but messed it up. I learned to dance with you, Tracy. Found that my feet weren't the stones I had always thought they were. And Jeffrey, your fruity brother. He didn't do my stock much good, either. Whine. Christ, how he'd whine 'bout how he had to go to war. Slaughter the Nazi bastards. And you, Tracy. You thought he was the only male in the world who'd ever had to fight. Served the pimp right that he got his ass shot off. What'd your ol' man's money do for him then? That time in scout camp, the bully jumped on my pack. Damned near tore my head off.

Max belched; his nostrils burned.

He held the martini up to the light. The olive, he thought. Never could understand why they put that Dago cherry in a good drink like a martini. Benny. Benny What's-his-name.

Max took the olive out of his drink, put it in his mouth and pulled on the toothpick. Turning his head, he spit the olive on the floor; the toothpick he put in his right raincoat pocket.

Back was sore for a week. Testing my pack, the snob.

Max wiped his forehead with the sleeve of his left arm.

Knew I didn't have a pack. Rope and string; he could see that. What was so hot about Jeffrey? Knew a lot a guys better'n him in the ring. Course, never fought him, or I'd a knocked the shit outta him. Shoulda put that in the letter, thought Max.

Your mother. God she was beautiful, Tracy. She was the one thing I had goin' for me. Only you said she said I shoulda been Catholic. Or that you couldn't get serious 'bout no boy that wasn't Catholic. Something, the bitch. But God, how she could wear the clothes. Furs and jewels! Fake jewels, knowin' that tight bastard, your ol' man.

Max set his martini glass on the bar. He searched his pockets. His pants. Then his raincoat. Finally, he found the toothpick and started stirring his drink. Stopping, he held the toothpick up and inspected it. That's what the olive's for, he thought. Toothpick's only to hold on to; never a dribble drip if you hold onto the swizzle stick. Or is it swivel stick? The olive.

Max looked at the floor where he had spit the offending fruit only a moment before. The floor was dark and splotched where the carpet was torn. Carefully, Max searched the floor around his stool with the toe of his left foot. Then he saw it.

Easing himself from the stool, he picked up the small black fruit and looked at it. Mine was green, though, thought Max.

"Playin' marbles?" asked Paula, an empty round metal tray in her hand as she went by.

Max ignored her. Seated again, he wiped the olive off on his raincoat and again inserted the toothpick. Then he dropped the olive into his glass and started to stir.

Suspiciously, Max looked at the people along the bar. No one noticed him. He looked for Adolph; the bartender was as the far end of the bar, talking. Max swirled the dark olive around in the empty glass. "Some smart . . . Adolph?" said Max, his voice loud and angry, "another martini, extra dry."

Max stirred the martini with the olive. Classy drink, a martini, thought Max. Sounds like a Dago drink, but what the hell! Tracy's ol' lady drank martinis. A martini, please, Hiram. The bitch. God, she was beautiful, though. Always wished Tracy'd had her looks. Her looks and Hiram's money. To have a mother that looked like that and who wore clothes like she did. Baxter, the flyin' bastard. She wore furs like his mother. Just to be one of those dogs around her neck would a suited me, I used to think.

Then he was warm again. He could feel it around his neck and hair. He was still wet under the arms.

Two days writing that letter, thought Max. Wonder if she even got it. Could at least have sent a Christmas card. No need to sign it. Just to let me know she was thinkin' of me. It was good to see you again, Tracy. How in hell could she object to a start like that.

He felt hot again. What parts had he thrown away. He tried to remember.

I musta been seventeen when I last saw you, Tracy, and went off to fight in the war myself. He'd put that in, he was sure. Off to war and maybe never to see you again. Off to fight the Japs.

That last night home. She coulda been more on my side, against her ol' man. *Pride of the Yankees,* and her and her family had to ruin it. I coulda told her that night how much I loved her. But, just like Dante and his Beatrice.

Max tasted the new martini. His mouth puckered. It's that damned olive, he thought. He picked up the toothpick and put the green olive between his teeth and pulled. Then he remembered: how to handle a martini, hold on to the olive. He spit the olive into his left hand and was again inserting the toothpick.

"If you speak gently to Adolph, he'll maybe give you a whole mitty full," said Paula, her face serious, as she slid a round metal tray of empty glasses across the bar, "and then maybe you can find some of the big boys in the back of the room and play keepies with them." Her voice was light but scronful.

Max wasn't listening.

I saw her at a party at the Thatcher House one time, Tracy. Her and your ol' man. A friend of theirs was havin' a party, a birthday party, 'cause I heard the singin'. Your mother was wearin' a white dress with large, soft blue flowers. I was washin' dishes in the kitchen and saw her. Your mother was really a doll the way she wore her clothes. It must be wonderful to have a mother like that.

Benny's mother was like that, too. Come all the way to San Diego just to cook his birthday dinner. All those weeds she put in that spaghetti salad. Damned Wops. Eat like animals. Dandelions! But she wore her clothes like that. And ol' Baxter's mom. Benny What's-his-name. Start with the A's. Aas, Abrams, Adams.

Max picked the olive out of the glass as he sipped at his martini.

B's. Baker, Banks, Beatrice. Dante coulda had her a coupla times . . . hum 52. That wasn't humanities 52. It was part a my distributed major after they booted my ass outta engine school.

Again he could feel the perspiration running down over his ribs.

I hope they give that course at the University of Nebraska, thought Max, his face hot, or she'll think I'm some kind a goddamned intellectual nut.

The martini tasted better without the olive. Max put the olive and toothpick in his right raincoat pocket.

And ol' Hiram McClosky. Dead. Deader'n a door nail. Dead as my ol' man. Her ol' lady and my ol' lady. Dead. Death, the great emancipator, the great equilizer, the great fraud. Read that someplace once. And Dante got his. Ol' Hiram. What punishment did ol' Dante give him down there?

You've changed, Tracy. That part had gone into the letter, that he knew. 'Cause I wanted to show her how much I'd remembered her the way she used to be. And I've changed, too, Tracy. Got a Cadillac, a good income. And I'm president of my own company. And I got my college degree, after they booted my ass outta engine school. Distributed major. Christ, what a reward! Ruptured duck and all. Ol' Dante. Served him right, gettin' his ass shot off. Shoulda taken Beatrice when he could and stayed outta politics. Goddamned Wops.

Max started to stir his martini. Classy drink. He looked up and down the bar and at the floor. "Another martini, Adolph. And extra dry," said Max, confidently. Again he looked up and down the bar. "And, Adolph," he called, his voice loud and friendly, "don't forget the olive."

Chapter 15

Max felt the nudge against his right leg as she sat down on the bar stool. She was dressed in a long, loose-hanging coat of Persian lamb, the gray-black curls of fur glistening wet from the melting snow. As she sat down, she laid her purse on the bar and, gently patting her hair into place, removed a black net scarf from around neatly set waves and placed the head scarf in her lap. Her coat was open at the throat. Around her neck was a black silk scarf, knotted in front, with a half walnut-sized broach, set with finely cut stones, forming an amber floral jewel in the scarf knot. Her hands were small but strong appearing and sheathed in black leather gloves. She reached for her purse, the black beads of the purse cover picking up the faint light from the windows and from behind the bar.

"Sorry," she said, again bumping Max and looking at him for the first time, "but I need a drink." The woman was small and slightly stooped.

"Make that one martini only and two olives, Adolph," said Max, his voice firm and authoritative. "A martini's just the thing for you, ma'am," said Max, nudging the woman with his right elbow. "You look like Christmas shoppin's 'bout got you down." Max laid a five-dollar bill on the counter.

"In Sioux City, Iowa, I usually drink a dachari when I need a drink," said the little woman, arranging herself more comfortably on the stool. She opened her purse.

"This one's on me," said Max, putting his hand over the woman's opened purse. "A token of Mountain-Plains' hospitality."

"A dachari is a woman's drink," she said, sitting back on the stool and looking into the nothingness over the bar.

"One martini and two toothpicks," said Adolph, noncommittally, placing the drink in front of Max.

"For the young woman," said Max, "with one olive for yours truly." Max took a toothpick and put one of the olives in his unfinished drink."

"You do have this thing for olives, don't you?" said Paula, this time laughing, but with a touch of sarcasm in her voice. "Two beers," she called out to the bartender. She reached across the bar for a cloth.

"Only way to handle a martini is to hold on to the olive," said Max, laughing and again nudging the little woman to his right. "A classy drink, a martini is," he said, still laughing.

"I needed a drink," said the little woman, picking up the martini and holding it in her gloved right hand. She didn't look at the drink but continued to stare across the bar. "Carl's brother gave the car to me for a Christmas present only last week."

"Yeah, it's one drink I can hold, it seems," said Max, pride and self-confidence in every word. "All things with moderation, of course, as ol' Crabnackle used to say." Max grabbed hold of the olive and began handling his martini. "But a martini every time."

Both were quiet for a moment as they sipped their drinks. Then it was Max speaking. "It was ol' AB that taught me to drink. Ol' Arzie Beatrice." Max paused, then turned momentarily to his new companion. "Do you know that Dante never did tell Beatrice he was in love with her?"

"No, not Beatrice," said the woman. "That's in Nebraska. Sioux City. Sioux City, Iowa." She licked her dry lips as she spoke. "Carl's brother has a car sales business there."

Again they were both quiet.

It was Max who finally spoke. "But he used the wrong approach," said Max, reflectively. His eyes were concentrating on his glass now. He sat with the fingers of both hands intertwined, toying with the stem of his martini glass with his thumbs. "He'd set out to get me drunk on cheap booze. Never could get on to that stuff."

They both sipped at their drinks.

"One time," said Max, warming up to his subject, "first time I ever came to Denver, ol' AB brought me here on a freight train. 'Gonna make a man outta you, kid,' ol' AB said. 'Learn to respect your kind.'" Max chuckled as he talked. "Just before Christmas, just like now, we hit Denver. Froze my ass off." He held the toothpick lightly between his right index finger and thumb, twirling the olive in the shiny drink.

"The man totaled it out, as the kids say," said the woman, without emotion, but factually. "And just before Christmas."

"Just before Christmas," said Max. "Spent Christmas day down there on Larimer Street, in one of the missions. Damn, what a feast that was, or seemed like." Max sat absently stirring his drink. "'Bout like they gave us in the Navy during the war."

"Carl's brother had a car agency in Des Moines, but he gave that to our son," said the woman. She held up her glass and looked at it. "In Sioux City, Iowa, a dachari is a woman's drink."

"Hell, on holidays," said Max, a broad smile on his face, "the Navy'd give you all you could eat." He twirled the toothpick around in his glass. "You'd think that they were out to kill you off, gorging you with all that food. Take what you want, but eat what you take. The bastards. You didn't see that in the officers' mess. Worked in the officers' mess a whole week once."

"Yes, it was a mess," said the woman, her voice calm and low. "The officer said he'd never seen such a mess." Again she sipped at her drink.

"Eat our crap and kill a Jap. Posters. Musta thought we were stupid." Max was quiet for a moment. "But, by God, they'd sure feed you on holidays in the Navy during the war."

"Carl's brother didn't have his car agency during the war. No, he bought out his boss right after the war."

"I remember one Christmas, we were down in the Caribbean. Used to fly submarine watch outta ol' Jacksonville, Florida. Did you know that the Nazis had Jacksonville mined up tighter than a gnat's ass during the war? At least twice, I heard. And I didn't hear this 'til after the war, myself. And I was there guarding the place."

"Carl didn't work in cars. He worked in furniture. He was a buyer for one of the biggest furniture companies in Iowa. Could have had a store of his own but didn't want all the worry about taxes and help and rationing during the war."

"Hell, rationing didn't bother me none during the war. Not in the Navy, it didn't."

"I wanted him to have a store if that's what he really wanted. He wouldn't say. First he did, then he didn't. But he wouldn't say. He'd be on the road a lot."

"As a matter of fact, speakin' of rationing, we enjoyed rationing during the war. Not rationing, exactly, but the shortages. Hell, we'd fly down to Cuba once every ten days or so. Fly back all loaded down with silk hose, cigarettes, rubber tires. The whole works. What the hell," said Max, laughing, "had to keep remindin' the 4-F's there was a war on."

"You've never been in Sioux City, Iowa. I can tell. If you had, you would understand what I'm talking about. The winters are beautiful in Sioux City. The summers are, too, but the winters are beautiful. We used to ice skate on the Lloyd River when we were kids, Carl's brother and his girl and Carl and I. We'd skate the old year out and the new one in. Kids don't do that any more, but we used to in Sioux City. That was before Carl's brother got into cars and Carl into furniture. Carl's brother always wanted his own agency, but Carl was against it. Too much risk."

"Risk, I guess. Have you ever been in Jacksonville, Florida, Navy Mainside? Christ, if you had, you'd never forget it. You fly those goddamned P-boats sideways across that river. Not sideways, I don't mean that. But across the river instead of down it. Across the goddamned river! You pick posies outta the trees goin' out and clean off the pontoons on the trees comin' in. And, half and half. Half your takeoffs are in the daytime, so half your landin's are at night. And vice versa. Risky, I guess."

"Yes. And Carl would tell his brother that and they'd argue and quarrel about it. But Carl was the weaker of the two. He wanted a store but just wouldn't say."

"A martini's a classy drink, wouldn't you say? Looks kind of oily if you get it in the wrong light."

"That's the way he always saw everything—in the wrong light. Carl, that is. Yes, he was much weaker than his brother, the poor dear."

There was a long silence.

"That's why I quit P-boats. Too risky. Torpedo bomber's more fun, anyway. Wanted to fly dive bombers, but they said I was too big. Me too big for dive bombers! But they were right. Dive bombers not for me. Always divin' through their targets. No car or gas to get to the race track so we'd go over to the field there in the Florida jungle and sit there on the fence bettin' on those dive bombers practicin'. One day, three in a row. Lost my ass that day. Even with dive bombers, who'd bet three in a row? But, that's why I quit P-boats. Too risky. If ol' AB only knew my side a the story, he wouldn't blame me for no one's death."

"Yes. Shortly after the war. On a buying trip in Des Moines. Had a heart attack, they said. The poor dear. But, he always was weak. And he could have had a store of his own, but he'd never say."

"How's the martini comin'?"

"The officer said someone would tow it away in just a few minutes. But I couldn't wait there and watch. Carl's brother will be just furious about this. Oh, no, not with me. No! No! But with the man who caused all the trouble. He hit several cars out there, I guess. I even heard someone was killed."

"Happened all the time. Benny got his. Benny? A's, B's. Beatrice. Hum 52. But that was before they booted my ass outta engine school. C's. Callan, Cortney, Clemens."

"Yes. That was Carl's middle name, Emmett."

"If ol' AB knew the whole story, he'd apologize for the way he acted. But that's why I quit the damned P-boats. Ever see a Catalina flyin' boat crash and burn? Well, I did and I saw it from a lily pad in the St. John's River. And the torpedo! Ever see a torpedo go off? Know what you're s'posed to do when you're in the water and a torpedo goes off? Stick your finger up your ass as far as it'll go, hold your balls with the other hand, and pray. Ol' Crabnackle. Like to see him prayin' like that."

"Twenty-five thousand dollars is what he paid. It was a family-owned agency. We felt it was quite cheap. Carl's brother wasn't as careful and cautious as Carl. Knew how to take a chance and learned from experience. Carl never did. He could have quit the road and made a home. But he just wouldn't say. When he died, it was too late."

"Drink up, mate. You gotta stir a martini to bring out the flavor."

"The crushed ice in a dachari is so cool. In Sioux City a dachari is a lady's drink."

"Ever been in Jacksonville, Florida? Ever during the war? It's one of few rivers in the Northern Hemisphere to flow north into the Atlantic Ocean. The St. Johns. Runs north right into the damned ocean, lily pads and all, I was told. And when the tide's in, it backs up the sewers all the way to the Georgia line. Tricky damned river. That, and havin' to land P-boats in there sideways. Ever land a P-boat? Now there's a tit wringer, especially bringin' 'em in sideways on the St. Johns. Just bring her in at about fifty feet, just enough to clear the bird nests in the goddamned trees, and then choke the engines. Not kill 'em, just choke 'em, and then piss and fart. Not me; the P-boat. That plane'd take on so much water. Every damned rivet hole. And those engines. Eleven men that night. Cooked 'em like steaks on a grill."

"Yes. The whole front end. I had to cry. But I just couldn't stand there and watch the wrecker tow it away. And new only a week ago."

"Damned lucky it wasn't thirteen. Might as well have been twelve. Ever see a guy stick a finger up his ass as far as it'll go, with a gaddamned hole in his back? And his pants wet to his skin? Ol' Eddie didn't have any lily pads. Shit-for-brains Eddie. Got a section 8. Eddie McKensey. Benny got it, too . . . A's, B's. Dante's Beatrice. Florentine but not a jelly bean. Callan, Clemens, Coleman, Comstock . . ."

"You must have known Carl. Emmett was his middle name. Everyone in Sioux City, Iowa, knew Carl. Do you suppose they make dacharis here?"

"This fruity Commander. Scrambled egg all over his cap. He gets on the plane that morning. In from Alaska, the Aleutians, wherever the hell that is. Gonna put some class in the squadron. How's the martini? Classy drink, don't ya think? 'A torpedo under each wing,' he says. 'On the hook, out past the engines.' That's how they slaughtered the Japs, I guess, outta the Aleutians. Come in, drop her, and then haul ass outta there. Christ, you shoulda seen that P-boat when it hit that buoy. Ol' AB would apologize if he knew my side of the story."

"Yes. There's sides to every story. But do you think people really care? Carl couldn't have children, I guess. He could have had his own store, but he would never say. But it was the only single indiscretion I ever made. In Sioux City, Iowa, you don't make indiscretions. We named him Carl, and Carl's brother bought a new car agency in Des Moines for him. Carl would have liked it that way. That's why we used his own life insurance money as the down payment on the agency in Des Moines."

"Half and half. Take off in the daytime, land at night. And vice versa. First torpedo, the one on the port side, lets go all right. Sometime after lunch. Think it was a shark, though. Ever see a hammerhead shark? The United States Navy sank more goddamned hammerhead sharks during World War II than Carter has liver pills. You're flyin' out there over that flat-assed Caribbean. Can't see the water, it's so flat. Only the sandy bottom. Then you see this shadow on the desert, it looks like. You take a sun fix and there he is. Sometimes it's a whale. And when that bomb goes off, you got cat food all the way from Havana to Halifax. Ever fly over the Cats at night in the dark—Big Cat and Little Cat? Bombed hell outta those islands one night just for the hell of it."

"I wouldn't travel with Carl. Always furniture and business."

"But the other torpedo, the one to starboard, wouldn't let go like they musta done in the Aleutians. Climb that damned P-boat, flip it 'til you're thinkin' your head's hollow. Then he'd dive. Ever see a P-boat dive? But that torpedo'd stick. Halfway 'round the world, seemed like, we're tryin' to shake that torpedo loose. All that weight to starboard and landin' sideways in that queer St. Johns at night. And that's the day I got AB's telegram. On the phone down in the hangar. 'Paul's dyin'', it says. 'Come home.' Lot a goddamned people died that day."

"Yes, I suppose. Only he was by himself, so they said on the telephone. A heart attack on a buying trip in Des Moines. The poor dear."

"You're not supposed to leave the plane after you've signed the yellow sheet. Ever sign a yellow sheet? Makes ya think it's your will. In San Diego they wouldn't let you fly unless you had a regular crew. If you wanted your flight pay, you paid for it. A fruity Commander was at the head. You gave him part of your pay, and he just put you on a yellow sheet. There were more goddamned crooks in the United States Navy during World War II than Carter has liver pills."

"Yes. But as I said, I didn't travel very much."

"So I'd already signed the yellow sheet and we're waitin' for the tractor to pull us into the water, and this fruity sailor pedals up on his bike. 'Emergency,' he says, 'on the phone back at the hangar.' Christ, they coulda court-martialed me for leavin' the plane after signin' the yellow sheet. But I ran all the way back and it was AB's telegram. As they tell it to me on the phone, I can see the tractor out through the window pullin' the P-boat to the ramp. Ever see 'em put a P-boat in the water? Well, I 'bout fall down the steps. They had that phone up in the eaves, up with the spatsies. And when I get to the ramp, the engines have started and the plane's startin' to take position to pull out into the river. I don't stop runnin'. The ladder's still down and I run and swim. I was 'bout drowned when they pull me up that ladder."

"I've never had a martini in Sioux City."

"If ol' AB only knew what happened that day, he'd apologize. I fell into a pile a lily pads, but Eddie got it in the back and in the water. I saw him later in the hospital. They gave him a section 8. Ol' Shit-for-brains Eddie. This Aleutian expert's gonna bring her in with that ton a powder under the wing. He yelled at everyone. He yelled at me when he found I'd signed the yellow sheet and had left the plane. He'd spotted my wet pants flyin' from the barrel a the port fifty. He yelled at me for bein' wet and standin' there in my skivies. Gonna break my ass. And what the hell's darkness? Sun doesn't even shine in Alaska. Bring her in over the trees, line her up between the standin' buoy lights, choke off the engines and, when he orders, throw out the port sea anchor to make up for the torpedo to starboard. He was a war expert. Only Eddie throws out the goddamned starboard sea anchor. Christ, you shoulda seen that ol' Catalina hit that buoy."

"I usually don't drink more than one dachari," said the little woman.

"How about another martini?" asked Max, stirring his martini with the olive.

"No, I must be going now," she said, resignation in her voice. "Carl's brother will just be furious."

She rose from her stool and was tying the black net head scarf over her neatly set hair.

"He'll get over it," said Max, smiling. "You haven't been here long."

"Well, it's always a pleasure to meet one of Carl's old friends," said the little woman. "If you're ever in Sioux City, Iowa, be sure to look us up."

Max raised his glass, a sort of toast. Then she was gone.

"Another martini, Adolph," said Max. "Extra dry."

Chapter 16

Torpedo bomber, more my style, thought Max. He was sucking on the olive. At least I'm alive. He thought of Eddie. What ever happened to Eddie? And Baxter, the flyin' bastard. What ever happened to his mother? Dead by now. Then Max remembered the bottle of perfume and the old woman who had bumped into him in the street. He felt his pockets; the bottle was still there.

"One martini," said Adolph, the bartender. He picked up a dollar bill from the change on the bar and turned to the cash register.

That guy in the alley, thought Max. That one eye. Max shuddered. What's a guy thinkin' when he's like that.

The drink was sharp and pulled at his tongue.

Life flicks past like a movie. See all the goddamned rotten things you did in your life, I supopse. Wanted to cry, he looked like. Wish he coulda cried. Nobody'd cared.

Max twirled the olive between the thumb and forefinger of his right hand.

Hamper and Adler. Max remembered his young insurance salesman and sales manager. Wonder what they would a done in that alley. Quittin' his job just when it's gettin' to be promisin'. The fruity bastard. Both gonna regret it when that Portland deal's all signed up.

Max breathed deeply; he relaxed, sighing as the air went out of him. Slowly, he rubbed his eyes with his left hand. Again, he sighed.

A feeling of despair swept over him. In the jumble of his mind a thought struggled to form a philosophy of life that would see him through this moment. The tragedy of man, thought Max, is the separation of life from body; or rather, the dual identification of man through body and life. The body suffers because of life, and life fails because of body. The body can be endured; life must be lived. The tragedy lies in the fact that body and life are alternately entombed in each other. Only in moments of experienced aestheticism does life escape the body, but always at a price—pain, guilt, anxiety or frustration. The physical body was born of a physical act, but the life was borrowed. The physical body fights a losing battle to save a life it did not choose to live.

A life it didn't choose to live!

Max liked that. Musta read it someplace, he thought. It absolved life of failure. This answer warmed him as he thought about it. He breathed deeply again. But that life is me, he thought. The despair that he had felt a moment ago gave way to a feeling of fear. Did the world really begin with me, my seeing it? he wondered. Is it all some kind of dream, and will it end when I end? For me, that's sure, but for the rest?

He looked into his glass. My world, he thought. Pain, guilt, anxiety . . . and death. Where does one's world begin? Death! My first death. I must a been a kid then. It was in the onion field, and it was the kids from the orphanage.

That's where it started. On the old Pforst place.

The slop boy, they called me, thought Max. Carried the slop to 'em and they ate it in the field. Eight or nine, I musta been then, he thought.

He rubbed his eyes again with his left hand.

Strange to think a bein' that young. And the young man in the alley. He'd been a boy once. But, that first death. Neither of those boys'd ever get to be a man.

"Put 'ore potatoes in," said a rasping voice from over by the door. "Those kids been 'orking hard. Put somethin' in their stom..s."

"I put in all the potatoes Mr. Pforst said to," said the boy, looking into the galvanized wash tub that sat in the middle of a large cook stove. Charred dirt rimmed the bottom of the small tub.

The boy wasn't tall, but was slender and slight of build. His hair was dark, the color of the gnarled bark of an ancient cottonwood tree in the cold of winter. The hair wasn't curly, but wavy, with a wide cowlick across the forehead, from left to right. His blue eyes were close together, under brows already heavy and dark. The pupils of the eyes changed to large black holes and the eyes themselves narrow slits when he was rebuffed or angered. Thin blue-red lips parted over well-set, flashing white teeth when he spoke. His cheek bones were high, but not unattractive; his chin was strong without being wide. The dark lips cut evenly across the opaque whiteness of his face. The nose, finely forged, gave a beauty to a common face. Drops of perspiration stood out on his forehead and along his hair line. His hand were small and delicate.

The boy picked up the flat, thin splinter of board and began stirring; the mass of watery soup bubbled in the bottom of the tub, about a third of the way up on the side of the blackened utensil.

"And anyway, Tosher, anymore wouldn't be cooked in time for dinner," said the boy.

"Now, Maxie, don't tell ol' Tosher how to 'ook," said the old man. He paused. "Too many years cookin' on the Burling..t..t..ton to be told by a kid 'ow to cook," he said at last, picking up a half of a head of cabbage from the basket on the floor beside him.

Tosher sat on a low, wide stool that had once been a chair. Round holes, with broken-off dowling chipped off even with the seating surface, formed a semi-circle around the top of the stool. He sat, his hunched back toward the patched screen door; his once-white underwear was buttoned down the front as far as his belt. Bare elbows, the skin like gray felt, forced their way through holes in the underwear sleeves. Wooly, white hair moved in and out around his neckline as he breathed. Formless, brown wool trousers draped protruding legs that rested, the right foot over the left, alongside the heavy oak pedestal of the round table at which he sat. The table was pushed back against the wall, by the screen door.

"Here, put in this 'abbage, then," said the old man, slowly.

"All of it?" asked the boy, looking at the cabbage and then at Tosher. "There's already lots a cabbage . . ."

"Just put enough 'alt and 'epper in it," said the former dining car cook, ignoring the boy. "When a man can't have enough potatoes," he said, the parenthesis wrinkles that began at the corners of his mouth spreading out from his pink lips, "then cabbage'll have to do."

Tosher's lips were thick and crinkled; a pull string in the back of his head sought to draw the lips closed as he talked. With effort, the muscles in his face worked against the pull string, biting off words before they were completed, or chewing them before they were fully formed. It was as though he tasted his words before sharing them with others. Dark brown teeth showed as he spoke.

Tosher's head was round like a turnip, and bald.

" 'Fore the car door fell on me, I was the 'est damned cook on the whole Burling..t..t..ton."

Tosher slumped over the stool now, his right elbow resting on the moist, scarred table top. His bent body appeared to rise out of the nearly empty basket beside the stool. "Stir it up a bit and then git the pots ready," he said, motioning with his head to the room beyond the stove.

The Pforst house was an involuntary gathering of rooms jammed together around a solitary chimney that stood at the far end of the cooking room. This room was long and narrow, with a wide door in the middle, on the east side, and with two tall, narrow windows at each side of the door. The windows were darkened; faded green shades, threadbare and torn along the edges, filtered out the sun. The door itself stood open, back against the wall, partly covering the window to the right.

Around the room, on the floor along the walls, were automobile seat cushions, tufts of cotton blossoming from tears in the rough mohair coverings. Leaning against the walls were long-handled hoes and rakes ready for use in the fields.

The west wall of the room was punctuated by two curtained doors, the one to the south leading to Angus Pforst's bedroom, the other to the dungeon, as Tosher called it. Here slept the boys on loan from an orphanage down at Hastings. The curtains were made of long strips of dusty army blankets, the tattered cloth hanging from fence staples pounded into the top of the door frame.

On a shelf near the chimney was a tall, two-mantle kerosene lamp, the bronze basin of the lamp scratched but shiny; the slender necked, inverted jug of a flue was dirty black, the top chipped around the rim.

The room was the knight's hall of the onion king of the Republican River valley.

In a little room to the north, beyond the chimney wall, was the apparently intended kitchen of the house, a shed-like afterthought of a room, that housed a tall rust-red pump and food storage bins and sacks. The long handle of the pump stood out at right angles to the pump and was almost flat against the east wall, just inside the kitchen door. For a kitchen sink, a large round pouring funnel was mounted, a foot or so beneath the downspout of the pump, to a triangle of two-by-fours, the base of which was nailed to the east wall. A black-taped red garden hose led from the bottom end of the funnel and into the wall.

To the left of the door, corners of cardboard boxes, piled to the ceiling, narrowed the entrance to the room to nearly half the width of the passage. Beyond the pump, in the corner, gunny sacks, some full and lumpy, were stacked high against the two walls. Without windows, the room was dark; the musty smell of rotting vegetables clung to the still air in the cooking room.

"Git the th--th--things ready, Maxie," said Tosher, his face struggling with the pull string in the back of his head and again motioning to the room beyond the chimney wall. "S---S ---Some a the kids'll be re---re---ready to eat."

Max stopped, setting the grease-stained white pot on the soft dirt; the heat from the vegetable soup in the pot burned the knuckles of his right hand. Shifting the flour sack that held the tin plates and wooden spoons to his right hand, he picked up the pot with his left hand and continued his slow march up the field toward the eating tree, a cottonwood whose extended, sinewy limbs stood sentinel over the fields around it and whose shade protected the tired workers while they ate.

Nearing a dirt farm road that cut east across the field at the north end, small hunched figures, straddling one row of onions and moving back and forth from the row to either side, were strung out in broken ranks, working their way north across the field. Here and there a bright red or yellow shirt would flash in the late morning light, but most of the backs were bare. The advanced workers were nearing the ends of their rows, to the north end.

The clear blue sky was hot now. Gone were the long shadows of early morning; only the cloudless sky and the sun. The humid air was still. Faint heat waves danced above the greenness of the valley floor, in the potato field beyond the end of the onion rows and on farther north toward the river. Far across the valley, in the hills west and north of town, the land lay alternately black and green, in an uneven checkerboard of the fallowed and planted fields of the divide.

To the east, visible above the trees along the river, where the channel bends a little to the north and under the two bridges that lead to Thatcher up on the hill, windmills and farmsteads, small islands of decay in the placid green, danced in the shimmering light of a distant prairie sea. On the south, the close barren hills brooded darkly over the irrigated farms of the valley.

The dirt between the onion rows was soft. The slick, slimy glare of dried silt mud mirrored the open blue sky between the rows that lay along the irrigation ditch. Here the dirt was crusted and hard. But where crawling, bare feet had wedged along the straight rows of onions, the dirt was soft and black. Perhaps a little too sandy in places, but loose and soft.

Bermuda onions. Big money down in Omaha and out in Denver. Cash crop.

A wide irrigation ditch ran on the left, coming in from the lateral canal that rimmed the bluff, across the creek to the south. From the abandoned pump house at the south edge of the property, the ditch ran north, past the house of the place, and on north toward the river, like the onion rows. Only the onion rows didn't go all the way to the river and neither did the irrigation ditch. A mile or so lay between the north end of the onion field and the Republican River. And the ditch stopped a half mile north of the onion rows, at the far end of the Angus B. Pforst farm.

When the ditch was running, the water not used in the fields along the ditch ran into a sump pond where it was collected and pumped into other fields of the Pforst farm or sold to the farms to the north and east. To the north of the onion rows was the potato field, the plants now only stunted suggestions of green in the well-tilled earth.

Half mile onion rows. A nickel a row. Three rows up before dinner and three back in the afternoon, with dinner served in the field.

"Every damned weed, you hear." Ol' Angus the Bull. It was the same speech every day. "Ya pull every damned weed. Ya don' break 'em off. Ya pull 'em out by the roots. An' the onions. Thin 'em. Ya think I'm payin' ya to drag your scrawny asses up and down those rows, mashin' those tiny plants. Ya don' mash 'em over 'til they're ready. Use the knife I gave to ya and thin 'em out. I'm watchin' every row. I see one weed, and no pay.

The finality in his voice had been certain; the voice had snapped like the beady brass clasps on the deep, soiled leather coin purse from which he paid the small boys who worked his fields.

Along the irrigation ditch, outlined in thick, stunted willows, hidden meadowlarks sang out anonymously to the fields and world their sharply noted yodel. The irrigation ditch, empty now, was mud-caked and silent.

"Hurry up with the shit bucket," yelled a voice from the shadows of the eating tree.

"That ain't what's in the pot, Flinty," yelled a second voice from the shadows. "It's our grub, Pforst class."

Max was almost to the tree.

"Hey, Potter," yelled the first boy, Flinty, "don't ya ever bother to wash it after the sonofabitch uses it?"

Max was under the tree now, in the shade of the reaching limbs of the cottonwood. The air was suddenly cool. A stool, a twin to the one Tosher used in the cooking room of the farm house, sat near the trunk of the tree, to the east. Max set the stained white pot of soup on the stool. The flour sack, with the tin plates and wooden spoons inside, Max placed on the stool, so that it leaned against the tree.

"Potter, the pot carrier." It was Flinty again. "Tell him, Poet."

"There once was a kid from Pottsburg,
Who said I believe I'm a bird.
I knew I'd regret it,
Cause it was me that fed it,
I'd rather be a turd than the bird."

Poet was by the stool now. "Give me Frog's plate," said Poet, fumbling in the flour sack on the stool.

Poet was dark; his face was shiny. Beads of sweat clung to the black hairs of his face. His eyebrows, and the dagger of long straight hair that cut across his forehead, were black and shiny. His well-set teeth were white and strong. Like Flinty, Poet was more than a head taller than Max.

"There's plenty a plates," said Max, reaching for the flour sack.

"Stay outta this, Potter," said Poet.

"Yeah, Frog's been askin' for it ever since he got to school," said Flinty. Flinty was blond and heavy; his shoulders were thick and stooped. His face, round and featureless except for the nose, was that of a melting snowman; the nose was a misplaced afterthought, flattened and pushed to one side, dropped and stepped on in the making but slapped on for last-minute inspection. "He's bad luck. They wouldn'ta sent us 'cept him fightin' Mouse. Then they sent us here."

"Hey, Frog's gonna lick ol' Bull's pot clean," yellow Poet to the other boys coming in from the field now. "A plate for everyone except Frog," said Poet, starting to hand out the plates. "Potter, where's the dipper?"

"On the tree," said Max. Max reached around the trunk of the tree. He took a tin drinking dipper off a nail on the tree and handed it to Poet.

"You're the pot dipper," said Poet, sarcasm in his voice. "I can't stand to look at the stuff and to eat it, too."

Max put the long-handled dipper into the pot. "Who's . . ."

Two clawlike hands grabbed a tin plate from Poet's grip. It was Frog.

Frog was without a shirt, the faded blue overall suspenders hanging loosely from his thin shoulders. His stature was straight but short; he was bulgy in the stomach but not fat of body. Two peg ears, tightly twisted into the pinched, cramped scroll of a face, gave prominence to his shrunken skull. A long sinewy neck, the muscles in the neck tautly strung, ended in a mis-shapened breastbone, the bridge to a large, animated violin. His skin was pale, opaque as river ice in March. Frog's arms were mere sticks wrapped in crinkled parchment, the red-blue blood vessels in his arms twitching worms that pulsed at the wrists as he breathed. His mouth was a long red slit; his nostrils flared with his breathing.

"I ain't afraid of you, Poet," yelled Frog, his breathing deep and even. He squinted his dark eyes as he spoke. "You got no reason to fight me, but I ain't a scared a you."

Without a word, Poet swung his right fist at Frog. Frog, shorter than Poet, dodged to his left, grabbing Poet's fist and pushing it aside with his own right hand. With a long sweep of his left arm, Frog struck Poet between the eyes with his left fist. Poet went down. Frog kicked at the fallen boy.

"Get him," yelled Poet, rolling away from Frog. "Long's we got him, we're gonna have to stay here in ol' Pforst's onions."

Three boys grabbed at Frog.

"I'll kill you," yelled Frog, sweat dripping from his chinless face. "I'll kill you."

His back was to the tree now.

"I didn't start no trouble," yelled Frog, kicking at the boys as they darted in at him. The opaqueness had left his face; his cheeks were red now. "You been pickin' a fight with me ever since I was sent to Hastings."

"Why don't you leave, then?" yelled one of the boys from the circle of faces, a boy in a red shirt.

" 'Cause I ain't got no place to go," said Frog, his voice nervous and trembling. He stood in the center of the circle, his long arms hanging by his sides.

The circle of boys was closer now.

"I don't wanta fight anyone no more, really, Poet," cried Frog, looking at the faces in front of him. Whirling, he stared at the others, the ones by the tree and the stool. "I don't wanta fight."

"The best part a you ran down your mother's leg," yelled Poet, jumping to his feet.

Frog turned, but not fast enough. Poet's arms were around his waist. The circle of boys closed in.

"Spit on his pecker," yelled a shrill, excited voice.

"Hold his legs. I got his overalls."

The circle broke open; a boy in a red shirt ran into the onion field waving faded blue overalls over his head. "I got his pants," he yelled, dodging back and forth in the field, throwing the overalls over his head and catching them.

"Spit on his pecker."

"I'll kill you! I'll kill you!" Frog's voice broke. He lay naked on his back, pinned to the ground by a boy on each arm, a quivering, gray mass in the dust. Darting in and out of the group, other boys backed up and spit on the naked Frog.

"Rub it in his eyes," yelled Poet, standing over the fallen boy.

Humping his back and rolling quickly to his left, Frog kicked at his tormentors. His body was slippery. As he kicked, he pushed himself away and jumped to his feet. He backed toward the tree. Panic swept over his face as he looked from the two boys on the ground to the faces staring at him.

"Watch me." It was Flinty; he had a curved thinning knife in his right hand. "Rake this through his crotch and we'll make a choir boy outa him." Flinty stepped over the two boys on the ground. "Now, watch this," said Flinty, laughing. Slowly, he started toward Frog, the curved knife in his right hand jabbing the air.

Frog backed up, bumping the stool. His eyes were wide now; he opened his mouth to scream but didn't. Looking down, he grabbed for the stained white pot on the stool. Lunging forward, Frog splashed the pot, mouth open, down over the charging Flinty's head, the hot soup basting the thick bare shoulders and flailing arms.

Flinty's body wretched and doubled over. Standing up, he spun around and around, grabbing at the hot thing that encased his head.

Poet, his eyes wide and staring, stood motionless, watching.

"Use a knife?" yelled Frog, mockery in his voice now. Picking up the stool, he beat on the stained chamber pot as Flinty struggled to free himself, hot soup splashing the ground with each stroke.

Flinty was on the ground now. Without a sound, he kicked once, then again. Then he was quiet.

"I'll kill the rest a you," yelled Frog, his nude and dust-caked body hovering over the fallen Flinty and holding the stool in both hands over his head. "I don't want to fight anyone but . . ." Looking down at Flinty, quiet now in a pool of watery vegetables, Frog began to cry. Turning, he smashed the stool against the tree, and without looking back, he ran across the potato patch, toward the river.

They found Frog's body, face down, floating in a stooped, meditating position in the irrigation sump pond, between the potato patch and the river. His body was clean and shiny. No longer were his arms crinkly parchment, but were soft like damp clay. The overalls clung to the wet body as they tugged on the suspenders, the faded blue fabric tearing where the suspenders crossed in back.

The boys watched as the quarter-ton pick-up truck worked its way noisily south toward the house and the road, down by the lateral canal. None spoke. Poet was the first to move. One by one they walked into the onion field.

The clear blue sky was hot. Faint heat waves danced above the greenness of the valley floor. The afternoon air was quiet. Then, somewhere in the willows along the irrigation ditch, a meadowlark announced himself in clear, sharp notes. Again the air was quiet.

Chapter 17

Benny and Frog.

No one wanted to fight.

But, Benny got his, too. Benny What's-his-name. L's, Landis. Lawrence. Lord. M's, Mason. Merrill. Mulvaney. N's. Nagel.

And Eddie. What ever happened to Eddie?

And Eddie Ox? Dead too, by now, I suppose.

The bell sounded, ending the second round.

Two boys, the one wearing faded blue dungarees and a once-white short sleeved undershirt, the other in trunks and bare-chested, were separated, the referee stepping in between the two and pushing them apart. The taller of the boys, the one in dungarees and undershirt, walked selfconsciously back to his corner. The other, the one in trunks, danced away from the referee and back to his corner.

"Ya made the bastard pay that time, Maxie," said a man in the southwest corner of the ring to the boy in the trunks. "Keep that up and the men at the plant'll be proud as hell a their boy, kid."

Panting hard, the boy in the trunks shook his head, all the while leaning against the corner post and the ropes of the corner, his forehead against the tall post and his arms braced against the ropes of the ring. The worn leather gloves were spotted with sweat from his own and his opponent's body.

"Remember, Maxie," said the man, shaking the boy and trying to look into his face, "keep on your feet. Long's you're on your feet they can't hurt ya. Grab on to him if ya have to, but stay on your feet."

The man was down on his right knee.

"Hurt ya, kid?" he asked, cupping the boy's chin in his own left hand and turning his head. "Naw, just a little blood in the nose, looks like." He turned the head back against the post.

"'Now, this kid's bigger'n you, Potter," said the man in the corner, his voice cold, "but you've murdered bigger one's than him."

The boy's breathing was coming easier now. He opened his eyes and peered into the almost dark grounds. No one from the Thatcher Artificial Ice Producers was out there, at least where he could see them. Only the man in the corner.

"Coupla more rounds and you'll have him, kid," said the representative of the local ice plant workers, Eddie Ox.

Eddie Ox wasn't his real name; it only sounded like Eddie Ox. The name his mother gave him was Ealey D. Dox, and he was production manager of the Thatcher Artificial Ice Producers, the chief supplier of sanitary ice for the domestic ice boxes in all of Thatcher, Nebraska, and for the refrigerator cars of the Western Division of the Burlington Railroad when the cars required repacking in Thatcher. The position of production manager at the ice plant meant that Eddie Ox was the only man on wages who wouldn't be laid off when and if the demand for ice threatened not to keep up with supply. Or, to put the situation more precisely, he was the son-in-law of the owner of the plant, Beverly P. Dodge.

Eddie Ox was a skinny man, tall and stooped. His eyes were a watery blue, with the opaque stare of cataract failure well advanced in his right eye, causing him to squint, as he listened, like a person who has been startled by the lightning and is only awaiting the thunder clap. His face was long and wrinkled, the lines creasing his face in deep, vertical whiskery grooves. Not bald, but with a high forehead, the skin above his eyes moved up and down as he spoke, the upward shifting underscoring a question.

"Ya sure you're not hurt?" said Eddie Ox, the skin of
his forehead wrinkling upward to the graying brown hair.

"No," said the boy, shaking his head. His breathing was
regular now.

"The bell'll be comin' soon, Maxie," said Eddie Ox, his
voice warm again, his thin face perspiring, "so remember!
Make him mad and save them punches. You're on top now
and can whip any goddamned Dago they can send up here."

The other boy, the one in undershirt and dungarees,
leaned against the post in the opposite corner, talking to the
three boys in the corner with him. The boy's face and head
were wet with sweat and streaked with dirt from the floor of
the ring.

The ring was a one-rope affair fastened at the four corners to long, up-right cedar fence posts set firmly into the
black dirt of the grounds. The floor of the ring was of dirt,
with wheat straws, their spidery roots still clinging tenaciously
to the loose soil near the corner posts and under the rope, giving the ring an air of friendly horseplay among the lads of
the West Thatcher Youth Center. No one bothered to measure the ring, and the one rope was settled upon as sufficient
to keep the contestants within the official boxing area.

There was neither chair nor stool in either corner of the
ring.

The ring was lighted by one of a string of five bare light
bulbs strung between two power poles, one at the street, just
in from the curb, along the sidewalk, and the other just stopping short of the southwest corner of the ring itself. The
lights danced in the rising wind, the shadows on the faces in
the ring and those watching jumping around as the light bulbs
jiggled in the wind.

Under the usual procedures, fights held on Friday night
at the Center would, if all went as planned, produce winners
who would, if they chose to participate in the new league
that was then forming, fight off the top contenders from the
East Thatcher Youth Center on Saturday night. The whole
idea was new and part of a program of the mayor's to keep
young boys, that is to say sons of the poor, out of trouble.

Since the program was new, and the brutal nature of the contest not generally appealing to even the sons of the poor, there was a decided lack of contenders for the recently created city-wide honors.

Tonight's contest, between Tony Amato and Maxwell Potter, was a grudge fight and therefore not officially to be considered within the usual rules of the mayor's program. Undaunted by, or ignorant of, this fact, or the grudge aspect, the fight had been billed around the YMCA and other sports areas and playgrounds as one of the important fights so far, with the hope that interest in pugilistic endeavors would justify the city council's faith in the mayor's seemingly gratuitous expenditure.

Grudge fights, honestly identified, were considered crude acts of violence, something carried out in the alley behind one of the town's several dance halls on Saturday night, and were, if acknowledged by the contestants, probably illegal. So, the error in billing the fight between Amato and Potter as part of the mayor's official program was understandable. Yet, a grudge fight it was.

Fights such as the one tonight had been regularly promoted for many years among the youth of Thatcher — from the less desirable fringe neighborhoods, to be correct.

Interest in this activity had been fostered by the production manager of the Thatcher Artificial Ice Producers and the men who worked the plant. As a challenge to all comers there was nailed to a bulletin board on the wall out front on the loading dock, at eye level, between the scales and the ice slicing machine, a notice, to wit:

OUR BOY, ——————————— CAN WHIP ANY CHALLENGER. TWO MINUTE ROUNDS WITH GLOVES. EIGHT ROUNDS. IF YOU DOUBT THIS STATEMENT, LEAVE YOUR NAME AND ADDRESS WITH ONE OF THE MEN INSIDE. $5 PRIZE TO THE WINNER.

For more than a year the name of Maxwell Potter had filled the blank in the notice at the ice plant.

Eddie Ox's fight promotion program had, over the years, if not from its inception, manifested a special forum for expressing public opinion on social questions in Thatcher. It was universally understood that the *our boy* contestant was always to be a youngster from an Anglo working class family. The challenge was expressly aimed at the boys in Dago Town, south of the tracks and along the bluff above the river.

The Potter family lived at The Fort, a hollowed-out square of a neighborhood, just west of the Burlington shops and south of the main rail yards, and was provided by the railroad for the families of the section, or maintenance, crew workers. Made up mostly of railroad box cars and unpainted clapboard shacks, the settlement was not part of Thatcher across the tracks to the north, nor was it actually an integral part of Dago Town, that wrapped around The Fort to the west and south. It was a purgatory wherein the sin of want could be expiated by the women of the compound scrubbing the floors of Thatcher and listening piously to their betters' advice on the virtues of not falling into the grip of Dago Town.

Fighting under the direction of the ice plant workers had offered Max not only an occasional five dollar prize but had forged a definite line that separated him and his neighborhood from Dago Town, at least in his eyes and those of the fight promoters.

There was the bell for the third round.

Max was out of his corner, stalking the taller boy. Fast on his feet, Max got in two body blows and then, dancing out of reach, circled his opponent, waiting for an opening and a possible kill.

Tony Amato was a tall, dark boy, with broad, thick shoulders. Not fat, but solid and with long, round arms, he appeared to be much heavier than he actually was. Weighing in at the ice plant on Wednesday noon, Tony had had it over Max by more than forty-five pounds. Much of this extra weight was due to height. Tony was more than a year older than Max and almost three inches taller. Tony was slower on his feet than was his opponent, but when his often wild swings did connect, they took their toll in welts to the other boy's body and increasingly painful looks in his eyes.

Tony had Max in the corner now, with his own back to the referee.

Max's arms were spread out on the ropes in the corner, his head back against the post. One, two, three blows to the body.

The referee moved in and separated the two boys.

"Keep away from him, Maxie," yelled Eddie Ox, the man in Max's corner. "Keep after him, now."

Max was dancing around the ring, sparring; a fast jab at Tony's head, missing.

Tony fell back, out of Max's reach, gloves palm open, protecting his face, his elbows low, covering his body.

"Goddamnit kid, finish the bastard off," yelled the production manager of the ice plant, the deep furrows in his face small rivers of sweat now, his stringy fingers gripping the ropes in the corner. "Make him wish he couldn't read English."

Tony connected, a powerful right to Max's face, the three boys in Tony's corner cheering. And a left to Max's body.

Max hit the rope, spinning as he fell, the other boy coming in to finish his work.

Max was on the rope now, trying to hold himself up, his knees beginning to sag.

The referee moved in, separated the two contestants.

"Breathe in deep, Max," yelled Eddie Ox, rushing up the side of the ring to his right.

Max was gripping the rope in both hands, taking the count. His head was down, almost to the rope, his breathing labored, and blood dripping from his nose.

"For Christ sake, Anty, where'd you learn to count like that," said Eddie Ox, grabbing his fighter by the chin and jerking him up off the rope. "Now, goddamnit, you're gonna lose this fight if you don't watch it. No goddamn Wop's gonna take my money, ya understand that, kid?"

Max tried to answer, to shake his head.

"Now, get in there and fight like ya intended to win."
He jerked the boy by the right shoulder and spun him around.

Tony was out of his corner now.

"Stay away from him 'til ya get your wind," yelled Eddie
Ox, again in Max's corner.

The referee was panting now, his own head and face wet
with sweat. His labored movements were more hops than
steps; he was an animated barrel pivoting and pirouetting on
two loose staves grinding in the dust that swirled around the
two boys in the ring.

Anton Reinhardt was the mayor's official sponsor of the
boxing program in the city-wide effort to give guidance to
otherwise idle youth. He came to the position well recom-
mended.

Anton Reinhardt was the proprietor of Anton's Restaurant, an aged and rancid eatery catering to the lay-over crews
of the Burlington and to passengers stranded in Thatcher
awaiting the next train on the spur line up to Wauneta.

Anton had inherited the establishment from his father,
Adolph Reinhardt, an adoptive American with proud and
strong Old World ties. The restaurant had occupied the same
lot since before the turn of the century, with only the front
frame structure giving way in the civic booster craze of the
mid-twenties to a rough brick veneer and plate glass exterior.
As owner of Anton's, Anty, as his friends knew him, had become a business success and a recognized diplomat of no un-
certain merit. Diplomacy was necessary because old Adolph's
ghost haunted, as it were, the business affairs of the restaurant
that had once boasted the family name.

Adolph Reinhardt had opened the restaurant during the
Spanish-American War and was looked upon as a solid citizen
and civic booster. Then the Kaiser marched into Belgium. As
proof that he had no liking for the theories of the Kaiser,
Adolph had purchased eight sets of duck pins and twenty-four
large balls from an Englishman, a salesman representing a
London firm with an office in Chicago. From then on,

Adolph's hatred of the English was exceeded only by his dislike for the game.

He had, however, continued to set it up on the floor at the rear of the restaurant. The game was popular with family men and their wives, and this was good for his food and beer business. Also, if he cancelled the game it would go to his most erstwhile competitor, the proprietor of the Leisure Hour pool hall, directly across Prairie Avenue to the west.

It would appear from the record that old Adolph had signed an agreement with the owner of the Leisure Hour that would have required the pool hall to take over the ownership of the pins and balls if and when Reinhardt's Restaurant quit using them. This had apparently been a dodge to stifle the old man's probably well founded anxiety concerning the expenditure of good American gold on trinkets of dubious patriotic value. To the old former Bavarian inn keeper, even peace with the Thatcher Kaiser baiters was not to be purchased with the possible loss of hard-earned gold.

When the game proved popular after the war, old Adolph faced a dilemma: give solace to his soul and unload his burden of English merchandise, or give in to the wishes of the Leisure Hour pool hall who now wanted the game. The latter was a two-edged sword: he would lose and they would gain.

It came to pass that Adolph Reinhardt died, leaving the Reinhardt Restaurant to his only heir, Anton, whose name was another concession to the Allied war cause.

Anton, a roly-poly, first generation American of German descent, remembering his father's grief, if not greed, concerning the duck pins, sold them, upon his father's death, to the proprietor of the Leisure Hour, an eighth-generation American of English descent.

But, as luck would have it, likes and dislikes on the part of the public had changed. The Leisure Hour pool hall didn't appeal to the wives of duck pin enthusiasts and the men did not come without their women.

This is where Anton acquired his reputation as a diplomat.

Not wishing to arouse the ill will of his by now aged competitor across the street, and yet desirous of honoring his dead father's deeply nourished feelings about the English, he bought back the pins and balls and used his influence with his uncle, Florid Reinhardt, a member of the school board, to introduce duck pins into the recreation program of the East Ward public school.

When the mayor had asked Anton to sponsor the boxing program he had said something to the effect that Anton could —"like the rest of us, goddamn well swallow your Republican pride and get in there and try to save the Republic." As an act of diplomacy, he had taken over the task.

The gusts of wind were strong now, the exposed light bulbs bobbing dizzily on the taut wire between the two power poles. The light bulb nearest the ring, to the right of the south-west corner, cast dancing shadows on the dusty floor of the ring, the ropes and contestants undulating back and forth in the sweep of the light bulb's arc. Dust from the ring and from the milling feet of the few remaining spectators swirled across the grounds to the street light to the south and on across the highway, the car lights flashing brief stabs of dirt into the passing traffic.

The bell ending the third round.

The referee ushered Max to his corner.

The boy's nose was no longer bleeding. Dried blood smeared his face, dust covered now and lined with sweat streaks of clean skin. Reaching the corner, he grabbed for the tall pole, holding on to it with the awkward boxing gloves. His knees sagged against the coarse grains of the wood.

"What the hell ya doin' out there, kid?" yelled Eddie Ox, his forehead wrinkling upward and grabbing his young boxer by the shoulders, as though to crush him. Then he shook him. "He's knockin' your brains out and ya just stand there and take it."

Max didn't let go the pole. His chest worked like a bellows. His right eye was puffed but still open.

"Now, get this, Potter," said Eddie Ox, his face red and perspiration standing out on his wrinkled forehead, "I don't fart around with just any punk that comes down the tracks down there." He wiped his face on his right shoulder. "Ya hear me, kid? When you come into this, or any other ring that I have anything to do with, you're supposed to stand up for what's decent in this town, for your old man's job and for the place ya call home. You're a symbol against those god-damned foreigners, understand? How the hell's that gonna look lettin' a stinkin' Wop beat the shit outa ya, huh?" Eddie Ox shook the boy. "Ya got that, kid?"

Max didn't answer. With his left hand still holding onto the corner post, his knees let go, his body falling backward into the dust of the ring.

The bell for the fourth round.

Max didn't answer the bell.

Chapter 18

Ol' Eddie Ox. Anton's Restaurant, gone now, too, I suppose, thought Max, twisting the toothpick in the martini glass.

The Pow Wow. Won that fight. And Geneva. Geneva Wilson, or Williamson, or something like that. Met her at the Pow Wow.

He sat at the soda fountain, watching them stream in and out of the drug store. Mostly young men and boys. By looking into the mirror on the wall in front of him he could keep his eyes on the door and sidewalk outside.

Impatiently, he looked up at the clock, a plain round clock with a clean white face and black numbers. Seven thirty-five.

Again, he looked into the mirror, watching the reflections of the out-of-doors. His view was limited to that showing through the long window and screen door.

The evening was hot.

Outside, the full rays of the setting August sun cast an orange-red glow over the town, the flaming light dancing off the windshields of cars angle-parked on Elm Street, at the curb alongside the Thatcher Pharmacy and Notions Store.

The steady motion of the black four-bladed electric fan above the notions counter mingled the odor of hot bodies with the scents of perfumes and soaps that were neatly arrayed on the five and dime rack that stood on the floor by the door.

Looking up, Maxwell Potter saw himself in the mirror. Selfconsciously, he pushed at the dark cowlick of hair that fell over his eyes. He looked at his collar. Maybe I should have worn my tie, he thought. With only limited success, he tried smoothing the open collar of his shirt out over that of his plaid, brown sports jacket.

The bell on the cash register up front on the candy and gum counter kept time with the moving of men and boys in and out of the store.

Young men stood in the narrow aisle of the store talking, their excited voices an unintelligible chatter above the noises coming in from the street. Shifting around to stare over the shoulders of their companions, they looked at themselves in the mirror, adjusting ties and brushing at their hair.

Max stirred his coke with the straw, poking at the chips of ice. Again he looked at the clock on the wall. Eight o'clock she'd be here. Twenty more minutes. Geneva Wilson. Or Williamson. Something like that.

He listened. The blare of a trumpet came in through the screen door.

The Emporium Dance Land, the Stepping Stone for the Big Dance Bands, said the sign on the door outside, where steep, narrow steps led to the dance floor above. The Jubilee Players, Thatcher's Own, read the weekly billings in the Friday edition of the *Courier*.

Walter Schwartz, or Walther as he pronounced it, was the leader of the Jubilee Players, an assortment of six musicians of varying talents and dispositions. Olga, Walter's wife, fat, with straight-hanging yellow hair and small steel rimmed glasses, played the viola. Unable to read music and without the benefit of a fancy Eastern education, as she liked to remind Walter, Olga had learned by heart a dozen or so pieces, and her playing of the viola was restricted to rambling versions of this curious assemblage of musical themes. When the last note had been bowed from her viola, she substituted Tiny, her younger daughter, at the piano, hammering out discor-

dant chords to the beat of the timpani and the bass drum under the sensitive command of Jimmy Unterwaldt, the morning fry cook at the Thatcher House, the town's most impres-
sive hotel.

Walter, so the story went, had met Olga at an amuse-
ment park in Denver some years before the Big War. They
had met at a musical show, *The Blue Lady,* then playing at
the summer theater in the park. Walter had been struck, as
he said later, by her interest in music and her knowledge of
the viola. It was here that she learned the last of the dozen or
so tunes of her repertoire.

Enraptured by the fair Olga, Walter had quit his touring
musical group and he and Olga were married the second day
of their acquaintance. He would return with her to the East.
On the road together! He writing music. She at the viola, and
with him on the piano or French horn, they would caress their
way to the big time, to Broadway.

He had neglected to communicate all of his ideas to his
young bride until three days after their wedding. Instead of
the East and Broadway, they moved into her modest room
above a pawn shop on Market Street in Denver. Instead of
writing music for his winsome wife, Walter played French
horn and trumpet nightly in the pit at the Tabor Theater and
waited tables in the morning and at noon in a dank little tea
room around the corner from the pawn shop, on Fifteenth
Street.

Olga continued to pick chickens in a produce house
down on Market Street on week days and to attend musicals
on Sundays. Thus, for nine years, life had passed for the musical Schwartz family. Then the discovery: Walter's brother,
Franz Joseph, owned a farm in the Republican River valley
below Thatcher, Nebraska, and the first mortgage on the
building that housed the Thatcher Pharmacy and Notions
Store.

Franz Joseph was, as he was wont to say, a confirmed
bachelor. But he liked family and so had welcomed to his
home his talented brother and his wife.

Immediately upon moving in with Franz Joseph, life for Walter and Olga had changed. Olga, barren these nine years, suddenly blossomed and gave birth, first to Virginia, a strange, dark cobble-stone figure of a girl, who now played the accordian and clarinet in the band, and then to Tiny. Tiny ate without restraint; when she sat at the piano other girls giggled and pointed at the round piano stool as it disappeared under her overhanging fat.

With the sudden changes in his life, Walter had decided to ask Franz Joseph to give him assistance in relaunching his interrupted musical career. But Franz Joseph wouldn't hear of Walter and his family leaving Thatcher. Was it not here that providence had smiled on Olga, not once, but twice?

It was then that Franz Joseph had exercised his lease option on the dance hall above the Thatcher Pharmacy and Novelty Store. And the Emporium Dance Land was born. Franz Joseph, the older of the Schwartz brothers, played the violin, mostly religious tunes, and it was he who had given the group its name.

For twelve years the Jubilee Players, in later years featuring the growing Schwartz daughters, had remained the prime entertainers at the Saturday night dances in the ballroom above the drug store on the corner of Prairie Avenue and Elm Street.

After the first hour the hall usually filled, and only the primitive beat of the large bass drum could transcend the drunken noise of the sweating and swearing revelers. The Jubilee Players were credited, not for their musical talent so much, but for their endurance, and their reputation had grown through the years.

The trumpet again. Then the clarinet, on the high notes.

Cars slipped by the window of the drug store, their passing mere flashes in the mirror on the wall across from the soda fountain counter. Local cars now, but by nine, ten o'clock Kansas cars would out number all others on the main thoroughfares in the town. Saturday night in Thatcher was Kansas night, and a Saturday night in August was a hairshirt for the entire countryside.

Again the sound of music from upstairs.

What was she like, the new girl? Comin' in with her family. Was her family like the other families? Would he be able to dance with her, or would she lead and he step all over her shoes?

Max was perspiring.

Four minutes to eight.

Max stared at the reflection coming in from the street. The band upstairs was playing now, not full tunes but bits of melody.

The drug store was nearly empty. Tramping feet on the stairs going up to the Emporium Dance Land muted the music coming in through the door. Then the blare of a horn rose above the noise on the stairs.

Chewing the last of the ice from the coke glass, Max worked his way to the ballroom upstairs, as far as the cashier's cage.

On the sign above the barred cage window: one dollar a couple. He felt the crumpled dollar bill and small change in his right hand pants pocket.

Watch for Geneva up here, thought Max. Stand out here and watch 'til she gets here and then be ready when she comes up the stairs.

The Jubilee Players, their wine-colored shirts and blouses already sweat-stained around the arm pits, stood, or sat on chairs, around three wooden music stands on a slightly raised dais along the right wall of the dance floor. A rear wheel from a farm wagon, suspended from the high ceiling by three log chains, formed a candelabrum of sorts, with bulbs of red and green turned down low and flashing alternately on the water-stained ceiling of the hall. Festoons of spiral-twisted yellow and orange crepe paper streamed from the wheel hub, in a wide spoke-fashion, to the four sides of the room. Up near the lights, cigar and cigarette smoke formed a wispy cloud that hung in shifting, white layers.

Hot and humid, the air in the cramped lobby at the top of the stairs was still. A single bulb hung from the ceiling of the lobby, overlooking the head of the stairs. The light from the cashier's cage flashed sporadically as people moved up to buy their tickets.

The men, clean shaven, with some sporting fresh razor cuts, stand in line before the cage. Some in coarse suits, their shirts open at the collar, brush nervously with their hands at the sleeves of their coats and at the hanger creases in the knees of their pants. Others, in striped or solid colored shirts buttoned at the wrists, adjust the pins in their neckties, the glassy beads in the pins picking up the dim light from the bulb at the head of the stairs.

The men look at the sign above the barred window and then in at the dance floor, not searching but attentive, like a land turtle with his neck out testing the wind.

Their turn now, they sort out a single dollar bill from the many papers in a crushed wallet and hand the money through the window to the door man making change out of the soiled cigar box. Feigning surprise, they jump back momentarily as the man at the door ink stamps the left wrist of the men as they are readied to enter the ballroom.

The women, the early ones the farm wives with the morning chores only a few hours away, are wide across the hips and stiffly corseted. They linger behind the men, congregating near the head of the stairs. Puffing from the steep climb up the steps, they make side glances into the uneven reflection of the full-length mirror on the wall at the head of the step and to the left, facing one as he turns toward the cashier's cage. Dark dresses, stretched and buttoned over moist bodies, are patted and pulled into place. Shyly, a finger adjusts a lipstick line. A white, crochet-trimmed handkerchief mops at the brow and is again tucked under the wide enameled cloth dress belt. Then a final toss of the head.

"Come on, damn it. I don't have all night."

The men's voices are gruff as they call back to their wives. Then, smiling at the man at the door, they step aside as the women, perhaps a suggestion of a skip in their steps, slip through the doorway into the open, welcoming ballroom.

Windows on the two street sides of the hall were open.
Dizzying shadows, their elongated bodies stretching across
the boards of the floor and with heads bouncing on the far
walls, filled the room as couples filed into the hall, the glow
of the setting sun flooding in through the opened windows on
the west. People milled around the open windows waiting for
the dance to begin.

Max stood on the corner in front of the drug store,
watching and waiting. Walking back to the door of the drug
store, he again looked up at the clock. Twenty-five minutes
late.

Would she even come?

Then he felt a hand on his arm. Turning, he saw her.

"Sorry, Maxwell," said the girl's voice, strong yet feminine, "it always takes us longer to get any place than we count
on."

Geneva Wilson was perhaps fifteen years old, tall, although shorter than Max. Slender of build and only beginning to fulfill her rich promise of womanhood, she walked
with the lithe step of an athlete. Her fair skin, freckled from
long days under the summer sun, appeared moist in the soft
light from the evening sky. Her lips, thin, yet not severe, smiled warmly, the mouth open and showing white, strong teeth.
Her nose, a bit generous in profile, fit well her rather long
face, the chin prominent but not unattractive. Partly obscured in the failing light, her brushed hair was dark, not black,
but the color of oak wood when it is wet. Pulled back off her
forehead and held by a small brass barrette, her hair fell
gracefully to her nearly exposed shoulders. She was dressed
in a peasant blouse with a low, half-circle neck line, and a
full flaired skirt, held tightly at the waist with a black cord
belt. Starched and ironed, the white, flower-figured cotton
still had a fullness of its own.

"Well, what should we do, Maxwell?" she asked, looking up Elm Street toward the entrance to the dance hall. "I
don't want to go up to that terrible place."

"Should we go to a movie?" asked Max, motioning with his right thumb and nodding his head toward the Fox Theater, up past the Thatcher House on Prairie Avenue. "It's cool in there."

"I'd better not do that," said Geneva, concern in her voice. "I might miss Albert if he decides to go home." Again she looked in the direction of the dance hall door. Then she laughed. "It's not easy getting Mama to make him take me with him when he goes out."

Neither of them spoke.

"Let's just talk," said Geneva at last, looking down Prairie Avenue toward the end of the street where it formed the parking lot in front of the Burlington depot. "Let's go down and watch the trains come in," she said. "I've never been on a train," said Geneva, her voice excited. "Let's go talk and watch the trains come in."

"You ever been to a Pow Wow before?" asked Geneva, her hands clasped behind her slender hips, her black patent leather slippers following a crack in the sidewalk. She didn't look at Maxwell but at the crack in the cement. "I've seen Indians before but never in their costumes and dancing like that." She turned her head, smiling at Max. "I think going places is lots of fun."

"My father works for the railroad and I got a pass," said Max, urbanely. He was walking near the curb. "I've been as far west as Denver and east to Lincoln," he said, matter of fact. Max watched the girl; not a beautiful girl, he thought, but pretty, like the girl at the First National Bank. "Next year I'm gonna go to Chicago." There was finality in his voice.

"You know what my dad did when he got married?" asked Geneva, looking at Max, the smile gone now, but her brown eyes warm and friendly. "He promised himself and Mama that at least every two years the family would take a trip together, even to the mountains once in a while."

"I've seen the mountains from Denver," said Max, his eyes on the curb, "but I've never been up in the mountains."

"But we've never been outa Kansas," said Geneva, dejectedly, "except to come up here."

"There's not much fun here," said Max, stooping and picking up an empty cigarette package and starting to open it down the side. "That's why I like to leave town — to Lincoln or Denver."

"Mama was in Topeka once," said Geneva, no longer following the crack in the sidewalk but walking beside Max at the curb. "She went there to have an operation. That's where the state capitol is."

"Did she see the governor?" asked Max, impressed.

"I don't think so," said Geneva, her voice serious. "She burned her left hand so bad and had to have it operated on. She spent all her time in the hospital when she was in Topeka."

"I had my left hand operated on once, too," said Max, holding his hand out, palm upward, so that the girl could see it. With the index finger of his right hand he traced the thin-lined scar across the base of the thumb into the palm wrinkles of his left hand. "Took it without ether, too."

"I'll bet that hurt," said Geneva, sympathetically, her mouth wincing as she said it.

"Some," said Max, shrugging.

Both were quiet.

The curbs on each side of the street were lined with cars and trucks, angle-parked in front of the open stores, open 'til ten o'clock on Saturday nights. Both doors on the trucks and the front doors on the cars were open as men sat in darkness, talking in muffled tones, watching the people on the sidewalk and spitting into the gutter. Small children, too young to be off on their own, darted from vehicle to vehicle and from the curb into the open stores, hiding behind benches and lamp posts, playing, waiting for the weariness that would put them to sleep in the back seats and boxes of the cars and trucks. Just inside the stores, or on benches along the front, under the wide striped awnings still down on the east side of the street, women sat, with paper sacks or packages at their feet, talking and sometimes patting small heads that tossed sleepily in their laps.

"Are you still in school?" asked Geneva, looking at Max, curiosity in her voice. "I graduated from the eighth grade last year. Passed the exams and I don't have to go any more."

"Three more years," said Max. "I'm gonna finish high school and then be an engineer and a pilot."

"Mama thinks that a girl can get too much education," said Geneva, noncommittally. "She says some men don't want a woman that reads and thinks a lot."

"My mother can read," said Max, pride in his voice, "and my ol' — father — don't care."

"But not all men are like that, I suppose," said Geneva.

They were down in front of the depot.

The western sky was blue now, the color of blue in the Monday rinse water. Blueing makes the whites whiter. In a few short minutes the sky would be black and the night and the town dark. Until then, the western sky hung like a lantern; a low wispy cloud on the horizon was no longer white, but turning pink.

Geneva and Max climbed the steps to the footbridge that joined Thatcher proper to the shops of the Burlington railroad and to Dago Town farther south, on the bluff above the river. Her flower-figured dress stood out clean and white on the faded red structure that spanned the tracks of the rail yards.

"A train every fifteen minutes," said Max, moving over to the railing of the footbridge and looking east, down the tracks. "Here comes one now."

An eye of light, bright but out of focus, was shining down the tracks below them.

"A cousin of mine that lives over on the divide," said Geneva, pointing to the hills southeast of town, "can sit out on their water tank and see the Denver Zephyr come down the valley every afternoon when the sun is shining."

The light was on the siding now, almost to the depot.

"Did you know a man committed suicide by jumping off this bridge once," said Max, examining the railing where they stood. "Tied a rope here somewhere, put it 'round his neck and jumped."

"I'm getting married next December," said Geneva, her voice low and her eyes staring at the train moving toward them, up the siding along the platform of the depot. "You ever going to get married, Maxwell?"

"I don't know," said Max, still examining the railing for the probable place where the man had tied the rope. "Maybe. Why?"

"No reason," she said, still watching the train. "I'm marrying the man that owns our farm." Geneva sighed as she spoke. "Mama says I'm lucky."

"Is it a big farm?" asked Max, his elbows on the railing beside the girl.

"Not as big as Daddy would like," said Geneva sadly, "but he has three others, all bigger than the one Daddy works on."

"Then I guess your mama's right," said Max.

The train was stopped now, a short passenger train. The locomotive was nearly under the bridge.

"We'd better move from here or the engine will get your pretty dress all dirty," said Max, moving back toward the steps.

"I wish I could ride a train sometime," said Geneva, following Max, but looking at the train in the partial darkness below.

"That's one good thing 'bout my ol' man's job on the railroad," said Max. "I get to use a pass." Then he looked at the girl. "Would you like to go to the dance now?" asked Max, walking beside her, his hands in his pockets.

"Not unless you do," said Geneva, laughing and turning to Max. "I don't get to town much. I'd just like to walk and talk."

Chapter 19

"Did you hear 'bout Kirby?" the man asked. He nudged Max in the side as he spoke.

He was a squat, lump of a man in a wet-smelling, faded plaid mackinaw. He sat to Max's left at the bar. His gray hair was wet and matted, flakes of white snow still clung to the twists of thick hair above his right ear. The man's face was lined, the skin wrinkled and loose-hanging under his chin. He ran his left hand nervously through his hair as he squirmed up to the bar. His legs groped for a place to rest. "A beer, Adolph."

"Kirby who?" asked Max, not looking at the man, but staring into the void behind the bar.

"The dead guy out in the alley a while ago," said the man, turning his head and looking at Max. "Didn't see it myself, but that's what I heard. Sorely sorry to hear it."

"I don't know no Kirby," said Max, dismissing the man.

The martini glass was almost empty; Max looked down at the wetness in the glass, at the olive in the bottom of the stemmed glass. Absently, yet methodically, he began to twirl the toothpick between the forefinger and thumb of his right hand, the fruit on the toothpick shriveled and puckered looking in the faint light. I don't know no Kirby, he thought. I don't know no one.

Not gonna look back, thought Max. Tear out the page and burn it. Don't look back. Not for an hour. Tear it out and burn it to ashes. Don't keep payin' for somethin' ya didn't buy.

"But, I heard you saw the accident," said the man, laying a handful of small coins on the bar. "That's what Fay said," motioning with his thumb over his right shoulder. There was persistence in his voice.

"What accident?" asked Max, looking at the man for the first time. "I seen lots a accidents! Which one ya want?" Max's gaze shifted back to his glass on the bar.

"The smash up out front," said Fay, critically, stopping in back of the two men. Reaching between them, she placed a round tray of empty glasses on the bar. "Two, Adolph," She was quiet then and waited.

"Right outa his shoe," said Max, his voice low, almost unheard. "Wanted to cry but couldn't."

"Ya can cry now, dearie," said Fay, dropping a damp bar cloth over Max's left shoulder. "But, he won't hear ya."

"Didn't make a sound," said Max, not noticing the sarcasm in Fay's voice. "He tried to cry but couldn't."

"Sounds like Kirby, all right," said Fay, picking up her tray with two full glasses, the suds still foaming over on to the dull metal of the tray. "Good ol' Warren." She grabbed the cloth from Max's shoulder. "If you ask me, he was askin' for it."

"Hustlin' the trade again, Fay?" It was Paula. She laughed, her voice dry and without emotion.

"Warren Kirby?" asked Fay, contemptuously and turning. "Hardly." She was gone.

Warren Kirby. The sharply spoken name struck like a clapper in Max's head. Warren Kirby. Wonder if he's one a our's.

The cars. Max closed his eyes. He could still see the Lincoln rickocheting off the cars along the street. He could hear the broken glass and metal. Hate to a carried their insurance, he thought.

Kirby, Warren. There'd be a number. He was young; number'd be a big one. *I will lay me down in peace.* Every morning in the *News.* Check every one. Hell of a way to start the day, findin' one that's gonna have a claim. Find out if it was suicide. Or maybe he lied on the medical. Warren Kirby. Irene can check.

"Drunk as a coot, I guess," said the man. "Christ, what a sorely way to celebrate Christmas — a tag on your big toe." The man turned to Max. "Your right one or left left one?" He laughed as he asked it.

Max wasn't listening.

Telephone. Max sat up straight. Unsteadily, he looked up along the bar to his right. Leaning forward, he gazed past the man on his left. On the wall by the door to the back room. Max pushed himself off the stool and stood up.

Watch your feet, he thought. Don't want Irene to think you been drinkin'.

Max started for the telephone on the wall at the far end of the room. Stumbling, he fell hard against the man on the stool beside his.

"Take it easy, fella," said the man, turning and brushing beer from the front of his mackinaw, "or they'll be sorely tying a tag on one a your big toes."

Warren Kirby, thought Max. 58 CSO mortality. Salesman's convention last year. Went over big, they said. Twenty-five. Wish he'd been twenty-five. Mortality rate at twenty-five —1.93 per 1000. Age twenty-five to twenty-six supposed to be eighteen thousand, four hundred eighty one outa ten million die. But he couldn't a been more'n twenty. The mortality factor for accidental death at age twenty-five is .46, assuming coverage to age 70. Math! Christ, that's where the future is.

Max picked up the phone. The coin chimed. Carefully, he dialed.

"Mountain-Plains Life Insurance. Merry Christmas."

"Warren Kirby," said Max, a note of excitement in his voice.

"Yes?"

"Yes, what, Irene?"

"I beg your pardon, I don't believe . . ."

"That is you, isn't it?"

"Yes!"

"Warren Kirby. Look . . ."

"I'm afraid we . . ."

"Look, Irene. I just offered your job to one of the Christmas helpers and . . ."

"Mister Potter!" Then she was silent.

"Irene, look up Warren . . ."

"I'm glad you called, Mr. Potter. I — we have been looking all over . . ."

"Warren Kirby, Irene. Look in the files and see if we have a policy on a Warren Kirby, white male, military now, or was, and . . ."

"Mister Potter, there is a meeting . . ."

"Irene, I am trying to trace down a most important fact. Please see if we have a file on a Warren Kirby. About twenty years old."

"Yes, Mister Potter." The line was quiet for a long moment. Then it was Irene again. "It will take a minute."

Old people wait 'til after Christmas, thought Max. He leaned against the wall, his right hand cradling the receiver up against the rough paint of the wall, the fingers of his left hand drumming unevenly on the mounting of the telephone. 'I will lay me down in peace.' Every morning in the *News*. Old farts give ya a new lease on life. Max shuddered.

The line clicked: "Maxwell?"

It was a man's voice, strangely familiar. Max snapped erect. The timbre of the voice searched his brain. Answer him, thought Max.

"Yes."

"Guthry, here," said the voice, friendly, the words sharp. "Like Santa Claus, I only come but once a year." There was laughter at the other end.

The voice! Guthry? It was an older voice than the Guthry he remembered.

"Come back to see the wife's family," said Guthry, still chuckling. "Try to do it every year."

Guthry, in Denver? Here to make a deal on the Oregon job, thought Max. Gotta be firm. No deals. Had his chance a long time ago.

"Guthry, what are you doin' in town?" Max's voice was high-pitched.

"Like I said, just passing through," said Guthry. The laughter was gone, but his voice was pleasant.

"Just checkin' on a possible policy holder," said Max apologetically. He licked his lips, then swallowed. Keep it natural, he thought. "A fella got killed in a wreck down here and name sounded familiar."

"Always liked your flair for business," said Guthry, approvingly. "That's what it takes today."

Always was a cool bastard, thought Max. Let him start the conversation and then pace him. Sneak into town on Christmas. No deals.

"Here's Irene, Maxwell," said Guthry. His voice was faint and distant.

The line clicked.

"No, Mister Potter," said Irene, matter-of-factly, "nothing close to that name."

"You checked the master listing, Irene?" Max was nervous now.

"Yes, Mister Potter."

"Very well, Irene." Max was quiet for a moment. "He was a soldier. Probably wouldn't have our kind a policy, anyway," said Max at last, relief in his voice. "I thought it best . . ."

"Mister Potter, I believe that you might want to return to the office . . ."

"I think I am the best judge . . ."

"But, they are most insistent that you be here," said Irene.

She was almost friendly, thought Max.

"Who's 'they'?" asked Max, curiosity showing in his voice for the first time.

"Mister Guthry, Mister Adler, Mister Worley and a man I don't know, someone from the Western Slope, a Mister Melton, I think his name is."

"Don't they know the office is closed?" asked Max, anger in his voice. "This is Christmas. Honor the Sabbath and keep it holy."

Goddamned Vince.

"They are most insistent, Mister Potter." It was a plea this time.

"Tell them I'm still Christmas shoppin'," said Max, no longer angry. Let 'em wait 'till I'm damned good and ready, he thought. Max breathed deeply, flexing his shoulders as he did so. "There's all of next week, and next year, for that matter."

"Very well, Mister Potter," said Irene.

"Oh, Irene. Did the boy from the parking garage downstairs bring my car keys up to the office?"

"No, Mister Potter," said Irene, diffidently. "I haven't seen your car keys."

"Merry Christmas, Irene."

"Merry Christmas, Mister Potter."

Max hung up the phone.

Arrogant bastards. Then he thought of the Oregon deal. No deals. Nice clean job. *Best's 400* next year for sure. And Guthry! Bastard's crawlin' for cover already. Must think he can get through me what he couldn't get on his own. He knows our company's not big enough for both of us. Max smiled. And Vince! Let him squirm, the horse's ass. Again he smiled. Haven't heard that term for a long time, thought Max. Losin' our grip on the language.

Max retrieved his stool at the bar.

He looked for the bartender. Down at the end of the bar.

"Adolph, call a cab for me, please," said Max.

Funny 'bout that term — a horse's ass — thought Max. Wonder why ya don't hear it any more. The etymology of the expression bothered him. Max looked at the man in the machinaw sitting beside him to his left.

"Would you get mad if a man called you a horse's ass?" asked Max, his voice serious, his eyes studying the man's face.

The man looked up, surprise on his face. Then he smiled. "Not if he bought me a drink first," said the squat man, chuckling. "You'd have to be a sorely horse's ass to appreciate this piss," he said, pushing back the partly finished glass of beer, a wry, bad-taste look on his lined face.

"Two, Adolph," said Max, holding up two fingers and looking up the bar past the man in the mackinaw. "Ever think 'bout that expression?" asked Max, his attention on the man beside him again.

"What, two fingers in the air?" asked the man, turning to Max, a new wrinkle across his forehead. "Not recently. No, can't say . . ."

"I mean calling a person a horse's ass," said Max, his eyes focusing on a spot somewhere behind the man's head.

"I suppose, since we use cars so much," speculated the man, now sipping at his beer again, "not many people have to sit there all day on the seat of a planter, or wagon, and watch that tail raise." The man in the mackinaw finished his beer and set the glass on the bar. Yawning, he pushed himself up straight on the stool. "Ten, twenty years a lookin' a horse in the ass every day made a man a expert of sorts on all kinds a people, I guess." The man looked at the bartender. "Speakin' of a horse's ass," he said, "this guy . . ."

"Know anything 'bout horses?" asked Max, curiosity in his voice. "Ten, twenty years . . ."

"Oh, not much," said the man, yawning again. "Bet on one once, twice a year, I suppose."

"I never bet on one yet directly but . . ."

"Used to ride once in a while myself. Ak-sar-ben, mostly," said the man, lifting the empty beer glass and absently drinking from it; his tongue licked at the beer drops on the rim of the glass.

The bartender placed two martinis on the bar in front of the two men.

"Here's to horses," said Max, a broad smile crossing his smooth face. He laid a five dollar bill on the bar and reached for one of the glasses. "Name's Maxwell Potter, president of . . ."

"Penderseth. Guy Penderseth," said the man picking up one of the stemmed glasses. Carefully, he tasted the drink, his upper lip, like the tip on an elephant's trunk, gripping the liquid before swallowing it. "Damned good drink, a martini."

"Classy drink," said Max. A man with class, thought Max, sipping his martini. "Used to ride, huh?" said Max, picking up the conversation again. "Always wanted to see the Runnin' a the Roses, myself."

"Ran in the Derby once. In '28, before the market crash," said the man, not looking up, but observing closely the drink before him. "War and Peace—called him Tolstoy." The man's voice was low, almost inaudible.

"Win?" asked Max, setting his glass on the bar, his eyes round, his voice high-pitched but not loud.

"Naw. Fell," said Penderseth, shrugging his shoulders. "Raining. Been raining for two days. Coming outa the backstretch, the horse stumbles, swallows its tongue and falls. The sorely sonofabitch." Penderseth pushed himself away from the bar, so that he was facing away from Max. He raised his right pants leg. "See that scar?" He paused, looking down over his shoulder and pointing a shaking right index finger at the calf of his right leg. "Damned near lost that leg. Had to operate," he said, shaking the loose, saggy pants leg back over the thin, white hairy leg. "Tolstoy—had to shoot the sorely sonofabitch."

Both men were quiet.

"Never rode much after that," said Penderseth at last, his voice still low, an edge of sadness lacing each word. "Bet on the longshots once in a while, but no riding."

"Longshots?" asked Max. "What's a longshot to you?"

"Fifteen, twenty, maybe twenty-five to one to win."

"Hit those very often?" asked Max. He edged over to the man at the bar.

"You have to know horses to hit on a longshot, remember." Penderseth shrugged his shoulders as he spoke. Carefully, he sipped at his drink.

"How many times have you hit a twenty-five to . . ."

"Now a mule is a better farm animal than a horse," said Penderseth, concentrating on his martini. "He won't founder on grain like a horse, and he won't let anyone get him over-heated. That trait in mules gave them a bad name. Men thought they were lazy and stubborn. Not so," said Penderseth, smacking his lips, his tongue searching out any liquid on his chin that might have gone astray. "A horse will over-heat itself."

"How do you figure out a long . . ."

"Professional," said Penderseth, stirring quietly the olive in his drink. "Got a niece that sends me money each month and I spread it out." Penderseth picked up the olive and sucked on it.

Both men were quiet again.

"A mule's a sorely complicated animal. When you under-stand a mule you pretty well understand a horse." Penderseth turned and looked over at Max. "Ever see 'em breed for mules?"

" 'Fraid they didn't teach that at the university," said Max, chuckling, a note of superiority in his voice.

"You don't have to worry about keeping the blood of the donkeys pure. They breed out, not in. You breed a mare horse with a jackass donkey to get mules. The mare can have a mule of either sex, but they're both sterile. How's that for nature?" Penderseth sipped carefully at his martini. Then he continued: "When you breed a jackass to a mare horse you gotta be care-ful. If the mare's not ready she can kick the hell out of a jack. And yet a jack won't help things out much. A jack won't tease a mare, so you have to bring in a stud horse to get the mare ready. When she's good and ready you bring in the jack."

"You do know your horses," said Max, the high pitch back in his voice.

"But you gotta be sorely careful breeding a mare with a jack," said Penderseth, excitement in his own voice now. "He gets ready and if he misses, your lost—the shot goes astray." Penderseth chuckled. "You don't get a jack ready again simply by trotting him around the yard once or twice. And you gotta be careful he doesn't rupture the mare by hitting her in the wrong place. A good jack, or stud horse, for that matter, can blow the ass out of every mare on the place if you're not careful. You gotta use what's called a teasing stick—a pole with a ring on the end—to guide the jack up to his target. Breeding for mules is a sorely interesting art." Penderseth relaxed on his stool, his shoulders sagging under the damp mackinaw. "You gotta know your horses to bet on a longshot."

A cold draft swept along the foot rest at the bar. "Somebody call a cab?" called a loud voice from the door.

"Here," said Max, waving his left arm and turning toward the door. Then he turned back to the man beside him at the bar. "Here's my card, Mr. Pender—Guy, and here's a fifty to put on a longshot for me. I gotta go, but put that on the horse and we'll split."

Penderseth took the card and looked at it. "Hmmm, president, eh?"

"Here, make that a hundred," said Max, handing the man five ten-dollar bills. "We'll spend it on martinis," said Max, laughing. "Twenty to one will do," he said, rising from the stool.

Penderseth looked at the card and the money lying on the bar. "Merry Christmas, Maxwell," said the man at the bar, his low voice trailing after Max as he left.

Chapter 20

"Where to?" asked the driver, slamming the door behind Max. The driver, a short man, slender and already beginning to stoop, circled the cab and slid behind the wheel.

"Gotta pick up my car," said Max, sitting limp on the back seat and rubbing his eyes with the fingers of both hands. "A Cadillac."

"Where, in Detroit?" The cab pulled away from the curb, heading south on Fifteenth Street. "Which bus depot do ya want?"

"I don't want a bus depot," said Max, angrily. "My car. I ran over a stop sign and put a hole in the pan or something. Gotta go pick it up."

"OK, let's go." The cab cut into the inside lane, then slowed, stopping for a red light. "Which garage did you go to?" asked the driver, looking up and watching Max in the rear view mirror.

"The dealer down there on Broadway, I suppose," said Max, still rubbing his eyes. "Been in that hole so long even this light blinds me."

"The one on the three-hundred block?" asked the driver, his voice sharp and inquisitorial.

"Yeah," said Max, "that's the one. Yeah, I remember that's where I got it."

"That's a used car lot and he don't do car work." The traffic light turned to green; the cab moved up Fifteenth Street going south. "You gonna try again, or you just want a ride out on Broadway?"

"Then it's closer up, somewhere in the six- or seven-hundred block." Max was pushed back in the seat now, looking out the window on the left. "Cadillac dealer. Long black —just got it."

"When'd you take it there?" asked the driver, nervously. Again he looked at Max in the rear view mirror.

"Sometime this morning, I guess," said Max, shrugging his shoulders, still looking out the left side window. "Told the attendant to call the garage and have them come and get it."

"Where's that, the attendant?" persisted the driver. The cab slowed and stopped. The WALK light was on.

"Over at the office." Suddenly Max sat forward on the seat. "What's the third degree for?" he shouted, rapping with the knuckles of his right hand on the glass partition separating him from the driver. "The seven-hundred block on Broadway." Max settled back in the corner of the cab.

Quietly, the cab moved through the traffic, going south; the gentle swaying of the vehicle worked on Max's stomach. He rolled down the window and stuck his face out, the fresh air cold, the snow flakes hard against his unprotected skin.

"Not in my cab, you don't," yelled the driver, again watching Max in the mirror. "You puke . . ."

"You're sure a belligerent bastard for being so close to Christmas," said Max, irritated but relaxing now into the corner of the car seat, his face still close to the window. Belching, he leaned forward and spit out the opened window. "I didn't spend all that time and money gettin' drunk just to give you the satisfaction a cleanin' up after me." Sniffing and coughing, he wiped his moist nose on the sleeve of his raincoat.

Both men were quiet. The cab turned east.

Max was the first to speak.

"Ever hear of a horse named Tolstoy," asked Max, sitting forward on his seat and looking into the rear view mirror.

"Ran in the Kentucky Derby in 1928, before the big market crash."

"No, I missed that one," said the driver, his voice quick, yet labored. "But I saw the movie, *War and Peace*, if that's any help." He took a fast glance at Max in the mirror, as the cab went through the intersection.

"Swallowed his tongue comin' outa the backstretch and they had to shoot the sorely sonofabitch," said Max, disbelief, etched in conviction, weighing on every word. "War and Peace! What a hellova name for a horse!"

"Yeah, I understand the book was even better."

Again the two men were quiet. The cab swung in close to the curb, turning.

Max sat back again in the corner of the cab, his eyes closed.

"Now, about your car, fella," said the driver, changing to the outside lane, on the right, "We're comin' to the eight hundred block now. You're sure this is the place?"

"Yeah, I oughta know. I bought it there coupla months ago," said Max, sliding over to the window on the right. The cab cleared the intersection. "Looks deader'n hell there now, though, don't it?"

The garage, with wide, tall windows facing Broadway, occupied the entire north half of the block.

"Sure as hell does, fella," said the driver, leaning over and looking out the right front window, the cab moving slowly along the curb. "If you got a car in there you're not gonna have it for Christmas."

"I'll get out and try the door," said Max, reaching for the door handle. "I'll just . . ."

"Oh, no, you don't," said the driver, slamming on the car brakes, knocking Max hard against the back of the driver's seat. "Get a free ride out here. Just like I thought."

"Damn, you get mean," said Max, ineffectually reaching for something with which to pull himself up off the floor of the cab. "Help me outa here," he yelled, his arms now braced against the two seats, "or I'll sue you back . . ."

The cab driver had the left rear door open and was pulling Max up onto the seat. "That's a buck twenty-five, plus tip," said the driver, anger in his voice, "and I'll whip it outa your ass right here if . . ."

Max was up on the seat now. Turning, and without warning, Max grabbed the driver's coat front in both hands and slammed the man's head and shoulders up hard against the top and inside the cab door. Max's arms, elbows out, blocked the driver's hands. He looked into the driver's eyes, now round and frightened. "What do ya think's gonna happen to ya, Cabby?" asked Max, his voice calm, his own eyes steady and close to the driver's face. He waited, staring into the man's eyes. "Huh?" Max asked, jamming the man's head and shoulders even tighter against the cab top, the knuckles of both hands deep into the other man's ribs.

The driver was silent, his face muscles fighting a cry of pain that was forming on his lips.

"Now, I'm gonna release this left hand," said Max, letting go of the driver's coat with the one hand. "And I'm gonna surprise you," he said, reaching inside his coat pocket.

The driver started to move his right arm.

"Know how easy a man's neck snaps, Cabby?" said Max, shaking only slightly the man's shoulders with his right hand.

Max withdrew his left hand slowly from his coat, not taking his eyes off the cabby's face. "See this," said Max.

The cabby tried to bend his neck, his frightened eyes looking down his nose from the stiff position up against the cab top.

"That's my wallet," said Max, holding it up before the man's face. Max could feel the cabby relax. "Now, go through it gently until you find three one-dollar bills and hand them to me." Max paused, but the cabby didn't move. "Go on!" said Max, again jabbing the man in the ribs with his right hand, still holding the vice-like grip on his coat front. "Nice and politely," said Max, still staring into the cabby's eyes.

Trembling, the cabby raised his right hand and, his eyes, like boiled eggs, peered into the wallet as his fingers searched for the small denomination bills. One by one he handed the bills to Max; Max held them between his thumb and the wallet. "Now, does that money look like the other money you been seein' lately?" asked Max, shaking his wallet and bills in the cabby's face.

The cabby tried to speak but couldn't. He raised and lowered his eyes.

"All right, then," said Max, his voice still calm, his gaze not moving from the eyes of the driver. "Know where the Professional Exchange Building is?" Max retained his tight grip on the cabby's coat.

Again the driver's eyes moved up and down.

"Will three dollars cover the bill?" asked Max.

The word 'yes' formed silently on the man's lips.

"OK," said Max, putting his wallet back into his coat, but still holding the cabby tightly with his right hand.

Traffic was heavy now; passing cars slowed down but didn't stop. A horn sounded as a car slowed, then pulled out and around the opened cab door.

"Get this, Cabby," said Max, again gripping the man's coat with both hands, the three one-dollar bills wedged between the thumb and index finger on his left hand, "your soul may belong to the Lord, but as long as I'm sittin' back here your ass belongs to me. Understand?"

Max released his grip.

"The Professional Exchange Building, please," said Max, handing the driver the three one-dollar bills.

The cab turned right at the next intersection, right again at Acoma and then headed north. Max sat with his head over against the left rear window, the air from the partly lowered glass fresh and cold against his face. A dollar's worth of respect for every dollar spent, that was his dictum.

The garage attendant's shack was deserted; the door was closed. Max rattled the door knob, but there was no response. He turned and looked back toward the street. The oil spill from his damaged car had been cleaned up; sawdust and a white chalky dust covered the driveway into the garage.

The garage was dark, except for the bulb in the attendant's shack. Keys are in the car, wherever that is, thought
Max. He stood in the garage opening, staring into the storm.

The cold air in the garage stimulated Max's lungs; he
breathed deeply. Christmas booze. Never could understand
the damned ritual, he thought. Pleased, he slapped his chest
gently with the open palms of both hands. Ten deep breaths
and suck in the gut and hold it. Good for the back. Max
breathed deeply, blinking his eyes, his mind lost in counting
the breathing exercises.

The door to the office building opened and three men
stepped into the garage. The first one, a tall, round man,
neatly dressed in a gray herringbone topcoat, held the door
for the other two. Then, quietly, the three men walked up to
the dark figure standing silhouetted in the middle of the
garage entrance. The figure, his back to the approaching
men, inhaled and exhaled forcefully, patting his inflated chest
after every breathing in.

"Maxwell." It was Vince Adler's voice.

"Eight," wheezed the figure standing in the garage
entrance. "Nine." Uncoordinated, he patted his chest as he
breathed. "Ten."

"Maxwell." Vince stepped up to Max, taking hold of
Max's elbow.

Max shook his arm free, taking one final long breath and
sighing deeply as he did so.

"Maxwell!" This time Vince's voice was loud and firm.

Max turned from the light of the street entrance toward
the voice. The other two men with Vince stepped forward.

"Maxwell, how good to see you!"

The voice was familiar, yet new, thought Max. It was
Guthry's voice, the voice on the phone when he'd called Irene
from the bar. The man who owned the voice was short, eye-
level height with Max. Shorter than the Guthry I knew,
thought Max. Thinning, finely combed hair betrayed a small
spot on the top of a disc-like head. Large ears formed axle
hubs for the disc; the nose and mouth were mere notches in
the rim of the otherwise thin, round head. The body of the

man was fibrous, the muscles in his neck giving a suggestion of tubular construction under a gauze-grained skin. His clothes were tight-fitting. When he shook hands with Max, the whiteness of the knuckles matched the coldness of his stare.

"Merry Christmas, Maxwell," said Guthry.

"A witches brew, if I ever saw one," said Max, surprise showing in his face, his voice low and calm. "What brings such tidings?"

"Your goddamned surly attitude . . ."

"I'll take care of this, Simon," said Vince Adler, his left hand outstretched, as though to block Simon Worley's access to Max. Vince's voice was strong and authoritative.

"Yes, Simon," said Max, looking at the attorney for the first time, his voice without warmth, "and what's wrong with my surly attitude?"

"I've taken it for the . . ."

"Damnit, Worley, I'll take care of this," said Vince, turning to his companion. The fat sales manager held a half-smoked but unlit cigar in his right hand.

Simon Worley was tall and broad shouldered. When he stood straight, his clothes fell in long lines, more the work of a tent and awning shop than a clothier. His face was pink and puffy, the cheeks smooth and only starting to show the small red veins that had already given a raw-meat hue to his thin, angular nose. Thick, short lips, more of a puncture than a mouth, accentuated the roundness of his head. His teeth, irregular and stained, added a russet color to the thin, neatly trimmed mustache that trembled when he spoke. His eyes, screened behind thick, metal-rimmed lenses, blinked rapidly when he spoke or listened, their wide, round exposure injecting a question mark into everything that was said. A shock of thin, wispy white hair, descending in long, fluffy sideburns to the jaw line, gave his stature the appearance of a giant milkweed having just gone to seed.

"You've taken more than we'll probably know, Simon," said Max, a warmth creeping into his voice. "But, then . . ."

"I'll come to the point, Maxwell," said Vince, standing in front of Max, between him and the attorney. "We . . ."

"You always do, Vince," said Max, contemptuously. "A characteristic of the salesman in you, no doubt." Max turned to leave.

"Not this time, Maxie," said Vince, smiling. Gently he grabbed Max's right arm. "Not this time." His manner was friendly but firm. "You'll hear me out this time, Maxwell."

"I'll take it up from here, Vince—Mr. Adler." It was Guthry speaking. He moved in closer, his right hand up, silencing Vince. "We've sat up there trying to find you," he said, addressing Max. "If you want to make this a power play, fine. We've got the money, the law and the votes on our side. And we intend to exercise them."

"Look, Max, it's over." It was Vince again. "Guthry, here's got the money to bail out the Oregon company. Christ, Larry Langdon's been tryin' to get hold of you all day to bring you up to date. We don't . . ."

"Guthry's got nothin'," roared Max, shaking himself loose, as though imaginary hands were reaching for him. "Mountain-Plains Life Insurance has . . ."

"There isn't going to be any Mountain-Plains, Potter." It was Worley speaking again; his speech was tempered, but harsh. He jabbed at Max's chest with his right index finger. "Because under the new proposal Sequoia National will absorb . . ."

"Let me put it another way, Maxwell," said Vince, again stepping between Max and the attorney, "I've been in contact with the Colorado stockholders for the last five, six weeks. They don't want things to go the way you want them to go regarding the future of the company. That is, a goodly number of them don't."

"What's with Simon," asked Max, looking at Vince but motioning with his left thumb to the attorney in back of him, "Guthry finally meet his price?"

Max turned on Worley, his own right fist shaking before the attorney's face. "Won't be no Mountain-Plains company!" he scoffed, turning up his mouth as though to spit. "Sure as hell not the same mouthpiece, but . . ."

"Look, Max," said Vince, his fat face creased into a frown as he spoke, "there was a meeting." He paused, the cold cigar shaking in his nervous right hand. "That's why we're here. Things like this," he said, struggling for the words, "should be done nicely, and under the right circumstances."

"Quit the soft sell, Vince," said Worley, stepping around Vince and again jabbing his opponent on the chest with his right index finger. "This bastard . . ."

"If I weren't drunk, Worley, I'd let the gas outa your bag for even touchin' me in anger," said Max, not moving.

The attorney jumped back, his wide eyes blinking.

"And, get this, Worley," said Max, moving forward, his voice rising, his hot breath clouding the face of the man addressed, "you think you have the money, the law and the votes on your side, eh?" The words hissed from his mouth, his hot breath smoking in the cold air of the garage. "But you don't have me yet. Guthry or no Guthry, you just try to unseat management."

Max stepped back, looking at all three men. His voice was threatening. "My record's clean as a hound's tooth. We know about some of the rest a you," he said, turning to Guthry. "The crudest goddamned twister in the Rocky Mountain Empire when I last saw you. But I'll see you bastards under a microscope in every commissioner's office where insurance is sold."

"Now, you . . ."

"Shut up!" yelled Max, again waving his right fist at the startled Guthry. "My toy, Vince says. The company my toy! You damned right it's my toy, and the territory's my circus. And you," he said, looking at the three men in one cold sweep of his eyes, "are my clowns." Max laughed, his face twisted, the mouth wreathing in scorn. "And I intend to be the lion a the whole goddamned show."

"It won't work this time, Max." It was Vince speaking again. Calmly, standing back in the garage away from the other men now, he lit a match, the flame lighting up his face; the flame flickered, almost died, danced, then died. He puffed nervously on the cigar.

No one spoke, waiting.

"I mentioned this earlier today, Max," said Vince. "It's not that you're slipping. That I won't bother even to document. And, it's not that you don't put in your time at what you do. No one even questions your sincerity of purpose most of the time. The problem, Maxwell, is that you don't really know anything about business, especially the insurance business. Gimmicks, yes. Your specialty. Gimmicks are all right when they pay off, and if you can keep coming up with them that pay off. But this last gimmick touches upon cost factors you can't even comprehend. You're through, Maxwell. The only question now is how to . . ."

"Even sober, I'd see through your little scheme," said Max, his eyes shifting from Vince to Guthry and finally to Worley. "Scare me and make me resign. Insult me and hope I'd run. Don't count me out yet, gentlemen. I may not know much about business, as you say, Vince," he said, turning to the fat man in the herringbone topcoat, "but I know men."

"There's an old friend of yours upstairs, Maxwell," said Guthry, ignoring Vince and the attorney, "by the name of Melton, from the Western Slope. He has about two-thirds a the Colorado stockholders' votes wrapped up. Vince's made sure of that. Now, we'll . . ."

Words! Words! Suddenly Max saw his insurance dreams crumbling before his eyes. You're on your feet, he thought. That's their first mistake.

"The king makers, three, eh Guthry?" said Max, smiling. "And Santa Claus, too?"

Make 'em pay, every damned word, thought Max.

"Wait 'till the stockholders find out that Mountain-Plains gave up the Oregon venture, and why," said Max, smiling. "And the effect that will have on their stock."

He didn't look at the three men. Then, turning on Vince: "Scaring hell outa Hamper and Langdon didn't help your stock either, Adler," said Max, laughing at the fat sales manager.

"I didn't get this job, nor hold it," said Max, looking at all three men again, " 'cause a the likes and dislikes a pissy assed has beens that hold meetings and contact shareholders."

Take it on your feet, thought Max. They can't get you so long as you're on your feet.

"And you, Guthry," said Max, his voice low. "Speakin' a power, you're gonna get a lesson in the use a power." Max stepped up close to Guthry, the thin disc face startled and pale. "Wait 'till the Oregon commissioner waves my telegram in your face," said Max, laughing. "I cancelled our offer hours ago," he lied, looking Guthry in the eyes, his own face calm, his expression noncommittal.

A telegram can still get there before business Monday morning, thought Max.

"And Guthry," said Max, staring the man down, "when you conspire, spend good money and buy better men than Mountain-Plains can apparently afford."

Max paused, standing erect. Breathe in deeply, he thought. Buttocks in.

"Come Monday morning, whoever holds Sequoia National stock will be in for a surprise," said Max, his voice mocking. "Take over Mountain-Plains, raid our cash position, and be home free, eh, Guthry? And from the kind a deal you must a put together, there'll be a lot a salty water flowin' into the Columbia River when the news gets out."

Without looking at the men, Max turned, started toward the garage entrance and the light. "Simon, what time is it?" he said, turning on the startled attorney.

"Seventeen minutes past three," said Worley, looking at his large gold wristwatch, his eyes blinking.

Vince shrugged his shoulders, black ashes falling from the dead cigar.

"Thank you, gentlemen," said Max, "I believe I am late for an appointment with a beautiful woman." Smiling, Maxwell Potter turned and walked into the afternoon light, his shadow falling in the sawdust and grit of the garage floor.

Chapter 21

The snow was no longer falling except for that blown from the trees and overhead wires along Sixteenth Avenue. The slush and snow on the sidewalk had frozen; an icy trail wandered through the brittle crusts, around low places in the broken sidewalk and the sloping surfaces of driveways partly hidden under the snow. Above, the cloud mass was breaking up, small patches of blue showing above the taller buildings to the west and north. The dark, brooding Colorado State Bank Building, an ungraceful giant, its sunglasses windows hovering suspiciously over the lights and traffic at its feet, blocked the view of the clouded hills to the west of the city. To the south stood the gold dome of the capitol building, cold, yet commanding above the government office buildings and small hotels along Colfax Avenue. The air was cold.

Maxwell Potter trudged heavily through the snow along Sixteenth Avenue, his shoulders bent into the cold wind now coming in from the west. His hands deep in the pockets of his light raincoat, his eyes downcast, Max stepped unsurely along the slippery path, laid out by others but followed uncertainty wherever the steps might lead.

At the corner, while waiting for the light to change, Max stood erect, his stomach in tight, buttocks pulled in, and breathed deeply. He counted the exercises. Seven. Good for the back, he thought. Eight. Don't think . . . Nine. Tear the page out and burn it. Ten.

208

The light changed. Max crossed the intersection, the path lost in the ground up ice of the street.

Double jeopardy, looking back, thought Max. Tracy! Why'd I have to look her up in Omaha? Should have left well enough alone. She's dead. Dead like my ol' man and her ol' man. Dead like Kirby and Benny. And like Frog and Flinty. And the kid with the golden gloves, and coach and Jeffrey. F D R and the Pride a the Yankees. All dead.

Scare me into resignin'. A two-bit company, and now look at it. Sellin' insurance in eleven states and soon be on the West Coast, in Oregon and California.

Catholic. Should been born a Catholic and then no problem. The accident a my birth, thought Max, smiling. A goddamned Wop and I'd a been all right for her ol' lady.

Ain't gonna be no Mountain-Plains, thought Max. He kicked at the icy path, almost losing his balance. He thought of the taxi driver; he could still see the fear in the man's face. What do ya think's gonna happen to ya, Cabby? Max chuckled. The fingers of both hands clenched, the hands hard fists in the pockets of his raincoat. Him president a Sequoia National and boot me out on my ass.

Two o'clock, at the Greek's. Phyllis. Don't look back. She's dead. Dead, Phyllis. Be there, Phyllis. Be there, waiting. She wasn't really important, Phyllis. Not like you. I don't even know her. I've always been in love with her, Phyllis, but not like with you. There must be room in us for loving more than just one, Phyllis. I'll make it up to you. Be there, waiting.

His mind swam in the mist of thought that blanketed his consciousness. Fear, long absented from his emotional awareness, isolated and held in check like a deadly bacilli in the lung of an aging body, now sparked to life in the periphery of his inner vision. It was not the fear of physical pain, that divine reminder that haunts and insults the mind until the body surrenders, once and for all, that mortal assence of oneself that enjoys the pleasures of life. This he had come to terms with long ago. Nor was it the fear of man for man. Strength and stamina insured against this. It was the fear of aloneness, the psychic acid that, once spilled, dissolves, in ever increasing sureness, the protecting shell that keeps one man from being like all others, yet threatens to loose another soul into the nothingness of the total of spent lives. It was a fear of self, unchecked and uncharted.

Don't look back, thought Max. His lower lip quivered. He slammed his right fist, hard and firm, into the palm of the left. The pain was reassuring. Only the present and the future, he thought. You can't change what's past. A page in a book. A page at a time. Tear it out.

The light changed. DON'T WALK.

Max stopped, breathed deeply. Stomach tight, buttocks in. His lips moved as he breathed in; his eyes blinked as he breathed out. Max shook his head; so light it felt. And his feet. Light and young. His mind skipped backwards, a child's skipping stone over a sea of time. Years! Years! And those special years, he thought. Where did they go? They disappeared as chipped pebbles dropped from a skimming boat, shimmering all the while but soon lost in the wet flashes of the moving stream. But what of those years? Why so special? Were they not bitter, terrible years? Of pain and torture and terror? Then why so special? Why these than other years? Because I was young and so was she.

The word ten formed on his lips.

WALK

They can have the company, thought Max, searching for the path in the ice and snow. The idea surprised him. A good place to start. Clean sweep. Find a new job, new life. Two years left on my contract and enough stock to keep 'em in line. And options good for another ten years. Max smiled. Never burn your bridges, that's my dictum.

And Phyllis, he thought. The thought warmed him. Take a couple a months off and get to know her again. Like it used to be, before we were married.

The path in the snow was wider now, and there were several paths to choose from.

And the city can go ahead and build their goddamned park.

DON'T WALK.

The flags waved briskly on the mast across Broadway, at United Nations Square, the snap of the cloth sharp and fresh.

Max watched the cars, without seeing them.

Traffic on Broadway was heavy now, moving south into Colfax or on farther past the front of the capitol, and on out toward Cherry Creek and other out-moving arteries.

He watched, his lips moving with his breathing, his face into the cold wind.

WALK

Twenty-two years, thought Max. Married to you at least twenty. Absently, Max counted the years, pressing cold fingers against the hand palms still thrust deep in his raincoat pocket.

Don't want to lose you now, Phyllis. I couldn't a been in love with her like with you, Phyllis. Her mother. She had class. Not like you, Phyllis. But she had class. I was in love with Tracy, but her mother was the one that had class. And my ol' man. Broke his ass every day on the goddamned railroad. Don't know what I'd a done if she'd a answered my letter. We'll never know that, Phyllis. But, it's all over now.

He was on Sixteenth Street now; he hurried to catch the WALK light at Court Place.

Max entered the Hilton hotel, the air in the revolving door warm, but stale. Crossing the entrance to the open elevator, he pushed LOBBY. He closed his eyes; the hammering in his chest frightened him. Suddenly he was weak.

The elevator door opened. Max hesitated, then stepped into the lobby.

She sat at the second table, her face a silhouette in the light from the curved glass of the tunnel-like roof. Not moving, she sat, her right elbow on the table, her eyes gazing far down Court Place to the east. Her back was to the restaurant entrance coming in from the department store. An empty chair was between her and the glass wall.

Max slowed, almost stopped. How young she looked, he thought.

Her blonde hair was not long; the slightly turned up ends just touched the gray mink cape she wore. The soft-luster depth of the fur gave relief to her features, a cameo in the curvature of the blonde hair. The cape was open at the throat. A choker of round black beads, three strands loosely strung, gave accent to the gentle curve of her neck. A golden wool blouse, visible at the throat, lent warmth to the delicate features of her face. Her skin was clear, almost pale.

Why have I avoided her so much for so long? he thought.

As Max approached the table, Phyllis raised her left arm, and her wrist, thin and sheathed in the long sleeve of her blouse, seemed to tremble. She pushed back the cuff of the sleeve, her black leather glove new and soft in the fading afternoon light, and looked at a small gold wrist watch.

Then she saw him.

"Why Max," said Phyllis, startled. Her face flushed. "I was watching for you but . . ."

"I know, Phyllis." He could feel his heart beat in his voice. "I've been . . ."

"I know, darling," she said, starting to rise.

"No, don't," said Max. He tried to pull the heavy chair out from the table.

The table, a rough opaque glass top set in a rectangular iron frame, was cramped yet adequate to the simulated garden atmosphere of the small restaurant. The chairs, four to a table, were of iron, with a grapevine motif wrought into the blackened metal. Foam-filled plastic cushions contrasted coldly with the plastic rose tree in the corner near the hotel wall. Bench seats with plastic cushions lined the wall along the glass where it curved upward to form the round-topped tunnel connecting the hotel to the department store. The two-foot glass arch sections that made up the roof were tinted and soiled, giving the snow mantle of the out-of-doors a coffee stain neglect. Along the ceiling of the glass tunnel gaily colored striped awnings for cutting down on the glare of the mid-day sun were suspended on wires. Uneven fingers of dirty ice and snow clutched the curved glass, extending below the curtain line. Twelve tables lined the east wall, a plastic orange tree, potted in brass-strapped red-wood pots and mulched with chips of white marble, adorning the space between every fourth table. Along the west wall was the service area; a large red wreath, soiled and torn, hung from the cash register.

Max sighed as he sat down.

"I'm late." He didn't look at her as he spoke. "I've had one of those days . . ." His voice faltered. His eyes wandered to the open plaza across the street on the May-D & F corner, where skaters circled in counter-clockwise motion around and around on the sunken artificial ice pond. Small seed electric lights strung in the trees that encircled the plaza twinkled now in the shadows cast by the May-D & F building. "I hoped that you would be here," he said at last. "I . . ."

"The garage called about eleven thirty and told me about your car," said Phyllis, concern and sympathy in her voice. "They brought it out to the house just before I left." Pausing, she reached over to the empty chair beside her. "Here are your keys," she said, opening a black leather purse and removing a red plastic key case. Handing the key case to Max, she closed her purse and put it in her lap. She licked her lips before speaking. "I didn't want to drive in, the weather being so bad," she said, hesitating. "I came in with a friend."

How to begin, thought Max.

Max felt hot; he wanted to take off his coat. He was perspiring. His clothes — what did he look like sitting here with his wife? Quickly, he tried to remember how he had dressed that morning. Sniffing, he could smell his clothes, musty and dirty. And his body, unbathed and unclean.

"I was late getting here myself, Max," said his wife, smiling across the table at him. "I hope you weren't worried."

"No. No. I wasn't worried." He fought for the right words. "I had some business to take care of downtown and . . ."

"I talked to Irene on the telephone — I called to see if I could find you and let you know that I was still coming — and she said you had just called in about a death. An accident." Again Phyllis' voice was warm and sympathetic. "Not even on Christmas does your work let up." She looked down at the table.

Both were quiet.

"I'm glad you did come in," said Max, at last, his voice low and calm. "I've needed very much to talk to you." His voice and manner were stiff. He paused.

"Let me begin, Max," said Phyllis. Then she was still, her nose and cheeks pale, her lips a thin, tight red line.

Max looked out through the glass wall at the plaza. The skaters were lined up along the railings of the skating pond, watching the ice cart sweeping and glazing the ice. The cool wetness of perspiration moved down over his ribs. He waited.

"You have your business, Max." Her voice had lost its warmth and was stifled, yet concerned. "You have always seemed to enjoy your work. I have never really been a part of it. There were times when I resented this, but now I know that I was wrong. It's your job and your life."

"I never meant to . . ."

"Let me go on, Maxwell." Phyllis had her purse on the table now and was toying with the zipper tab. "I know that a discussion on love," she said, her voice almost lost in the cold-ness of her face, "between two adults who have shared as much as we have must sound trite, but an act of love must never become trite if two people who truly respect each other are to do what they know is right." She paused, her attention concentrated on the zipper of her purse.

Max didn't move but sat looking across the plaza and at the tiny lights twinkling in the trees beside the icy pond.

"We should never have married in the first place," she said, her soft voice straining to go on. "But we did." She swallowed. "And I'm sorry, Maxwell."

Slowly, Max pushed back his chair and started to rise. His face was red now. His hands trembled as he pushed on the table.

Phyllis looked up.

"Oh, not sorry for me, Maxwell," she said, her breath rushing out. "Oh, Maxwell. Never sorry for myself. No. No. Maxwell. But sorry for you. I should never have married you. I did so under false pretenses, and knew it."

Maxwell was nearly to his feet now and was starting to sag on the chair. The muscle in his right jaw began to twitch.

"Please, Maxwell, sit down," Phyllis pleaded, reaching her right hand across the table. Gently taking his left hand, she pulled Max back into his chair. Breathing deeply, Phyllis continued: "Just before I started to college I thought I was in love with a boy in the Springs. And he thought he was in love with me. He was two years older than I, so he left me at home. He went to Annapolis. That was during the war. The war in Europe had just ended. When he graduated from Annapolis he joined the Air Force, new then. He married a girl from Maryland right after graduation. I was a junior in college when that happened, or would be in the fall. Then I met you, Maxwell." She still held his hand; she squeezed it as she spoke.

Maxwell listened, the words seeping into his being, through the shell that encased his soul. She understood, he thought. I'm not alone. She understands. It's happened to her too. He didn't speak; he put his right hand on top of hers and pushed it down hard on his other hand.

"I married you, I guess, on the rebound," she said, her voice still soft and low. "I didn't think so at the time. My mind was still on him, but I married you. I've cheated you, Maxwell, by loving him and marrying you."

He gripped her hand.

"I'm sorry, Maxwell."

Tell her it's all right, he thought. It's all right. He wanted to scream it. The weakness he had felt come over him in the elevator was again upon him.

But she was still speaking: "He's an officer in the Air Force and is stationed at the Air Academy." Phyllis started to cry, but didn't "His wife was killed in an air crash a few years ago in Newark, New Jersey and he's been alone ever since." She gripped Max's hand. "I called him today and told him I couldn't hold out any longer." She rushed the words, to get the message out, completed.

Max sat staring across the table at his wife, his eyes round, his face sagging. He tried to speak but could only clamp his jaws together, tightly. Then it came, the crushing humiliation of loss, the loss of love, or worse yet, the loss of a love he believed he treasured but never possessed.

"He had called me last spring when he was first . . ."

Max tried to listen but couldn't. Twenty-two years, he thought. And Roger?

"And Roger?" asked Max, aloud, his eyes looking up at his wife's face, his mind still groping.

"That's probably why he didn't come home," said Phyllis, biting her upper lip. "But he'll get over it, Maxwell."

Both were quiet now.

Maxwell sat staring across the table, not moving. Phyllis sat, her right hand held tightly in both of his, her left hand clutching her purse.

"I couldn't do it before, Maxwell," she said, finally, squeezing his hand. "I was worried about what would happen to you." She relaxed her grip. "But, when I started finding notes around that you obviously intended for someone else, I felt that now was the time." Her voice was warm again and friendly. "I don't blame you, Maxwell. I have been unfair to you all these years. I'm glad that you have found another woman to love you. It will work out for the best for both of us, you'll see, Maxwell."

Max let go of her hand and sat back in his chair. Trembling, he tried to speak. "It's all right, Phyllis." He clenched his fists, then opened them wide, flexing the fingers. "It's all right."

"I moved my personal things out of the house today, Maxwell," said Phyllis, not looking at him. "It will be best that way." She pulled her hand away from his. "I'll be staying here in the hotel tonight."

"It's OK," said Max. Get to your feet, he thought. Take it on your feet. Slowly, he pushed himself free of the table and looked out through the glass wall, across to the plaza. An elderly couple, the man's bare head gray and both wearing glasses, were performing on the ice, the other skaters watching and clapping their hands.

"It's OK, Phyllis," said Max, turning. He felt faint. He was about to vomit. "It's OK."

Chapter 22

Keep on your feet; keep movin', thought Max. Walk around; keep on your feet. Don't think about it. You got it straight. No excuses. Straight between the eyes. She didn't owe you anything. Thought she was doin' ya a favor.

A long line of taxis waited at the curb, along Court Place to the east, to the right of the hotel entrance. An airport limousine, its front wheels pulled in toward the curb opposite the revolving door, blocked traffic in the outside lane, alongside the parked taxis. Cars were jamming up in an uneven line behind the limousine, those closest backing up and pulling around into the next lane.

Horns blared as the afternoon traffic moved by the hotel, under the tunnel restaurant that joined the hotel to the department store across the street.

Max looked up the street to the east.

Keep going, he thought. Walk. Keep on your feet. Get down and the pain'll kill ya. Keep movin'.

He pulled his coat up tightly around his neck.

Over. No gettin' used to it. No plannin'. No preparation. It's over.

Max tried to swallow, but the lump wouldn't go down. Suddenly his eyes were watery and hot. Not here! Oh, Christ, not here, he thought. He turned up the street, to the west.

Cars maneuvering around the airport limousine in front
of the entrance to the hotel swung left, into the lane along
the curb, accelerating to make the light at the turn-only sign
on the corner of Fifteenth Street. The gritty ice of the street
softened the surface noise of the tires. Fumes from the fast-
moving cars sweetened the cold Christmas air.

Quit flounderin', thought Max.

He stopped, turning toward the shop window. Not here;
can't cry here.

Get your mind off it.

He looked into the window. Oriental art. Max closed
his eyes.

Flounderin'.

He leaned against the wall, his left hand cold against
the glass.

A chicken. Cut off its head and jump back. Blood spur-
tin' and clottin' the dirt and paintin' the wall a the fence, the
chicken tryin' to jump over the fence. And the feathers; white
and all soaked in its own blood.

On the guillotine they strap ya down. Eyes blink twice
and that's all. No flounderin'.

Keep on your feet.

Think 'bout somethin' else.

He looked into the shop, at the oriental art works.

Goddamned Japs won the war, he thought.

The jade tree, leaves, flowers and fruit all jade. Denver
has one a the greatest jade collections in the country. That's
what the book said. Guard said the book was wrong. And
everybody writin' on jade keeps copyin' the same wrong goddamned book. Only jade collection in Denver is the whores
up town during the conventions. The guard was an old man.

Art. Lots a sleepers in Japanese art. Article in the *Jour-
nal*. Especially woodcuts.

Twenty-two years. Married to you, Phyllis, for twenty.
Coupla months together, to get to know each other, like before we were married.

Rode in with a friend, she said. The thought stabbed at
him. Here in the hotel tonight.

Again he tried to swallow.

Then he thought of Tracy.

How would I have broken the news to Phyllis 'bout her, he thought.

Suddenly Tracy was a shattered toy, a trifling thing of his childhood, of his youth. She was a stranger, unknown to him as a woman until only a few weeks ago. Left to gather dust for twenty-eight years along with his pump twenty-two and the old bicycle that he'd used on the *Courier,* Tracy had remained a guardian of his fanciful children's dreams, inspirer of a groundless faith in a life that might have been, but never was. How many of us, thought Max ruefully, looking back on this girl of so long ago, go to our graves as old men and women, with our child selves inside screaming to be let out, to try again, promising to succeed.

Keep movin', thought Max. Can't stay here.

Max turned, stepped to the curb. Looking east, past the entrance to the hotel, he raised his right arm. The headlights flashed on; a taxi moved up the gutter and stopped.

"The Professional Exchange Building, please," said Max, his voice heavy, but strong.

Traffic going west on Colfax and turning left around Civic Center slowed, pausing before the holy creche and Christmas tree display in front of the City and County Building. Another line of traffic moved out from behind the new Denver Art Museum on the south to circle the park, pausing before the Christmas display.

Max watched as the taxi worked through the crowded street.

The lights were on in the display, the street in front of the City and County Building pulsating with people on foot and the two-way automobile traffic, especially patrolled to assure safe, yet cautious, advantage for viewing the civic ornamentation. A large creche, with the wise men and the star, occupied the grounds in the forefront of the scene. Splayed red, blue, green and amber lights, in a regular, preset order, transfixed the masonry structure of the government building into a waterfall of moving, muted light. Families and other small groups milled about the open space across the street from the display. Bundled babies in strollers and agile young men with cameras on tripods mingled with the passing curious pedestrians, all intent upon the illuminated commemoration of the coming of the Christ child.

Max let himself in through the building entrance to the underground garage.

The corridor lights were on.

Max paused, opened the door. The coffee room was dark; the vending machines, boasting luxurious but quietly bubbling and demanding ads of contrived pleasures, blinked and stared along the far wall. The floor looked clean-swept, the chairs and tables in place.

The building was quiet.

Christmas Eve, thought Max. How many Christmas Eves does a man have? Max looked back. Too many, he thought. And the future? Would there be enough? Could there ever be too many?

He pushed the button and waited.

And Roger.

He'll get over it.

The Christmas display, he thought. Every year. Same place. That summer a the Colorado centennial — a hundred years a somethin'. Pioneer town and the Martin missile? Same place. Christmas display every year. Same place. He'll get over it.

Max leaned his head against the wall; quietly he wept.

The elevator clicked; the doors opened.

Please don't throw lighted cigarettes on the floor.

Max stepped inside.

The preset pause; the doors kissed.

Twelfth floor.

Max pushed the twelfth floor button.

What to do? thought Max.

Is there an elevator that doesn't stop? he wondered. One that goes on for ever, taking you where you want to go but never stopping.

Floundering again, he thought. Like a fish. A carp. Shiny carp. Catch 'em by hand in the Republican River, when the water'd dried up. Only holes along the banks. Carp'd try to run the shallow current between the holes. Creep up on 'em, surprise 'em and throw 'em out on the sand. Flounder, flippin' their long silver tails, the one gill smackin' for air. The eye watchin', long after the gill and tail stopped.

The elevator stopped.

Max stepped out.

He was trembling. Suddenly, he was chilled.

Stay in the office tonight, he thought. Get drunk. But the old man at the bar. The one without a face, in the straw hat. Once a wino, always a wino. Again he shuddered. Something sweet. Then he remembered: nothing since breakfast. It's the sugar you're after, the doc said. The best for both of us. He'll get over it.

Mountain-Plains Life Insurance Company.

Enter.

Send that telegram to Oregon first thing in the morning, thought Max.

Max fumbled with the key case. For the first time, he was tired. The pain in the stomach that had bothered him earlier in the day was back.

Sleep, he thought. In the office tonight. Can't go back to the house. Twenty years, married to you, Phyllis.

The office door swung open. He flipped on the light.

Then he saw it.

First, the Indian oil painting in the outer office, then the trail of glass shards into his own office, the door partly open. The head of a large claw hammer, the handle standing out as a soiled make-shift hanger, was imbedded in the panelled door. A note, typed, was stuck to the door, below the hammer. The tape tore the paper as Max pulled it from the door.

Friday: P.M.

Dear Mr. Potter:

A lady delivered a picture to the office. She said it was for you. She became upset. I am sorry, Mr. Potter. I suggest that you report this incident to the police.

Merry Christmas,
Irene

On scratch paper, too, thought Max, turning the paper
over. A ditoed message — a Christmas party. Max dropped
the paper on the floor.

Sighing, Max walked into his office.

He turned on the lights.

Each print had been smashed, one blow of the hammer
shattering the protecting glass and tearing a deep dent in the
print and straw-matted wall behind the frame. Like the foot-
print of some giant cog wheel, or perferator, the spaced holes
in the wall measured the stride of the angry wielder of the
claw hammer.

Max stared at the wreckage.

Munch. The face of the little girl had disappeared under
the blow of the hammer. Only the hair, neatly brushed.

Strange man, Munch. In love with his sister, or somethin'. She died a TB, or somethin'.

An' The Weavers. Kollwitz. A doctor of somethin.' Before Medicare. Kid dyin' a consumption. The boy in the crib
was gone; only the mother lookin' down, sad.

Barlock. Smashed. The window a the cathedral gone.
Skeleton still there, climbin' the cathedral.

The accident a my birth, thought Max, not bein' born a
Catholic.

Fakes, the whole bunch of 'em, thought Max. Maybe
they never really lived the things they painted. All fakes.

He'll get over it.

The oil painting in the outer office was leaning against
the wall of the sales manager's office, a chair, two legs still
sticking through the canvas, hid the sun from the field of
battle. The frame was still intact; the canvas had pulled loose
and had ripped through the sky above the sun.

He'll get over it.

Benny, thought Max. He got over it.

Max closed the door to the hall and turned off the light
in the outer office. Then the lights in his own office. The glass
crunched like ice under his feet.

Used to skate the old year out and the new one in, he thought. Kids don't do that any more. Sioux City, Iowa. The winters are beautiful in Sioux City, Iowa. Carl could have had a store of his own, but he would never say.

Max stood at the window, the small one on the west.

Lucky to get this office when I did, thought Max, for a moment lost in the lights and traffic that blinked at his feet. Someday, somewhere out there, I'll make it. Make it the way I was meant to. Make it big.

Max thought of the men who'd built the city. Parks named after them. Airports. Streets. And fountains. Potter Fountain.

Goddamned stump, he thought. Be able to see . . . Max couldn't say it.

Tonight in the Hilton, he thought.

Max shuddered again. Why not?

It's been there all the time, he thought, amazed that it hadn't occured to him sooner. Death, the emancipator. Predistination, he thought. That's what I got it for.

Mechanically, Max crossed the office to his desk. The top drawer to the right of the knee hole. On top of the pile. He felt better already. Nasty little job up close. Feeling around in the drawer, he took it out. 25 caliber. Wonder where the license is, he thought.

Max weighed the gun up and down in his right hand. Kicks like hell, the man said, but nasty little job up close. He looked around the office, at the broken glass on the floor, bits of the splinters picking up the faint light coming in through the windows. Then at the prints on the wall.

Morbid bastards, thought Max.

Pocketing the gun, Max felt his pocket for his key case. The terrace. Won't be found up there 'till after Christmas.

Standing in the door of his office, Max turned. One final look. The hammer. Max pulled the claw hammer loose from the door, inspected it, the claws barely visible in the dark. Then, cautiously, he adjusted the hammer into the hole in the door.

Turning, Max opened the outer door and left the office.

The terrace door slid closed; Max dropped the key case back into his raincoat pocket.

Unrestricted now, Max had a panoramic view of the city, to the north, west and south. This city that he'd visited in his youth, the mother city of the entire front range. He sucked in the air, cold and still now. His mind grappled with the magnitude of the night. In a bed of twinkling jewels lay the Queen City of the Rocky Mountain Empire.

Max looked for Pike's Peak far to the south and Long's Peak to the north, both obscured in the blackness of the storm-set sky. Lookout Mountain to the west, its TV antennae blinking their warnings to the planes approaching and leaving Stapleton Airport to the east, hovered mysteriously at the end of a string of lights that started out as Colfax Avenue before it lost itself wandering into the distant hills.

Seeing the city, Max forgot for a moment the tribulations of the day. He forgot the gun in his pocket and the fear that had so recently begun to haunt him. He was now part of something alive, something beyond his own imperfections, his own success or failure. The city at his feet, alive, pulsating. Living because its builders and sustainers lived. Living even when they died. The city. An assembly of a multitude of nothingness, but as a city a thing alive. Greater than the sum of its parts.

The whole city a Christmas display, awaiting the commemoration of the coming of the Christ child.

Max listened.

The Cathedral of the Emaculate Conception. The chimes drifted up through the clear night air.

Max felt the pull of a distant beat, a childhood belief, an adult denial.

The chimes waned, then strong again.

Quietly, Max let himself out the front door.
Two blocks, he thought.
Not a Catholic, but nobody'll mind.

The figure of a man moved south down Logan Street toward the Cathedral. Body erect, stride brisk, he seemed to outdistance the two figures that darted after him, sometimes in the shadows along the west side of the street. In front of the residence behind the Cathedral they caught up with him. The lone figure in full stride, the length of heavy pipe hit him, above the left ear, just alongside the head. Unaware of his assailants, the man went down in the icy whiteness of the street.

"Yeah, he's the one," said the bigger of the men. "Flashin' all that money around down there in the bar."

Quickly, the man's hands went through Max's pockets. His wallet first; he handed it to his companion.

"Would ya look at that," said the other man, taking the money out of the wallet. "There's a Santa after all."

"And look at this!" said the bigger man, pulling out the gun. "The sonofabitch's bigger time than I thought." He stuck the gun into his own pocket.

Then they were gone.

He felt their hands and then they were gone.

Reaching out, Max could feel the snow on his hands; then it was on his face. Must a fallen, thought Max. He was on his knees now. Slowly, he rose to his feet. In a bed a twinkling jewels. But the jewels were gone. For a moment the world was dark; total darkness. Then he vomited.

He stumbled to his feet again. The darkness was gone. The traffic on Colfax Avenue. He could see it. The darkness was gone. Max lunged toward the traffic, stumbling as he ran. His feet; there was nothing to walk on.

Lady! Max waved his right arm but it wouldn't wave. He looked at the woman until she was gone. The left eye was all light. It exploded. Then darkness. Puzzled, Max stopped, reached for his head, his left arm lifting the right, the right arm falling. Then he saw the blood and the sticky fingers of the left hand. He tried to cry.

Max grabbed for the sign on the corner, the one with the announcements, by the Cathedral. Gripping the post nearest the curb, he looked up at the people crossing the street, his good eye staring into their faces. Their eyes never met. They don't see me, thought Max, again trying to cry.

Max looked up at the tall spires of the Cathedral. Death climbing the Cathedral.

Like a candle before a hot flame, Max melted, falling to the sidewalk on the corner in front of the Cathedral.

He felt the thing in his pocket; he tried to move it. That'd be the perfume. Like before we were married.

Max lay on his back, his feet outstretched. Keep one leg bent, he thought, good for the back. Then he was numb.

It ain't so cold, the snow.

His right eye still open, Max watched the jet cross the narrow sky above, the spewing black exhaust visible in the glow of the city's lights.

Baxter, the flyin' bastard.

And, Benny. W's. X's. Y's. Z's. Benny Z. Then he relaxed. Knew couldn't forget him. Benny Zancanelli. Benny the Wop.